---

# ALEXA'S DOM

---

## RENEE MARKS

Published by Blushing Books
An Imprint of
ABCD Graphics and Design, Inc.
A Virginia Corporation
977 Seminole Trail #233
Charlottesville, VA 22901

Renee Marks
Alexa's Dom

eBook ISBN: 978-1-64563-884-1
v1

## Chapter 1

Alexandra Mills was seated in the vast office building, waiting in the lounge, and everything was so dark. It was a bit uncomfortable. She played with a strand of her long, straight brown hair while her leg bounced, making her light blue stiletto heel, which matched her light blue skirt and her light blue blouse, plink against the gray tile. Her eyes darted around as she took in the gray walls, gray furniture, gray everything. It wasn't a very friendly place. How did they get to the top?

She had to seriously reconsider applying for the position of MAEP at Mackenzie and Andrews Editorial and Publishing. She had what it took for the job. It wasn't her first rodeo, but the place was cold, and she didn't seem to belong there. It was a waste of time.

There were at least thirty-five people in the lounge with her, but nobody seemed cramped. Some seemed so poised, calm, cool, and collected. Others were even more nervous than she was.

Thankfully, she had a job to fall back on if she didn't get this job. She had already been working in the small publishing company, BAP, Brandon Adams Publishing before MAEP posted the job ad. She had been at BAP for almost three years, even did her internship there during college. She had over-loaded herself with courses to obtain her diploma more quickly. She also completed some college courses while in high school, because she knew what career she wanted for a very long time. She loved reading, even dabbled in writing some of her own work, but no one knew. She didn't want to leave BAP, but she thought it was time to broaden her horizons and look at options.

"Alexandra Mills!" A woman shouted from the office behind her seat.

Alexandra rose and went towards the woman, her heels clicking against the gray tiles as she proceeded toward her. The knot in her stomach got worse when she saw the total bomb, Sandra Carpenter, coming out of the door she was walking towards. Why was Sandra there? She was really good at BAP. Why would she want to leave? She had everyone eating out of the palm of her hand there.

Alexandra began to freak out, what was she doing there? She was no match for Sandra. She was magnificent, incredible references, and had a lot more experience than she did. She nearly turned around and took off.

*'No,' she thought, 'you've got this. You're just as good."* Alexandra eventually arrived at the woman who called her by name.

"Ms. Mills, I'm Carla James, HR, let's go," the tall woman said, flipping her fiery red hair over a shoulder.

As Alexandra followed her, Sandra came out of the office. The next thing she knew, Sandra grabbed her arm. "Good luck, little girl, although I have it in the bag." She snarled a little and let go.

Alexandra began to walk in to the room, while glaring at Sandra, when she was suddenly sprawled out on the floor after her foot caught something. All her papers fell from her hands, and were strewn across the floor.

"Thanks, Sandra, real professional, next time why don't you try to be nice and not be a total bitch." The last word died on her lips as she looked in the office, her face paling. Well, she just shot herself in the foot. But instead of the frowns she had put on the faces of the occupants, what drew her attention the most was the bronzed, very tall man with dark hair who was slowly coming towards her.

While he approached her, he picked up the papers she had lost. He squatted and held out his big hand towards her. "You okay?" he asked in a deep voice.

She did nothing but nod. She was frozen when his hazel eyes locked with her own hazel eyes. Only his had more green with little flecks of blue in them while hers were more blue and had flecks of greens and gold.

"My name is Dominick Mackenzie; come on, why don't you let me help you?" He smiled in a perfect row with perfectly white teeth.

Alexandra's heart began to race. She couldn't move. But his big hand wrapped around her hand and as he stood slowly, he pulled her up with ease. She chewed on her bottom lip a little as she stood, barely reaching his chest even with the two-inch heels she had on. She swallowed hard as she stared at the tall, sexy deliciousness.

"Dom, can we wrap this up? We still have thirty-four interviews to do before our meeting." The male voice asked, breaking the moment between the two.

"Yes, Patrick," Dominick answered, then turned and brought her right along with him. He held up the papers. "Are these for us?"

Alexandra nodded her head one more time. And she had thought she was nervous before.

He smiled at her again and moved to the other side of the

long, dark conference table. "Please," he glanced at the paper, "Alexandra, have a seat."

She gulped loudly. "Alexa, please, Mr. Mackenzie."

"Please, Alexa, just call me Dom. Mr. Mackenzie is my father." He smiled again.

"Yes, Mr. Mackenzie." She flinched inwardly. *'Great, you just showed him you can't do what you're told.'*

Instead of frowning, he grinned even more and laughed. "Well?" He nodded at the chair.

*Oh. Right. A seat.* Alexa took the chair across from Dominick Mackenzie, *the* Dominick Mackenzie, the man who made this publishing house bloom.

After what seemed like an eternity of him going over her resume, accomplishments, education credits, and everything else, he finally looked at her.

He jumped in, and she responded as sincerely as she could. She'd probably tell him everything if he asked for it.

The interview seemed like an everlasting one. How long until this is over?

---

The minute the little woman literally fell into the conference room and burst out at the stupid blonde, he was immediately intrigued by her. Short and a spitfire. He just had to smile at her.

Her paperwork was well organized, just like her clothes had been before the fall. Something had drawn him to help her up, and he wasn't usually nice to people. Most were afraid of him, and he didn't mind it until her beautiful hazel eyes rounded in fear at him. He wasn't trying to frighten the poor woman.

She seemed capable of managing herself, but that did not stop the immediate need he had for her. He wanted to protect her, help her flourish even more in the publishing industry. Hell, he just plain wanted her. That wasn't making any sense. She was far from his usual type. His type roamed more toward the stupid blonde who just left. But this woman, sitting across from him, was definitely gaining his interest.

His gaze stayed glued to those full pouty lips of hers, and the only way he knew she was done talking was by seeing those pink lips stop moving. He'd rattle off another question, and he'd wait for those lips to finish moving.

He was biting the inside of his cheek while attempting to control his libido. He felt Carla and Patrick getting tense, but he asked the last question anyway. "How soon would you like to begin?"

---

Alexa froze when he asked when she wanted to start. She had never had an interview and had never had a job offered by a business owner. She had always done business with the human resources manager of BAP. She turned her eyes to the woman, Carla, who had a deep frown on her face and then to the man sitting next to Dominick, who seemed equally distraught.

Then she heard the gentleman by Mr. Mackenzie's side. "She's too inexperienced, Dom, we don't want a person like her."

"That's not your choice at this point, is it? She's fresh, young, we could have some very new, good ideas from her, couldn't we, Alexa?"

Her skin covered in goosebumps at the sound of her name from his sexy mouth. "Yes, Mr. Mackenzie, if that's your wish," she answered innocently.

Carla interrupted. "We will let you know, Ms. Mills, good-bye," she said dismissively.

Dominick's eyes went straight to Carla. "We should not be

rude to employees, Carla, as Alexa pointed out to the woman who preceded her." Those sexy eyes turned toward her. "Tomorrow, I want you tomorrow."

She widened her eyes in shock. "Yes, Mr. Mackenzie, um, what time?"

"At six, I can go over more things with you tomorrow."

"But, Nicky, I usually do that." Carla whined a little.

"Not this time." Dominick smiled at Alexa. "Tomorrow at 6 a.m. in this room."

"Yes, sir, thank you," she responded as she stood. Was that a gleam in his eyes? It felt strange. And too good to be true. But she'd take it. She slowly left the room in case he changed his mind, but it didn't happen. All she heard was, "Send the others away. I found who I want." And there was definitely an emphasis on the *I* part.

She swallowed hard again as she left the building, now she had to talk to Brandon. She owed the man so much, but it was time to grow. He would understand, she hoped.

---

Dom glanced at the few people who surrounded him. Patrick and Carla were seething.

"Nicky, why'd you pick her?" Carla whined out the nickname not very many people used, but she did, and he hated it.

Patrick chimed in, "She wasn't that impressive."

Dom leaned back in his chair steepling his fingers. "Well, that's where you're wrong, Patrick, she has a backbone. I feel she won't let our clients walk all over her and will tell us what she really thinks of any work that comes our way. She is young, we can shape and mold her into our perfect editor."

Patrick and Carla shot a glance at each other. "I believe Mr. Mackenzie is thinking with a different part of his anatomy, rather than his brain." Patrick sneered a little.

Dom stood, and went around the conference table. "Nope, not my type." He left the room and retreated to his office, carrying Alexa's papers in his hands. What had he been thinking? Trying to blend business and fun?

He couldn't help thinking with that other part of his anatomy Patrick had mentioned. He could not even stand and shake her hand, or he would have had an embarrassing situation on his hands.

He had to get his body under control. She wasn't for him. She was soft, a spitfire, but needed gentle handling and probably love. He didn't do love, it was not on his priority list, but they would see. He hoped she didn't prove him wrong with his feelings about her work.

───────

Alexa made her way back to BAP. Her heart was racing, she couldn't believe the man was giving her a chance. And he had looked at her like no other man had before. Was that part of the reason she got the job? Or had he actually been impressed by her?

Well, he had another thing coming if he thought something could possibly happen between them. She had sworn off men years ago. And she wouldn't change her mind just because Mr. Mackenzie looked at her like she was something to devour.

It just wasn't in her. She walked through the doors of BAP and headed for her mentor, boss, and friend, Brandon Adams. She knocked on his door and heard him say, "Come in."

His voice washed over her in a settling wave, he would understand. He just had to. "Brandon?" she called uncertainly.

Brandon looked up from his desk, pushing his glasses up his long, thick nose. "Lex, my dear, how are you?" His somewhat wrinkled face broke into a huge smile. "I thought you were on vacation."

"I am, I just need to run something by you," she answered as she walked into the room.

He pushed his glasses up into his salt and pepper hair. "You look awfully dressed up to be on vacation."

"I know, Brandon. I've really got to talk to you." She paused, biting her lip, unsure.

"Go ahead, darling."

"Well, I'm sure you've heard MAEP is looking for a new editor."

"Yes, quite a few gossipers have mentioned it." He leaned back in his desk chair.

"I love you, Brandon, like the father I've never had. You've given me so many opportunities, and I will never forget I wouldn't be where I am today without you." She paused again, twisting her fingers in her lap.

"Come on, Lex, spit it out, sweetheart."

"I applied for the job, and I just came back from the interview. I just thought it would help me with my interview skills since I am terrible at those, I never expected the outcome, they hired me." Her eyes darted up to his soft brown eyes.

"Really? Are you taking it?" he asked, leaning forward, placing his arms on top of his desk.

"Will you be mad if I do?"

"No, of course not, when do they want you to start?"

"Tomorrow, I just didn't have the ability to speak except to answer the questions."

"Yeah, that woman can be such a hard ass." Brandon chuckled a little.

"Woman?"

"Yes, the HR, Carla James, she does all the interviewing over at MAEP." He gave her a strange look.

"Oh, yeah, her. She didn't really do the interview."

"Really, who did then?" His eyes narrowed a little bit.

Alexa swallowed hard. "Mr. Mackenzie."

"That old goat?" Brandon let out a laugh as he seemed to think about the older Mackenzie.

"No, his son," she whispered slightly.

Silence fell across the room. You could have heard a pin drop. Alexa's heart rate picked up instantly. She listened to the pounding in her ears grow louder.

"Dominick Mackenzie, huh?" Brandon began, as he leaned back in his seat and placed his forefinger over his lips. "He must have seen something exceptional in you, which I saw three years ago. If you feel you are ready for this challenge, then go for it, love." He leaned forward becoming more serious. "But I will warn you, that boy is a player, so just be careful."

She reached forward to clasp his hand in hers. "You don't have to worry about that. I am never letting a man close besides you, Brandon. He won't get to me. I'm going to do my job, and that's all."

He stood up and leaned forward, pressing his lips to her forehead. "You'll always have a job here, Lex. But if this is what you want, then spread your little wings and fly, but stay very sharp around that young man."

"I will, sir, thank you." She stood up from the desk. "I'm so sorry for the short notice, Brandon."

"It's okay, this is a great opportunity for you, and I'm not letting you miss out on it."

She bobbed her head a little then headed out to her desk. She sat in her chair. She was leaving this place behind, not for good, she would visit Brandon as much as she could. But this was good, a new adventure and chapter in her life.

As she finished cleaning her desk, she caught Sandra out of the corner of her eye. Her gaze darted over, and Sandra was heading right over to her. *'Oh no, not now.'* She bit the inside of her cheek.

Sandra sat on top of the desk like it was no big deal. "Aww, did Brandon find out about the interview and decide to finally get rid of our weakest link?"

Alexa glared at Sandra. This woman really got under her skin. "No, I have his blessing for a new job I got."

"Well, then good luck, can't believe this place will lose both of us at the same time, such a shame we never found out which one of us was truly better."

Alexa let out a breath and pasted on a smile. "Oh, I'm sure we'll find out soon. Well goodbye, Sandra, and please don't try to trip me this time." She stood up from the chair and walked away from Sandra and BAP. This was what she wanted, and it would flatten Sandra when she never got the phone call she was expecting.

Too bad, she was going to miss it.

## Chapter 2

Dominick was at his mansion by himself, as usual. These nights got boring and lonely sometimes, but it was the life he had chosen. Only tonight, his thoughts were racing about Alexa Mills, he wanted to see her again so badly, he didn't think tomorrow would be soon enough. He tried his usual strenuous workout, tried to pound her out of his mind with music. Nothing worked.

He was sitting at his large oak desk, tapping his fingers, racking his brain about Alexa instead of looking over one of the manuscripts from a long-time client.

His eyes kept flicking over to the stack of papers with Alexa's number, email, even her scent of peaches and strawberries all over it. He picked up his iPhone and dialed her number. It rang only twice before her melodic voice answered.

"Hello?"

"Alexa, how are you?" His heart picked up speed at the sound of her soft voice.

"I'm fine," she answered hesitantly. "I'm sorry, but who is this?"

"Oh, Alexa, I'm hurt, it's Dominick," he answered easily

and heard the sharp intake of breath on the other side of the phone. He wondered if she'd make that same noise if she were beneath him.

"Mr. Mackenzie, sir, I'm so sorry, what can I do for you?"

"Well for starters, call me Dominick, I feel so old when people call me Mr. Mackenzie and two, I just wanted to make sure we are good for tomorrow at six."

"Yes, of course, Mr. Mackenzie, sir."

"I was very serious when I told you I think you'll be good for my company."

"Thank you, sir, your HR and co-owner don't feel the same way though."

"Eh, they are older, too old-fashioned, they also forget how it is to be new and needing a start. I'm still young, as well, and have made a lot of changes to this company which has made it flourish, I need more people like you to see things my way," he explained in his deep soft voice.

"Well, I appreciate the opportunity, Mr. Mackenzie."

Dom chuckled, he wanted to hear those sexy lips say his name, not Mr. Mackenzie, but he'd let it go for now. "Are you okay from the fall earlier, it had to have hurt; what exactly happened?"

He heard her swallow hard, right before she answered, "I'm fine, and young, I bounce back quickly. I worked with her at my last job, she's always treated me like that, she gets a kick out of getting under my skin, I slip with the profanities around her sometimes. It makes her, well, giddy."

"Well, then I am glad I could get you away from her, she seemed like a real ditz." Dom chuckled. "Pardon the put-down."

"No, that's okay, is there anything else, Mr. Mackenzie? I still have quite a bit to do to get ready for my first day tomorrow."

He didn't want the conversation to end, he could talk to

her all night if she'd let him, but he couldn't come up with an excuse to keep her on the phone. "Hmm, no I think that's it, don't forget to meet in the conference room, not my personal office." He knew if he got her in there, he would probably never let her go.

"Okay, I will be there at six, good night, Mr. Mackenzie."

"Good night, Alexa." He hung up the phone and couldn't help the smile that spread across his lips. He couldn't wait until he got to spend most of the day with her tomorrow.

---

Alexa hung up and stared at her phone, that was just weird. Why did he just call her? Was it only to make sure she was reassured about the job or was it something else? She put her phone on the charger, laid it on her bed stand then went to take a shower. She couldn't get his deep voice out of her ears. But she couldn't go down that path. No one would get past her barriers.

Once she got out and dried, then dressed, she headed to her bed. She collapsed on to the flower printed comforter. As her eyes closed, her mind was invaded by those gleaming hazel eyes.

She huffed and rolled onto her stomach and stared at the plum purple wall in front of her. *'Don't let him in, don't let him in.'* She kept repeating to herself as her finger absentmindedly traced the scar along her arm. Let him see the imperfection, and he would lose interest. That would be the plan, she had other scars, but he'd never see those. He wouldn't have to.

She finally fell asleep.

---

Alexa jerked awake at the sound of her alarm. She woke up so many times the night before with Dominick invading her dreams. She shut the alarm off, then headed into the bathroom. She threw her hair up in a bun and began to shower.

She struggled with what to wear. She wanted to look perfect for her first day. She decided on the black skirt that was flowy around her thighs and knees. She got her black stilettos, three-inch today, she needed all the height lift she could get to be around Dominick. It was bad enough she purposely gave herself a lift with those heels just because she was short, five-two to be exact, then with him around, she felt even shorter.

She grabbed her favorite dark purple buttoned blouse. She pulled her hair out of the bun, brushed out her long hair, and did a quick sweep with some very light pink lip gloss. Ready. She could take on anything today.

She grabbed her computer bag, phone, and purse and began to walk to MAEP. New day, new life here she came.

It was such a short distance for her, just like BAP. She began to wonder about Brandon. She'd miss seeing his face every day.

She arrived at MAEP, she pulled on the door, but it was still locked. Five-forty, oh well, it was only twenty minutes. She spotted the bench beside the door and sat down. She crossed her legs as she pulled out a full manuscript from BAP, she began to go over the last few pages she had to read and then would drop it off to Brandon after she got done at MAEP.

She was so engrossed with the pages she didn't feel someone sit down beside her a few minutes later. She finished the last page and made her final mark when the manuscript was pulled from her hands. She jumped and moved away quickly, and fell off the edge of the bench.

Alexa looked up and met the hazel gaze. She swallowed. *'Oh, no,'* she thought.

"Alexa, are you okay?" He moved to the edge of the bench and helped her up. "I'm sorry."

"That's okay, Mr. Mackenzie." She stood up slowly and began to brush off any dirt from the back of her skirt.

"What are you doing sitting here by yourself?" he asked sternly.

"I was too early. I figured I could wait for you, sir," she said meekly, averting her gaze a tad.

"Why didn't you stay in your car?" he demanded.

Her cheeks flamed. "I don't have one. You're in walking distance of my home, so I just walked. I prefer it anyway."

"I see." His gaze roamed over her and stopped when they reached her feet. "You walked here in those?" he demanded, his tone becoming even sterner.

"Um." She glanced down at her feet. "Yes, Mr. Mackenzie."

His gaze narrowed at her. She was a little closer to his shoulders today. Bigger heel lift. He put the manuscript beneath his arm and headed toward the door to unlock it. "Right this way, Alexa." He held the door open for her, and she walked into the building in front of him.

---

As Dominick walked in behind her, his eyes glued themselves to her nice, round ass as it shook back and forth as she walked in those ridiculous heels. He felt a clench of desire. Boy, was he in trouble. As should she be, a silly woman walking the streets by herself, and sitting on that bench by herself. She wouldn't be able to get away from someone in those shoes of hers.

He followed her to the conference room, and threw the manuscript on the table as he sat down in the same chair he sat in the day before, facing the doors. "So, what's the meaning of that?" he asked, pointing to the stack of papers.

Her face reddened. "That's the last project I had to finish for Brandon, I only had a few pages to finish," she explained, still standing in front of the table across from him.

He steepled his fingers. "I see." He leaned back in his seat, making it tilt back a little. "The things I expect from my employees are loyalty, not doing side work, and not giving my business away to competitors of mine."

"Yes, Mr. Mackenzie, it won't happen again." She squirmed underneath his gaze.

"But you also showed me you could be loyal. You finished this project. You didn't drop it because you left BAP." His gaze raked over her. He noticed her rubbing a spot along her arm with her tiny fingers. His gaze zeroed in on the spot when he caught a glimpse of the puckered skin. It ran almost the whole length of the inside of her arm.

His eyebrows arched a little as he looked at her, it almost looked like she was about to start trembling. "Alexa?"

"Yes, Mr. Mackenzie?" she asked, looking up at him.

He let out a breath. "Why don't you sit now so we can get more of the necessary issues hashed out." He wished she would have sat beside him, but instead, she sat across from him again.

They dove into everything at full speed. They were so caught up in everything they hadn't realized morning slid into the afternoon.

Alexa's stomach growled loudly.

Dom looked over at her with raised eyebrows. "A little hungry, are we?"

She blushed, man that color looked good on her when he made her acquire it. "Maybe a little, I may have skipped breakfast this morning."

"Why?"

"Nerves," she answered simply and began to go over more paperwork.

He reached out for her hand. "Lunch first, then we can finish when we get back."

"Are you sure, Mr. Mackenzie?"

He chuckled. "You like making me feel like an old man, don't you? Yes, I'm sure, let's go." He stood and walked around the table. He caught her hand before she went for that scar again. He pulled her up out of the chair and close to his body.

He put his hand at the small of her back and ushered her out of the room, then the building. "There's a small sandwich shop just down the street."

"Mabel's," Alexa said.

"Have you been there?" Dom asked, keeping his hand against her back, loving the feel of her soft body against his, he almost pulled her closer to him but refrained from doing so.

"Yes, Brandon takes me there all the time," she answered casually.

"Brandon?"

"Adams," she answered, in a tone like he should have known whom she was talking about.

"Isn't he a little too old for you?" he whispered, as he bent his head down to get close to that delicate little ear of hers.

She jerked her head up and turned to look at him. Anger was written all over her face. They both stopped moving as their eyes collided. She glared at him and after a couple of heartbeats turned away from him, not answering.

Dominick rushed after her, his hand returning to her back. He hadn't meant to make her angry. He'd said it as a joke, unless she really was screwing her much older ex-boss.

Just the thought made his blood boil.

They reached the sub shop and headed in. They ordered

the same thing and made their way to a little table in the corner. They ate in silence for a little while.

———

Alexa stewed over what Mr. Mackenzie had said about Brandon, it was absurd and made her so angry. "He's the father figure I never had," she blurted out, staring at her half-eaten sub. She began to stroke the scar on her arm. It wasn't to show Mr. Mackenzie how imperfect and broken she was. It was because of the memories of her no-good father.

She felt his strong hand touch hers and pull it away from the scar. She looked up and locked eyes with Dominick.

His fingers trailed along the scar. "I didn't mean to make you angry, it was meant to be a joke. So my rival Brandon Adams is like the father you never had? I can definitely see that in him. What happened to your real dad?" His tone was gentle, as were his fingers stroking the scar.

"My parents divorced when I was fifteen, fifteen years too late, but they did it," she answered, and pulled her arm away from Dom. The touch of his fingers sent chills, then hot flashes across her body.

"Ah, I see," he said and pulled his hand back from her.

He didn't see. A man like him couldn't possibly understand.

"My parents divorced when I was thirteen," he commented.

"Really?" Now that spiked her curiosity.

"Yeah, my mom wasn't satisfied with just my father, she was very flirtatious with other men."

"Oh," she whispered, she saw his eyes darken a little. She reached out to squeeze his big hand. "I'm sorry, Mr. Mackenzie."

He looked at her quizzically. He was never going to win

with her. "Ms. Mills, what's it going to take to get you not to call me Mr. Mackenzie? You call Mr. Adams by his first name, why not me?"

"Well, I've known him since my junior year in high school, while I was taking as many college courses as possible. He was a speaker at one of the courses, and he had me hooked on editing, he gave me the road to the path I'm on now, he's an important figure in my life, has been for the last six years of my life, it took me a while, but I finally warmed up to calling him Brandon."

"Well then, I guess I'm going to have to warm you up to calling me Dominick, Nick, or Dom, hell, I'd even let you call me Nicky if you wanted." He smiled at her.

"Carla called you that yesterday during the interview."

"Yes, she did, and I don't care for that name too much, especially from her, but I'd let you call me that in a heartbeat." His gaze darkened again, and this time it wasn't from sadness.

Alexa pulled her hand back quickly. *'Don't get close to him, watch your back with him. He's a player.'* She averted her gaze from his and began to pick at her sandwich. Brandon's words echoed through her head. And yeah, Dominick looked like one. He was used to smiling and getting precisely what he wanted or needed from someone. She glanced at him under her eyelashes. He was just staring at her with his forefinger covering his lips, leaning back from the table.

Alexa felt so awkward all of a sudden and stood. She headed to the counter to get a box for her sandwich. She would just finish it later.

As she headed back, she felt his eyes on her, and sure enough, she glanced up and met his eyes. She hurriedly looked away.

She packed her food, grabbed some money out of her purse, and tossed it to him for the meal then rushed out of the shop. *'Keep the barriers up, keep the barriers up.'* She kept repeating as her heels hit the sidewalk and headed back to MAEP.

---

Dom grabbed the money and rushed after Alexa, unable to get to her fast enough. He hated thinking about her walking alone.

He wondered if he could get her to agree to let him pick her up in the mornings and drop her off in the afternoons. Doubtful, but he could try.

He finally caught up to her wiggling ass, he managed to slip the bills back into her purse since he had already paid for lunch, then laid his hand on her hip this time.

---

As they walked into the office, he was ambushed by Carla and Patrick. His hand tightened on Alexa's hip as she tried to walk away.

Carla began first. "Sir, these need to be looked over." She held out a folder full of resumes. "Surely, someone better will catch your eye." She looked at Alexa with some disgust.

"Dom, we have a meeting to take care of today," Patrick said next.

Dom glared at Carla as he moved Alexa to his other side and tucked her against his body, then shoved the folder out of his face. "Sorry, she's who I want, and you can take care of the meeting today, Patrick, I am too busy with Alexa."

He moved past Patrick and Carla and headed back to the conference room, which would soon be in use. He grabbed his stack of papers, and the manuscript, and led Alexa to his office. Once inside, he guided her to the small table, placed the stack of papers on the table and pulled out a chair for her, which got him a whiff of that peach and strawberry smell of her's as she moved to sit.

God, she smelled delicious. He reined in his desire and made his way over to the chair, right beside her. He pulled out a single sheet of paper from the stack. "These are the people I want you to contact, stay in touch with. The list is short, but that doesn't mean I am unsure of your abilities, what I also want from you is to focus on scouting out new and upcoming talent, reach out to them when you find them, work with them."

"Okay, where do you want me to find this new talent?" Her gaze collided with his.

"Anywhere you can think of, this is your project," Dom answered, smiling.

"Why are you searching for new talent? I mean, you're already flourishing and at the top for reputation and everything."

"I want to give new talent an opportunity to blossom and to have a chance."

Her eyes darted to his. "Like you did with me?"

"Brandon gave you your chance, you're obviously great, or you wouldn't have been working for my rival. I am just helping you spread your wings, see what else is out there and find out if you like doing this kind of thing. I think you will and that you have what it takes," he answered calmly.

Her hand went to that scar of hers, he reached his hand out to stop her. "Alexa, you won't let me down, I know it."

"What if I do, though?"

"Then, we try again," he answered simply.

"Okay," she replied, some of her courage restored, and they continued to go over everything.

As the afternoon slipped to almost evening, Dom stood and stretched his long limbs and tall body. His gaze still lingered on Alexa. She was so beautiful, especially the way she bit her full pouty bottom lip or pursed those lips together when she was deep in thought. "We can call it a night, Alexa," Dom said softly as she continued to work.

He laughed a bit when she kept going over things on the table, he leaned down next to her and pulled the papers and tablet from her.

"Hey!" she cried out and looked up, their lips inches away from each other.

All he wanted to do was turn slightly and move forward a little more, and he could get a taste of those delicious looking lips. "Come on, Alexa, let me take you home, we've done enough for today."

"It's okay, I can walk. I have to stop by BAP before I go home and drop off that last manuscript." Her voice sent tingles along his body. She would be a great seductress. She was already doing it to him without trying.

Neither one of them moved away from each other. He dipped his head a little more when he saw her eyes flick to his lips. "All the more reason for me to take you. We'll stop at BAP, drop off the manuscript to Brandon, then I can take you to supper, and afterwards I can drop you off at home."

She nodded her head in agreement.

All he wanted to do was get a little taste of her. He was so close. He dipped his head, about to succeed when his office door flew open, and he jerked back away from her.

"Nicky, I've found someone perfect, she'll blow you out of the water!" Carla's high-pitched voice exclaimed in excitement.

Dom turned from Alexa and glared at Carla.

"Oh, I'm sorry I didn't know she was still here," Carla said, her dim green eyes narrowed as they landed on Alexa.

Alexa scrambled to get everything into her computer bag and stood up quickly. "I was just getting ready to leave," she muttered, and made a break for the door.

"Alexa, wait," Dom called after her, but she kept on walking. His eyes hardened as he looked at Carla. "I don't want anyone else, Carla, she's going to do great, and she's who I want."

The argument began after his last statement.

---

Alexa couldn't leave fast enough. She sat there like an idiot, and she almost let him kiss her. That couldn't happen. No way. No how. He wasn't right for her, and she wouldn't be good for him or any other man. She had to give him respect as her boss, but that was all.

No more giving information about what he wanted to know if it had nothing to do with publishing, or any other part of the job.

She made her way to BAP as quickly as possible. She pushed open the door when she finally arrived and almost ran to Brandon's office. She barely gave him time to answer before she walked in.

He turned around behind the desk to face her, he stood up immediately. "Alexa, what's the matter?" He reached her and brought her to the chair in front of his desk, as he sat down on top of it.

---

"You are not the boss here, Carla. If I tell you I don't want someone else then that is what it means. I want Alexandra Mills, and she will be staying here, end of story!" he shouted, grabbed his suit jacket, and left his office. He scanned the spacious lobby, no sign of Alexa anywhere. Shit. He rushed to his blue twenty-sixteen Camaro and got in, making his way toward BAP. He hoped she was there.

Alexa sat in the chair, staring blankly at the floor. She almost screwed up, she almost let him in, almost let Dominick Mackenzie, the playboy, kiss her. She read the thought in his eyes, and she didn't stop him.

She couldn't bring herself to tell Brandon what she had almost let happen. She began to finger the scar again.

Brandon didn't know what to do. He hadn't seen her this upset in a while. He got off his desk and crouched down in front of her. He placed his hands on her knees. "Darling, tell me what happened, did someone hurt you?"

In a way someone had hurt her, Carla smashed her feelings of hope. She had to pull herself together, but Carla was worse than Sandra, especially for it being her first day on the job. She nodded her head but choked a little, trying to hold back the tears.

Everything came flying back, all the hits, the negative sayings from her birth father.

Brandon patted her back a little. "Did it happen at MAEP?"

She jerked her head in an answer.

"Hold on, honey. I'll be right back." He kissed her forehead and rushed to the break room to get her a bottle of water. As he walked out of the break room, he froze when he saw the tall man shove open the main door quickly.

Dominick Mackenzie, in the flesh, was walking through his building. Blood boiled through Brandon and he confronted Dom before Dom made it to his office.

"What'd you do to my poor sweet Lex?" Brandon demanded, glaring up at the younger man. Only being five-seven, he had to tilt his head up a bit but wasn't backing down from the jerk.

Dom held his hands up, fingers splayed in a nonthreatening manner. "Is she here, Brandon? I need to talk to her."

"What did you do to my girl?" Brandon demanded, glaring at Dom.

"It wasn't me, honestly. Carla came in while Alexa and I were working, she was spouting her mouth off negatively about Alexa. She didn't know Alexa was there and before I could say anything Alexa took off, I already put Carla in her place," Dom explained. "Please, can I talk to her?"

Brandon could see the sincerity in his eyes and heard it in his voice. Brandon looked him over once more, then motioned to his office and led the way inside.

He took a deep breath as he opened the door, and walked over to Alexa and laid a hand on her shoulder. "Sweetheart, someone wants to talk to you."

As soon as he finished trying to prepare Alexa, Dom came over and crouched down in front of her. "Brandon, can we have a minute?"

Brandon waited for Alexa to look up at him, his brown eyes locked with her shadowed filled eyes. "Is that okay with you, sweetie?"

Her eyes darted from him to Dom, then back again, but she nodded her head. He gently squeezed her shoulder. "Okay, I'm close by if you need me, don't ever forget that." He walked out of his office to wait.

## Chapter 3

Dom's heart finally slowed down the minute his eyes landed on Alexa and shoved away the need he had to paddle her rounded ass for taking off the way she had – alone and in the dark – but grief sliced through him when he saw the pain in her eyes and her stroking that scar on her arm continuously.

He heard the door shut before he began, but she wouldn't look at him, so he placed his forefinger beneath her chin gently. Their eyes met. "I am so sorry about Carla, I set her straight, she shouldn't be bothering you anymore. You can do this, Alexa. I believe in you. If I didn't, I wouldn't have taken over the interview as soon as you sat down in front of me. I want you at MAEP and what I say goes, okay?"

Her eyes moved slowly as she looked into his, but pulled away. He made her look at him again. "It's more than Carla, isn't it?" he asked softly. "I'm sorry I almost kissed you, it won't happen again. You don't want someone like me anyway, my reputation is not spotless, and I am sorry I tried to make a move on you."

Alexa tugged that bottom lip of hers in between her white teeth.

He felt the desire start to rise again. No, he couldn't do this, she wouldn't be happy with a couple of times, if that. She'd want more. He pulled that tempting lip from between her teeth then rubbed his thumb against her chin. "I promise, Alexa, I really am sorry. I don't want you to leave MAEP yet, I need you there."

She nodded her head a little.

---

Alexa felt terrible for running out, but she hadn't known what else to do. She didn't want verbal abuse from anyone ever again; maybe it had been a mistake taking the job. But she had to try, she couldn't just throw the opportunity away. "I'm sorry," she whispered.

Dom brushed her chin again with the pad of his thumb making it heat up under his touch, then he squeezed her knee with his other hand. "Not your place to apologize, the fault is all mine. I didn't even take the chance to find out if you were taken before I even came that close to kissing you. Come on, let me take you to dinner then home." He stood, grabbing her computer bag, he plucked out the manuscript that needed to go to Brandon.

He held out his hand to her, and she placed hers in his slowly, could she really keep her heart from getting hurt because of this man? Just the feeling of his hand on hers made her whole body tingle.

Then again, tonight proved she could never deal with getting yelled at or treated as cruelly as Carla had treated her. She was safe in her own world. It was for the best.

She let Dom take her toward the office door, she locked

eyes with Brandon right away and pulled her hand from Dom's. She didn't want Brandon to think anything was going on between herself and Dom.

Alexa stared at the floor after pulling away from Dom. Then she heard Brandon say, "I want to talk to you before you take her home." She looked up at Brandon, confused. Why would he talk to Dom before they left? And how did he know Dom was taking her home?

Dom touched her shoulder, and she looked up at him. "Don't leave without me this time, Alexa, I'll be right back."

"Okay." She headed over to a white cushioned dark chair in the lobby to wait.

Dom hated himself as he watched Alexa move. The only way he was going to be able to keep his lips, hands and other central body part away from her was distancing himself from her. He supposed that was what he was going to have to do.

Brandon nudged his shoulder, then motioned toward his office.

They walked in, Dom shut the door. "What's up, Brandon?"

"Dom, I've known your father for a long time, so in turn, I have known you for a long time, I know what your reputation is. I've already asked her to be careful around you, she deserves better."

"Couldn't agree more, Brandon. Tonight will be the last interaction I will have with her for the most part. I kept her way too late tonight, so I am taking her to dinner before I take her home, nothing else, though."

Brandon nodded his head. "She puts up a brave front, and she can come off as one hell of a spitfire, but inside she is still a scared little girl. I never expected her to be treated so horribly in your agency, if I had had an inkling of that happening, I would have talked her out of it. I know Carla can be difficult, but a woman like Lex needs to be treated with some caution and fairly."

Dom ran his tongue between his teeth and lips. "Like I said, I dealt with Carla. She'll back off. If not, she will not have a job anymore."

"She'll do great work for you, Dom, she just needs to be given a chance to prove herself. I hated to lose her to you, but I also feel she is ready for more. I wouldn't have let her go if I didn't feel that way."

Dom sat down in the chair. "She tells me you are like the father she never had, but her parents didn't divorce until she was fifteen, what do you know about that?"

Brandon's face and brown eyes hardened a little. "I can only tell you I broke that asshole's nose once, and it wasn't even close to what he deserved. Just make sure there are no more instances of Lex getting verbally attacked by Carla."

"You won't tell me more?" Dom asked, almost pleading.

"No, Dom, I'm sorry, it's her story to tell. If she wants you to know she will tell you." Brandon's body relaxed a little.

Dom stood up. "Okay. Oh, she wanted to bring this to you tonight. That's how I knew she was here." He handed Brandon the stack of papers.

"Oh, she finished it?"

"This morning before work, before I even got there to unlock the office, she was outside waiting."

"You're not mad at her for finishing this for me, right?"

"Of course not, it showed her loyalty to finish a job, and I told her so. I'll try to take better care of her, Brandon. You love her like a daughter, don't you?"

"Yes I do, ever since the first time we talked for hours

about her going in to editorial as a career, among other things."

"Then, I have to work harder, so you don't break my nose." Dom smiled, then headed out. She was still sitting in the chair he had left her in when he went in with Brandon.

What had happened to make her this way and had made Brandon break her father's nose? But he had to distance himself so he'd probably never know.

"Are you ready for dinner?" Dom asked as he got closer to her.

"You really don't have to, Mr. Mackenzie. I'd be perfectly fine with going home." Her voice was less seductive and less soft.

"My treat, Alexa. I kept you late tonight, so this is my repayment for you being such a trooper today, come on, please?" He held his hand out to her pleading, but she didn't take it and stood on her own. He dropped his hand, but stuck close to her as they walked out of BAP.

He led her to his Camaro and opened the passenger door for her. He needed a little more time with her before he pushed himself out of her bubble as much as possible. He was glad when she sunk into his car instead of taking off to go home.

He went around to his side, trying to push the image of her creamy smooth legs out of his mind. Not being around her would be difficult, but he'd do it for her. He didn't know what all he could actually give her. She needed the happily ever after that he didn't believe in anymore.

The drive was painfully silent, and the car was too dark to see her face, so he couldn't even guess what was going through her mind.

He couldn't help the grin that played on his lips as he pulled up in front of the five-star restaurant, Machello's. Yeah, she deserved this after this evening.

She grabbed his jacket sleeve as he went to get out. "Mr. Mackenzie, I'm not going in there, it's too fancy for someone like me."

"Sweetheart, nothing is too fancy for someone like you. Honestly, you will make this place fancy. Everything is drab compared to you," Dom reassured her squeezing her hand.

Her eyes were round. The confusion was written all over her face as he opened his car door, and the light popped on. He reached a hand out to her cheek, but she cringed away from his touch a little, but he kept going and softly cupped her cheek. "Don't be afraid of me, Alexa, everything is going to be okay." He rubbed his thumb over her bottom lip, making her lips part a little. "Let's go have a very nice supper." He got out of the car and walked around to her side and helped her out. As he shut the door, he pulled her close to him. One last night to touch her this close and this much, and by God, he was going to do it.

As he walked in, the maître d' hurried up to them. "Mr. Mackenzie, good evening, what a surprise, the usual seating?"

"Yes, that's fine," Dom answered and pulled Alexa more into his body as the maître d' glued his eyes to her. "As little interruption as possible, as well."

The man nodded his head. "Of course, Mr. Mackenzie, right this way." He gestured as he grabbed two menus.

They followed him to a secluded area of the restaurant that was lit by mainly candlelight. The typical soft setting he liked to enjoy when he was out eating.

"Two glasses of wine, red and an order of your breadsticks as well. We'll need a little bit to look over the menu for our meal, though," Dom began, he caught Alexa staring at him as he ordered. "Is that okay with you?"

She barely nodded her head.

Dom dismissed the maître d' and gazed at Alexa. "Are you really that mad at me?"

"No, Mr. Mackenzie, I just don't understand why you're doing this."

"Well, I like your company, and you deserve a good supper, and I don't want to lose you and your talent due to my arrogant asshole ways and Carla's bitchy ways."

"Oh." She fell silent again.

"So what's the deal with your real father? Must be pretty bad for Brandon to have broken his nose once." Dom gazed at her from the other side of the table, wishing he could be right beside her.

She glanced at him. "He told you about that?" She turned red and looked away quickly.

"I asked a little bit about him being a father to you and asked what happened to your real dad, he told me he broke his nose once, but that wasn't even close to what should have happened to him, so what's the story?"

She shrugged her shoulders. "He made Brandon upset."

"How?"

"He was a jerk." Alexa glanced back up at him. Her eyes shadowed again with pain and pleading for him to change the conversation.

He moved to the seat right beside her, and laid his hand on hers. "Well, he doesn't know what a great girl he is missing out on, totally his loss."

---

Alexa stared at Dom, he was wrong and couldn't have a chance at being right, he knew nothing about her. "You don't know that," she whispered.

"I've spent most of my day with you. I'm usually a good judge of character, and I've discovered you are amazing, hard-working, and adorable when you are deep in thought." His thumb brushed against her hand.

She looked up into his eyes and smiled slightly, unable to fight it.

She was in so much trouble with this man. She could let her guard down with him, but would that be a horrible idea?

## Chapter 4

"I can't shake him from keeping that useless bimbo. She's going to drown the company, we needed someone experienced, but she is not. The minute she fell into the conference room Dom was instantly smitten with her, I don't get what he sees in her." Carla was with Patrick at Machello's. "He actually yelled at me today, like really yelled at me. I haven't seen him that angry in a very long time."

Patrick dug his fingers through his blond hair making it stick up in places. "I don't know what's gotten into him. I mean she's pretty, I guess, but she's not stunning like his usual type. She wasn't that impressive during the interview, and it sucks I can't do anything about it. I don't have a say like he does, I am so tired of being below him when he's younger, I have more experience and have given so much to MAEP, but I can't do anything. Anything we say, he'll just overrun us and do what he wants anyway."

Carla's dim green eyes met his brown eyes, they had such different goals, but she had to get him on her side. "I think with her attitude problem it'll be easy to get rid of her, due to insubordination, we make her so angry she'll snap."

"It's a possibility…" Patrick began, but froze when he saw two people walk past them. "Or it may not work."

Carla turned, and there they were, close together, and Dom had his hand on Alexa's waist. They looked so weird together because of the class difference and height difference.

That couldn't happen. She'd make sure of it, and she'd get Patrick to see it would indeed work. Alexandra Mills would be nothing but a memory at MAEP.

## Chapter 5

A lexa had relaxed after her third glass of wine. Being tucked up against his tall, hard body felt amazing as they walked out of Machello's.

She let him lead her out to his car. He opened the door for her. She managed to get in without making a fool of herself. She settled in her seat and snapped her seatbelt on as her eyes stayed glued to Dom as he walked around the front of the car and got in.

---

Dom looked at her as he got in the car. The wine had relaxed her some, and he liked it, she wasn't as cold, but if she would have drunk even just a little more, he would have had to intervene. He liked his women to act a certain way and getting drunk was not one of them. He froze his thoughts instantly, she wasn't his woman but he couldn't help wanting to instill how he wanted her to act. He almost reached out to lay his hand on her knee but stopped. He put it on the gearshift instead and began to pull out of the parking lot. "Where am I going?"

She told him the address, and he headed towards it. Close to his office, his ass. It was like fifteen blocks, at least. He sighed as he pulled up to the curb in front of the gray duplex. Surely she could do better than this place, why would she stay in a slummy neighborhood like this? It was barely safe for her to take the trash to the curb after dark. He wanted to take her across his knee, thinking about her wandering out here at night by herself and walking to his office.

As she went to get out, he placed a hand on her knee this time. "Alexa, I can pick you up in the morning and drop you off after work if you'd like me to." His tone did not match how he was feeling at all.

She turned in her seat to look at him. "It's okay, Dom, I can manage. I do my best thinking when I walk, so it's okay. Thank you for dinner, Dom, I appreciate it," she said quietly.

Their eyes locked and he was sure he had a stupid smile on his face, she didn't call him Mr. Mackenzie, how long would that last?

But she was smiling back at him softly and leaning toward him. He moved his other hand to cup her cheek, rubbing her cheek with the pad of his thumb. The tension and chemistry were so prominent between them. He moved a little closer but was going to let her come to him the rest of the way. Even while his brain was yelling at him that this was a terrible idea and wasn't what he was looking for at all. She was too delicate to be drawn into his world.

She laid her hand on top of his and was so close to sealing their lips when all of a sudden a knock fell on the passenger window.

They jerked apart, and the door was flung open. Alexa was yanked from the car. She let out a startled gasp. "Dad?"

Dom got out of the car fast and was around the hood in

four strides. He pushed his way between Alexa and the man who pulled her out of his car.

———

Alexa couldn't believe he would show up now of all times. She thought her father, Tate Mills, had left her alone for good, but here he was in the flesh. A bit wrinkled, the same hard brown eyes she grew up with. His black hair streaked with gray. She hadn't heard from him in months and even when she did, it was only because he needed money.

"Um, excuse you, I'm Tate, and I need to have a word with my daughter, then you're free to use her any way you'd like." Tate glared at Dom.

She didn't know what to do, she stepped between the two men. "What do you want?" she demanded through gritted teeth as she glared at the man who gave the sperm that created her.

"Now, is that any way to greet your old dad?" He gripped her chin harshly. "Some respect from you would be a nice change, but I won't hold my breath," he snarled out.

Dom reached out and gripped Tate's wrist and squeezed hard, making him let go of her.

Alexa laid her hand on his arm. "Mr. Mackenzie, don't, it's fine, I'll handle this. You can go," she said firmly.

"The Mackenzie, from the publishing company?" Tate asked. "Finally, able to bed a real man who can actually pay you pretty well, looks like I stopped by just in time."

Alexa turned to spout off to Tate but was met with a harsh slap, but she stood her ground. "How much did you drink tonight?"

"Not enough to drown you out." Tate glared hard at Alexa.

Dom threw out his fist and slammed it into Tate's nose, hard. Now he saw what Brandon was talking about. "Get the hell out of here. Don't come near her again, or I will call the cops." He pushed Alexa behind him away from Tate, daring the older man to try to hurt Alexa again in front of him.

He felt her shift behind him and saw her hand over a small wad of cash. He reached out to stop her, but she grabbed his arm tightly.

"Here, two hundred, that's all I have right now, please just take it and go," Alexa said quietly.

Dom watched Tate snatch the money from her hand and take off. He turned to Alexa when the asshole was far enough away. He laid his hands on her arms. "He was an abuser." He looked into her eyes, but she looked away from him.

His fingers went to the scar on her arm. "Did he do that to you?"

She didn't answer, but bit her bottom lip.

Dom rubbed her arms. "Did he?" he asked softly.

She nodded her head a little.

He pulled her into his arms to hug her, but she stepped away from him. He didn't know what to do or what she would want him to do. "Alexa?" he questioned as she moved away. If he wanted her in his life, this was going to be a rough hurdle to attempt to get over.. He slowly scanned her face and body, she wasn't looking good to him at all.

"Please, Mr. Mackenzie, just go home. Thank you, again for the wonderful dinner. I'll be at MAEP tomorrow."

"Alexa," he tried again, as she stepped away from him and walked up to her house and rushed inside. He leaned back against his car. He could go after her, but that would just make her afraid of him, and he wasn't the right man for the job either. "Alexa," he whispered as the door shut loudly, the sound was a statement, shutting him and the world out of her life.

What was he going to do? He knew he wasn't what she needed, but he wanted to be, for some stupid reason. He made a step toward the house, then rushed up the steps, and knocked on her door.

---

Alexa broke down into tears as soon as she shut the door. She was leaning against it, unable to make her legs move, her arms wrapped around herself tightly trying to hold herself together, when she heard the loud knock that made her jump. She was afraid to open the door, what if Tate came back? He would be furious after Dom punched him in the face.

"Alexa, open the door." Dom's voice sounded muffled from the other side of the door.

She sighed and turned to open it. "Mr. Mackenzie, please just go home," she pleaded.

He somehow managed to squeeze himself in through the slightly opened door. "Not yet," he whispered as he shut and locked the door. He scooped her up into his arms and headed over to the couch, where the entry to her home opened up into the small living room.

He took her shoes off the minute he sat down with her in his lap.

She tried to fight him, but the tears began again as he wrapped his arms back around her. "It's okay, Lex, just let it out."

---

She buried her head against his shoulder and let it all out, unable to hold back anymore. She tightened her arms around

Dom's neck as she comfortably curled up into his lap and arms. She cried hard, just like every other time after a confrontation with Tate.

Surprisingly, Dom just held her and rubbed her back gently. His other hand stroked her thigh. "It's okay, Lex, it's okay," he said soothingly.

She curled up into him more, shaking her head. It wasn't okay to be losing herself in her boss' arms. She only met him yesterday and started working for him today, and he already took her to lunch and dinner and found out about her dad. Everything was falling apart around her. It couldn't get much worse than this.

---

Dom didn't know what to do for the poor woman in his arms, so he held her close. She was so tiny she fit almost completely in the cocoon of his body. He just held her and rubbed her body gently as she cried on his shoulder. This wasn't distancing himself, but after seeing her *father* hit her, he knew he couldn't do that right now.

He would pick her up in the morning and drop her off after work. Hell, he'd be her chauffeur on the weekends if she'd let him. He couldn't leave her to her *father's* violence anymore. He just hoped he wouldn't hurt her emotionally any more than she already was.

Dom squeezed her thigh gently. "Where's your bedroom?" he asked softly.

She jerked back from him so fast that if he hadn't been holding her, she would have fallen from his lap.

"Hey, easy, not for that reason. I was going to take you and draw you a bath, let you have another glass of wine, then tuck you in." His hand moved up her thigh, over her side, and arm then cupped her cheek. "Is that okay?" he asked softly, even though he didn't want her to get drunk, but she deserved one more tonight.

"I don't have any wine," she admitted, looking away from him.

"Hey, it's okay, how about just the bath then?" he suggested calmly.

The only thing he could get out of her was a shoulder shrug. He let out a sigh, and stood up with her cuddled close to his body. "Come on." He found the only bedroom and walked into the bathroom that was off from her bedroom. He placed her on top of the vanity. He turned the water on to let it warm up, then pushed the stopper into the drain.

Dom turned back to Alexa. He saw the horrible red mark where Tate had slapped her, he walked over to the closet and pulled out some lavender smelling bubble bath. He began to pour it in.

"No!" Alexa shouted. "I can't use that!"

Dom turned to look at her. "Lex, what's wrong?" He couldn't help but let the nickname slip out again, he just thought it was adorable when Brandon called her it. He wanted to see if she would let him call her it too.

"He hates that smell. I can't use it." She jumped off the vanity top, walked up to Dom, and tried to grab it from him quickly.

He pulled it back from her and grabbed her wrists with one of his hands. "Honey, look at me, do you like it?"

Her head snapped up, and her eyes moved slightly as she looked into his. "It doesn't matter."

"Yes, it does. Do you like it?" he asked gently.

She nodded her head a little.

"Then that's what matters. He won't hurt you anymore, I'll make sure of it." Dom just didn't know if he could protect her from himself.

Alexa looked at him, narrowing her eyes a little. "You're not going to be able to keep him from doing anything."

"That's where you're wrong, I have plenty of resources, and I will use them to keep him from you, he will not touch you again." He set the bottle down on the back of the toilet then shut off the water. "Why don't you get in the tub, while I go make some calls real quick." He brushed his thumb against her bottom lip softly.

The feel of his thumb against her skin made goosebumps rise along her flesh. She shivered a little as he walked past her and shut the door lightly. She made sure he wasn't coming back in, then unbuttoned her shirt, unfastened her bra and skirt, and got into the tub. The water was just right. How did this man know exactly what she wanted?

———

Dom paced the floor in the bedroom as he made a call. "I need around the clock protection for this woman, okay maybe not around the clock, she'll be with me at MAEP at least eight hours out of the day Monday thru Friday. So sixteen hours' worth during those five days but twenty-four hours Saturday and Sundays. I don't care what the cost is, just do it. And dig up as much as you can on a Tate Mills. The job starts tonight, she's at her apartment, and learn his face, he doesn't come near her ever again." He hung up the phone and sat on the bed, staring at the bathroom door.

She'd hate being looked after like this, but it was for the best, and he'd try to make it so she didn't know what was going on. It was becoming all clear why she was in a dump, didn't have a car, and pretended to be okay and happy with this life. That bastard wouldn't get another penny of her money. He'd make sure of it.

He heard water move and her body as she obviously

shifted in the tub. What he wouldn't give to be in there holding her. He ran his hands over his face, he felt so drained all of a sudden.

He could only imagine how Alexa felt. He sighed as he fell back on the bed, his feet still touched the floor, and his head was barely on the bed. It was ridiculous how much she went without. He'd give her so much she didn't have, but deserved, if he could find a way to give her forever.

He heard the water move again as he stared up at the ceiling. If he had known what she'd been through all of her life he probably wouldn't have brought her on at MAEP. She'd put up such an attitude toward the blonde bimbo he thought she was like that all the time.

Dom lay there thinking how he could get her to trust him and believe he wasn't intentionally going to hurt her. Even though the possibility was there that he would. He had to keep reminding himself he didn't do serious relationships. It was better that way, and she needed serious. He let out a rough sigh and ran his hands over his face and raked them through his black hair. What was he going to do?

He heard the knob turn on the bathroom door, and he turned his head. His stupid body reacted instantly. She was in only a towel, even with her being so tiny it barely made it down her thighs. It clung to her pale skin like he wanted to do. His member strained against his slacks even more.

"I'm sorry," she whispered as she stared at the ground. "I have to get clothes."

Dom sighed, as he sat up. "Alexa, come here for a moment, please?" His gaze followed her every move as she walked toward him slowly. She stepped in front of him. "Yes, Mr. Mackenzie?"

He chuckled, shaking his head, he laid his hands on her bare thighs and pulled her closer to him. "You never have to apologize to me, especially in your own home, okay?" Which wasn't entirely true, he would expect an apology if she acted out or took risks that weren't necessary.

"O-okay," she stuttered out then pulled her bottom lip between her teeth.

The action made his body tighten even more, what he wouldn't give to pull her on the bed with him and make love to her all night, until her skin glowed from pleasure. Make love? He didn't do that. This woman had him all sorts of fucked up. He would prefer her to be tied down below him as he pleasured her, but that wasn't what she deserved.

Dom's thumbs slowly brushed against Alexa's bare thighs. The next thing he knew, she climbed onto his lap, laying her head on his shoulder. He took a deep breath. The lavender scent on her invaded him. It smelled so good on her just as good as the peaches and strawberries.

He turned his head into her neck. His lips brushed her skin. He was in deep shit.

Alexa took in a deep breath when she felt the brush of Dom's lips on her neck. Goosebumps rose against her skin, she didn't know what possessed her to sit in his lap, practically naked, but she felt safe in his arms. His hands roamed up her back a little and didn't stop until they were on her exposed skin above the towel.

She let out a little moan at the feel of his fingers against her skin.

"Alexa, you should get dressed, then we can talk, okay?"

"About what?" she asked as she pulled back from him a little, the movement made her sink in his lap a little more and she let out a gasp when she felt a bulge of hardness beneath the material of his dress pants.

"About a lot, I think." He reached down to the small of her back and pulled her closer to him, getting her away from the hardness beneath her.

She gazed at him for a moment, was he like that for her or

45

was he thinking of someone else as he'd lay on her bed? Surely, it couldn't be because of her.

His hand came up to her cheek. His fingertips brushed against the bruise that was now showing up. She drew her lip back between her teeth.

"I wish you wouldn't do that right now." His voice laced with want, his eyes clouded with desire.

She let go of her lip. "I'll get dressed," she whispered. She climbed out of Dom's lap and went to the dresser finding a pair of sweat pants and a baggy t-shirt. She scurried to the bathroom to get dressed.

What was it about this man that she felt so safe? But he couldn't keep her that way nor would he, he was a player, a different woman every night and this was just the same to him only she'd be the different woman, and that's not what was going to happen. She would not give in to the man, she'd stay strong. Like she always did and put on her mask of no pain.

She got dressed then walked out of the bathroom. "You can go, Mr. Mackenzie, I'm fine, and there's nothing to talk about. I need to get to bed, early day tomorrow and for you too."

"There's plenty to talk about, Lex."

"No there's not, nothing out of the ordinary happened, it's my life, my business, and it doesn't concern you. I'll be fine, I just want to go to bed now." She met his eyes; urging him to go was for the best.

Dom stood up from the bed, the tent in his pants still noticeable, but she tried to keep her gaze on his eyes instead. "Okay fine, Alexa. Get some sleep, I'll be here in the morning to pick you up."

"That's not necessary, Mr. Mackenzie, I can handle myself."

"It is necessary, goodnight, Lex." He headed out of the room, but before he went out the door, he stuffed two hundred dollars into her purse since she had given it to Tate to leave her alone. He closed the house door slowly.

Alexa rushed to the door as he finally shut it and began to lock the deadbolt, chain and door lock. She let out a shaky breath, grabbed her purse and headed to her room. Great, just great, now he was going to act like a baby sitter. She didn't need anyone, and it would stay that way.

She got into the small, lonely bed, and began to fall asleep.

## Chapter 6

Dom did as he promised, he went to pick Alexa up from her place.

He watched her walk out of the house, she started to walk down the sidewalk like she didn't even see his car. He quickly checked his side mirror then got out. "Alexa!" he shouted as he rushed over to her. She looked so beautiful in another black skirt that didn't flow out like the day before and an aqua silk blouse, and her heels matched the blouse. Today she had her hair pulled up into a tight ponytail and was wearing a pair of square-framed glasses with multiple shades of purple.

Wow, she even looked sexy with glasses on instead of nerdy. He smiled at her as she turned around. She wasn't smiling back.

"What are you doing here, Mr. Mackenzie?" she demanded, crossing her arms over her breasts tightly.

"I came to pick you up like I said I would." He rolled his eyes, a little upset with her. "Come on, Lex, for me, so I know you're safe," he added when she didn't move.

She shook her head at him but made her way over to him. "You really don't have to do this."

He reached his hand out and wrapped his arm around her waist.. "Yes, I do, I need to keep my investment safe," he teased.

"Investment?" She looked at him, frowning.

"I'm teasing, Lex. I may be an asshole, sometimes yell at people a little louder than I should, and not have a spotless reputation. But I can care about people, there are very few, but you are definitely one of the few." He turned towards the car and led Alexa over to it.

He opened the door for her. "So are you ready to officially start being on your own today?"

"I'm sure I can handle it," she whispered as she opened her purse to pull out her phone. As soon as she dug in to get her phone, her hand touched a stack of papers instead, she pulled it out. "Dom, what is this?" She held up the money.

She watched his eyes dart over then back to the road. "What's what?"

"What's this money doing in my purse?" She narrowed her gaze on him.

"Honestly, I don't know, how much is there?"

"Two hundred," Alexa answered after she counted it. "The exact amount I gave to Tate last night."

He just shrugged his shoulders and continued to drive.

"Dom, I can't take this." She went to hand it to him, but he pushed it back toward her. "Dom, seriously."

"Just take it, Lex, it'll be our little secret, no one will know but me and you, I promise." He smiled at her and laid a hand on her thigh, and he continued to head to work. "And you don't have to put on the brave face with me either. I want you to trust me, Lex."

She sighed and laid her hand on his. "Small steps, Dom, can't have it all at once."

"Well, so far, only Mr. Mackenzie once, so it's a start, and I'll take it." He smiled at her.

Her heart skipped a beat when he smiled at her, he didn't move his hand from her thigh, and she didn't move her hand from his.

She took a deep breath as she leaned her head back against the headrest.

"What's wrong?" Dom's deep voice flowed over her like a lover's caress.

"Just a little tired is all. I didn't sleep too well last night." Between the past creeping into her dreams and Dom, it had been a little challenging to get any sleep.

"Want to talk about it?"

She thought about it for a moment then shook her head. "No, that's okay." She heard him sigh, but he didn't say another word.

He was quite angry when he saw the bruise had darkened overnight. He wanted Tate found and dealt with. He had meant to ask her how often she gave him money to go away but also didn't want to push her into telling him things she wasn't ready for. Like she said, one step at a time, day by day, things would get better, and as soon as Tate made another move to try to hurt her, he would have the man locked away so fast he wouldn't be able to say the word two hundred.

Once they got to the office, Dom showed Alexa where she could set up her own space.

"Okay, I'll let you get to work. If you need anything just let me know." He squeezed her shoulder, then headed to his office. He wanted to spend the rest of the day with her but knew if he did, he wouldn't get any work done.

Alexa watched Dom walk away. She couldn't believe she

let herself call him Dom instead of Mr. Mackenzie, she could have smacked herself in the head, but she decided it was pointless.

She sat down in the chair behind her desk and began to get her notebook, pen and tablet out of her bag. *'Well, here goes nothing,'* she thought. She started her search on Apps and websites for new writers who deserved to have a chance like she'd been given.

The early morning slipped into late morning, and unfortunately, she hadn't found much that stuck out in her brain. She covered her face with her hands after sliding her glasses to the top of her head. Why was no one sticking out in her mind? She was already letting Dom down.

She let out a little aggravated groan. Then someone came in and leaned against her desk. She looked up, expecting Dom, but no, it was Carla instead. *'Great.'*

"Is the job taking its toll on you already? Just because you may have slept with Nicky doesn't mean your job is secure." The woman glared at Alexa, no life in her eyes at all.

"Really?" Alexa began sarcastically, "I didn't know that. I thought employee performance was based on looks only, huh, good thing I don't sleep with my bosses nor do I plan to nor want to."

Alexa glared back at Carla and stood. "And for someone who's in HR, you aren't very perceptive of people, and you don't treat them very well. Or is it just me because Dom went against your wishes and hired me? You really should work on your people skills, or better yet stop being crazy about a man who clearly does not want you." She leaned over and grabbed her purse and headed out of the room that was supposed to be *hers*. She needed some caffeine. And quick.

She was used to spouting off to Sandra and a few others at BAP but never an HR manager, Carla was just as bad as Sandra though, if not worse. She pushed her glasses back down onto her nose and headed out of the office to get some coffee. Maybe once she got some caffeine in her, more ideas would come. She headed down the sidewalk toward the Starbucks that was a couple of blocks over.

---

Dom's stomach growled as he ended the meeting he had scheduled with Patrick and a prominent client, Angela Lane, she was definitely one of their most popular clients.

As the three said their goodbyes and went their separate ways, Dom headed to where he left Alexa earlier that morning. As soon as he saw she was gone, dread fell around him. He yanked out his phone and began to call her. "Where are you?" he demanded, almost shouting into the phone.

"Umm, Starbucks?" she answered in a questioning tone.

"You stay there. I'm coming to get you." He ended the call and headed to his Camaro. He got in and flew to the Starbucks closest to his office. He couldn't believe she had taken off without talking to him first. Why didn't she understand he cared about her and her safety?

One of these days she was going to understand, even if he had to pull her across his knee and turn her ass red. He'd be calm and worried for her, completely different than what Tate used to do to her.

He whipped into a parking spot and rushed into the coffee shop. He scanned the crowd of people. Finally, his eyes landed on her, sitting in a corner alone. He made his way through the people and finally got to her table.

She looked up at him right before he yanked her up from her chair and pulled her against him. "Don't ever do that again," he whispered roughly against her ear.

She tilted her head up to look at him. "Do what exactly?"

"Take off like that without telling me. I would have

brought you, and I would have known where you were and that you were safe." He stopped hugging her and framed her face gently in his hands. "Don't forget I care, Alexandra, more than I should, but I do care."

"It's not good to care about me, Dom, not good at all. It's already starting things at work with Carla, and I've only spent three days there and the first day was only an interview. I'll just drag you down. You don't have to care, I have been taking care of myself for a while now, I'm okay to do things by myself, and I can't stop living just because he came back to town to get money."

His thumbs brushed her slightly reddened cheeks. "Well, it's too late for me not to care, and I don't give a damn what Carla says. I'm sorry, I don't want you at the mercy of your father ever again, he's done enough to you to last you three lifetimes," he reassured.

"It doesn't hurt anymore nor does it last as long. And I do care about work, I'm not really liking the idea of everyone thinking I have my job, or can keep it, because I'm sleeping with my boss." She pulled her face out of the gentle grip he had on her cheeks.

"But we haven't slept together. Hell, I haven't even kissed you yet, even though every time I look at you I want to."

"Well, don't, Dom. Now can we go back to work since I've had my caffeine pick me up?"

"How about lunch first, then we head back?" he suggested, instead of ordered.

She rolled her eyes and huffed. "Fine." She left Starbucks and made her way to his car.

He followed after her bouncing, wiggling ass, his eyes glued to it and thinking about turning it red after that eye roll. He shook his head clearing the thought and began to think on other things. So people thought he'd picked her because he was attracted to her. They weren't entirely wrong. But it wasn't the only reason, and why people didn't see that reason was beyond him.

He got in on the driver's side and groaned when his phone began to ring. "Mackenzie," he answered dryly.

Alexa was watching him as he talked.

He glanced over at her. "Oh really, she did, huh?" He raised an eyebrow at her, which made her redden and look away quickly. "I'll deal with it, Carla. No, you will not, I said I'd handle it. I'll be back at the office within the hour, yep, bye." He hung up the phone and turned in his seat. He cupped Alexa's cheek in his hand and turned her to look at him.

"I'm sorry, I understand if you want to fire me," she whispered.

"Oh, Lex. Stop saying sorry about everything, and no, I'm not firing you." He tilted her head up a little more. "I want you to tell me what happened."

"Lack of sleep makes me really irritable," she began after she sighed. "I was getting a bit frustrated because I wasn't finding anything good that stuck out to me. I'm failing at the major task I have at MAEP already. I was getting angry at myself when Carla came in asking if the *job was already taking its toll on me and that just because I slept with Nicky didn't mean my job was secure*." She quoted Carla exactly.

Dom leaned back against the door of his car. "And what did you say?"

"I said, 'really gee, I didn't know that, here I thought the company was based on looks only, good thing I don't sleep with my bosses nor do I plan to or want to,' then I also added, for her being an HR manager she wasn't very perceptive of people, and she didn't treat them very well or if she just treated me that way because you went against her wishes with me and that she needed to work on her skills or stop being crazy about a man who clearly didn't want her."

Dom's hazel eyes widened in complete shock. "Alexandra," he gasped out, not knowing what else to say.

"What? The way she calls you Nicky, the way she whines thinking she'll get her way from you, the way she detests the fact I am around and possibly sleeping with you, it's obvious." She narrowed her eyes at him.

"I think someone's a little jealous," he teased, his lips breaking into a huge smile.

Alexa scoffed a little. "No." She narrowed her eyes even more.

He chuckled and started the car, then headed to a little diner for lunch.

---

Alexa finished her coffee as they pulled into the parking lot of Lola's Diner. She let out a sigh; was she jealous? She didn't want to admit it out loud, but she wanted to lose herself in Dominick Mackenzie, even if it was just for a couple of minutes, but she couldn't do that.

She glanced over at the delicious playboy, and that was the problem, playboy, only she had been shown a different side of him. He was gentle with her, but that didn't mean he wasn't sleeping with someone else. A man like him had particular needs she didn't know if she could satisfy.

The thought burned her blood. She refused to share that he finally broke the ice around her heart, but he wouldn't change. She closed her eyes tightly. *'Stay strong. You don't need or want a man. He'll be just like Father was, once he finds out how annoying you can be.'*

"Alexa?" Dom's gentle deep voice pulled her from her thoughts. She looked at him. "Come on, let's go get some lunch."

They headed inside, Dom got a burger with everything on

it, it was so thick she didn't know how he wrapped his mouth around it to get a bite off of it, while she decided on a chicken strip salad with ranch.

Dom broke the silence. "So how often does he really come around, Lex?"

She looked up at him a little confused. "Who?" she asked, raising an eyebrow above the frames of her glasses.

"Tate."

"Dom, do we have to talk about that?"

"Lex, I just don't want him hurting you anymore, how long will that two hundred keep him away?" He reached across the table and placed his hand over hers.

"I don't know, the last time I gave him two grand, and that kept him away for a couple of months, until last night."

"Lex," he whispered, brushing his thumb in tiny circles on the back of her hand. "So needless to say, that two hundred won't keep him away very long."

"Probably not, and I won't have much to give him when he shows back up." She shivered at the thought.

She looked up when Dom pushed his plate next to hers, got up and moved into the green vinyl booth seat beside her.

Her eyes were locked with his, unsure what he was going to do. She soon found out as he wrapped his arms around her and pulled her close into his chest.

She let him and didn't fight the need to be held. The only people who ever held her like this were her mother and Brandon. Tate would always hold her down just to give her the lashings she deserved when she was younger.

She laid her hands against Dom's chest, but then slid her hands around him beneath his suit jacket. Her hands pressed against his hard, rippling back, heat flew through her whole body.

"I can make sure he will not hurt you again, and I *will* make sure. You won't be thrilled about it, but you deserve to be happy and not have to always look over your shoulder worried that he's coming for you, will you let me help?" he asked as he rubbed her back making the muscles in his back move beneath her spread hands.

She stared at the ugly green tabletop for a minute, it would be nice not to feel scared all the time, but what would it cost him to do that? She nodded her head, then pulled back from him slowly and looked up into his eyes. "I'll pay you back for everything, Dom."

His hand came around to her cheek and gently cupped it. "No need to, I don't want to see another mark on you, so it'll be the least I can do. But, you have to promise me no leaving the office without me, you let me pick you up in the mornings and drop you off in the evenings, the rest of the time I will have a bodyguard follow you, you won't even know he is there unless you need him." He rubbed her cheek with the pad of his thumb.

She pulled back a little more. "A bodyguard?" Of course Dom couldn't follow her around all the time, he was far too busy and had other things to keep him occupied.

He smirked at her. "I'd love to follow you everywhere and anywhere, but I'm already having issues keeping my hands to myself."

She averted her gaze and pulled away from his safe, robust and tall body. "Okay," she agreed and began to finish her salad.

They finished their lunch and headed back to the office.

Dom walked her back to her office, and he went to his.

Alexa hated herself as she watched him go, wishing she could be near him. She logged back on to her tablet and got back to work.

Dom had a happy edge to him the rest of the day now that she agreed to his help. Small steps, Dom, small steps. He'd do whatever he could to keep her. No matter the cost, no matter the sacrifice, he'd make it. He'd prove to her he cared about her one way or another. Then maybe just maybe he could change his ways, but that was very unlikely. He, at least, wanted her friendship.

# Chapter 7

Alexa walked out of her duplex apartment. There he was waiting as usual. Week three, and he was still always on time. By day five of coming to get her, he didn't even text her to say he was on his way. He was just there at the same time in the same spot.

She was feeling even more for him now. Especially since every morning, he showed up with either a Smoked Butterscotch Frappuccino or a Mocha Cookie Crumble Frappuccino along with either a blueberry muffin or banana nut bread.

He was always so thoughtful. She headed down the steps quickly. She stopped suddenly when someone stepped in front of her. Her chin was gripped harshly.

She tried to yank back, but she was pulled forward roughly, making her stumble a little. "That measly two hundred wasn't enough, you know I want more now, you owe me."

She glared up into the man's face, that sometimes still haunted her at night, and reached up to shove him away from her, but he pushed her to the ground, making her let out a high-pitched scream.

Dom was waiting for Alexa, but he was on the phone with the bodyguard he had posted at Alexa's the night before.

His head jerked to the passenger window when he heard the scream. "Shit, call you back." He hung up the phone and threw it down in the seat as he got out of the car quickly.

He saw Tate pull his fist back to strike Alexa. Dom caught it before Tate could move to connect and yanked the old man off of her, he stepped between the old man and Alexa. "The broken nose I gave you wasn't enough?" he demanded.

Tate got in Dom's face, but Dom shoved him back quickly, the older man reeked of alcohol, it was disgusting.

"She's my whore of a daughter," Tate slurred out.

"She's my girlfriend, so I will protect her from the likes of you." He glared at Tate, then felt a small body press up against his back and clutch his gray suit jacket. "I suggest you get out of here and never come back, unless you want to spend the rest of your life in jail."

Tate glared back at Dom. "It's kind of you to lie to protect her, but you really don't have to. I know what kind of whore she is, sleeps with rich men to get what she wants then pretends she has no money."

Dom took a step toward Tate, but felt Alexa's hands tighten in his jacket. "Get away from here or I will call the cops, and just so you know, I have an eye on her at all times, so try me, asshole."

Tate glared harder at them but left down the sidewalk quickly.

Dom turned to look at Alexa, his arms wrapped around her pulling her close to him. "Are you okay?"

"I guess so, except he made me break the heel on my shoe," she mumbled into his chest.

Dom shook his head. "Come on." He scooped her up into

his arms and headed to the house. She unlocked the door, pulled her heels off her feet, and he set her down on her bare feet. He looked down at her. He loved seeing her out of those dangerous shoes.

He watched her go to her bedroom as he leaned against the couch. He was angry with himself for not paying more attention and being on the phone with the bodyguard instead.

His gaze flicked up when he saw her come down the short hallway. He smiled faintly at her. Then his smile got more prominent when he noticed the flat silver shoes she was wearing. They matched the skirt and blouse she was wearing nicely. "Well, that's a nice change," he teased.

She blushed as she looked down at her feet. "Yeah, my ankle hurts a little bit, so these seemed more sensible."

"Are you okay?"

"Yeah, I'll be fine, come on let's get to work. I've already made you late." She headed toward the door with a little limp.

He followed her out the door and put his arm around her shoulders, he opened the passenger door. "Your coffee's in there, also some banana nut bread, Butterscotch today."

"Thank you, Dom," she said as she slid onto the seat, careful with her ankle.

He leaned into the car and kissed her forehead. "You're welcome." He shut the door and went to his side of the car, and headed to the office.

Alexa sipped her Frappuccino quietly for a few minutes then he heard her sigh. "Why'd you tell Tate I was your girlfriend?"

He glanced over at her. "Well, you're definitely not my whore. I got angry when he called you that, so it was my only option, he also needed to know I am not letting him mess with you anymore."

She smiled at him a little and continued to drink her coffee. She always waited until they got out of the car before she'd eat either the muffin or bread he would bring her, even though he told her time and time again that she could eat it on the way. But she insisted she didn't want to get crumbs in his car.

They parked, and she got out, favoring her right ankle still. He let out a sigh as he got out and went around to her. "Do you want to go get it checked out?" he asked, softly putting his hand on her hip.

"No, I'll get a bottle of water from the break room and take some Tylenol, I'll be okay," she reassured him.

"All right, if it gets worse, let me know I'll take you to get it looked at." He walked with her to the break room and then her office. He leaned his forehead down against hers. "If you need me don't be afraid to get me, and don't forget the meeting we have with Patrick and Claude Benson.

"I'll be there even if I have to roll there in my chair."

Dom chuckled as he pulled back from her and kissed her forehead. "If it comes down to that, I'll carry you to the conference room."

He headed out of the office, leaving Alexa behind. If she had actually been his to take care of, he would have rushed her to the hospital. But, considering she wasn't his and was too bull-headed, she wasn't going to let him take her.

---

Alexa was touching base with her list of clients, which took almost all of her time until the meeting. She got up from her desk. Her ankle didn't want to support her weight right away.

She stumbled out of her office and landed surprisingly into a pair of arms. She looked up quickly into a pair of light blue eyes. "Mr. Benson, I'm so sorry."

He smiled at her. "No problem, you okay?" He helped her straighten up.

"Yeah, just hurt my ankle a little. I'm okay, though. Well should we head to the conference room?"

"Actually, I'd like to talk with you first if that's okay?"

"Claude, there you are!" Patrick Andrew's thunderous and deep voice practically yelled from the other side of the room.

Claude and Alexa turned. "Um, yeah, I'm here. I wanted to talk to Alexa before the meeting."

"Oh, we don't have time for that, you can chat after." Patrick came over to them. "Plus, I've pretty much taught her everything and told her what to focus on." He clapped Claude on the back as they made their way over to the conference room.

Alexa was frozen to the floor at what Patrick had just told Claude. He did nothing to help her with Claude, it was all her hard work, alone. She glared after the two men. Maybe she'd just skip this meeting.

"Alexandra, you coming?" Dom asked as he walked over to the conference room and stopped in the doorway.

She huffed and limped over to him. "Yep, here," she said shortly, her temper getting the better of her.

"You okay?" Dom asked, laying a hand on her shoulder.

She pulled away from him. "Peachy." She walked in, dropping her notes on the table hard and quickly. Then she sat down, crossing her arms and legs. Her blood was boiling from the insult from Patrick. How dare the man be that much of an ass that he wouldn't even let her take credit for things she had taken care of with Mr. Benson.

Dom sat down beside Alexa, looking her over a little. "So what have we come up with, Lex?" he asked as he clamped down on wanting to correct the attitude she got with him. They were definitely going to have to talk about that one.

She began to talk, but Patrick pulled the paper out of her hands.

Dom frowned as she shot a harsh glare at Patrick. "What are you doing, Patrick?"

"Oh, you didn't know, this work was mostly mine, she came to me one afternoon begging for help."

"No, I didn't," Alexa argued right away.

"Excuse me, what's going on? I've worked closely with Alexa all week," Claude interrupted.

"Thanks to me, giving her ideas and help." Patrick shot a look at everyone, almost daring one of them to challenge him.

And of course, Alexa was the one to do it, she stood up quickly. "You're lying." She glared at Patrick. "I never talk to you except during these meetings."

Patrick stood, coming very close to Alexa. "I'd suggest you sit down right now, Ms. Mills." He moved slightly.

Alexa jerked away from him and stumbled back into her chair.

Dom got up quickly. "Don't ever touch her, Patrick, if you touch her, you'll have to answer to me." He rolled her chair to where he had been sitting and pulled his chair into her spot.

He sat down and laid his hand on Alexa's knee, knowing she was furious and had actually gotten a little afraid, which he understood after what happened this morning.

---

As the meeting continued, Alexa's mind kept running. She never wanted to deal with Patrick ever again. She felt stupid for challenging him, and then when he moved slightly, she really thought he was going to hit her. She felt like a complete moron.

She was an idiot. No one believed in her. She should just go back to Brandon. He listened to her and knew what she was capable of.

"Alexa?" Dom's voice interrupted her thoughts. "What do you think?"

She shot a glare at Dom. "Oh, now you want my opinion? You let Patrick take over the meeting, I think that pretty much sums everything up to me." She got up from the chair and limped out of the room, leaving all three men sitting there looking at each other.

Mr. Benson broke the silence first. "She is one hell of a spitfire."

Dom shot a look at him. "Hence why I hired her so things like this wouldn't happen, what were you thinking, Patrick?"

"You are going to believe a woman you've known for three weeks over your co-owner you've known for twenty years and have worked with for eleven?" Patrick demanded standing up, and Dom stood up too.

"Yeah, I think I am." Dom turned to Claude. "We'll be in touch soon, Mr. Benson, after I talk with Alexa. Thank you for coming in today." He reached out his hand. "And sorry about the little drama episode."

"Hey, I get it, and for the record, I did do all my dealings with her and loved all her ideas."

"Thank you, sir." Dom left the room and headed to Alexa's office. He poked his head in. Anger simmered inside him when he saw she wasn't in there.

He began to search for her. She was upset enough to leave, and he didn't blame her. He pulled out his phone to call her, but she didn't answer. He let out an aggravated sigh. She had to start keeping her phone on her and learn to answer his calls.

What was he going to do with her? He racked his brain, trying to figure out where she would go being this upset. He let out a huff. He spotted Carla over by the lobby receptionist, Ashley. He walked up to the two redheads. "If either of you spots Alexa, will you send her to my office, please?"

"Is everything okay, Nicky?" Carla asked, meeting his gaze as she laid her hand against his chest, moving closer to him. "We could hear you yelling all the way out here."

"Everything's fine, just send her to me if you see her." He turned away quickly, trying to push the sick feeling he felt from having Carla touch him. Strange, it never seemed to bother him before Alexa came to work for him and pointed out Carla indeed had a thing for him.

He sat at his desk after slamming the door of his office shut and dug his hands through his black hair.

Alexa knew she couldn't leave the office without Dom, and she didn't want to make him even angrier with her than he already was.

She went to the rock oasis they had behind the office. She sat on one of the concrete benches and stared into the unmoving pond. Then the large Koi fish popped up from the water. Alexa smiled, the fish was so many different shades of oranges, from pale to dark to white. For some strange reason watching that Koi swimming around made her relax some.

She finally supposed she was relaxed enough to face Dom. She took a deep breath and got up from the bench to head back inside. She wrapped her hand around the knob to pull when she was yanked to the side and shoved up against the brick wall.

Her eyes met hard, brown eyes. "Patrick," she gritted out through clenched teeth as she glared at him.

His hand reached up, latching his fingers on either side of her mouth, squeezing hard. "I don't appreciate being made a fool of in front of my clients."

She tried to pull her face out of his hard grasp. "That was your own doing. If you want your clients to be impressed with you then here's a hint, do the work yourself. Don't throw them away on to someone else because you are too busy."

He jerked her head up higher and squeezed tighter. "That attitude of yours is going to get you in trouble one of these days, little girl, and I'm sure Dom didn't appreciate his little toy giving him an attitude either. I will not put up with the disrespect you showed us today even if you are a toy to Dom, although I don't really get what he sees in you." His index finger trailed down her chin, down her neck just above her top, and popped the top button clean off the blouse. "Although with cleavage like that, it could be interesting. Have you ever done two bosses at the same time?" He chuckled as she tried to move away from him.

She glared at him. "If you don't want to be embarrassed, then earn the respect and I will give it, take care of your clients better and stop shoving them off on me. And no, I have never done a boss, now let go of me!"

His hand caught her chin again. "You shouldn't forget your place, and it's not here." He shoved her back against the wall hard and headed back into the building.

Alexa had to fight the vomit that threatened her. She slowly sank to the ground, trying to get her breathing under control. She felt on the ground for the button he had ripped off her blouse but nothing. She shook uncontrollably for a few minutes.

She finally got her breathing under control and went back inside. She was headed to her office when Ashley waved her down.

"Hey, you okay?" Ashley asked, concern written all over her face.

"Yeah I'm fine, what can I do for you?" Alexa answered, trying to straighten her attire.

"Mr. Mackenzie wants to speak with you. He asked me to send you to his office if I saw you," Ashley explained, her gaze flew over her, and it wasn't in disgust. It was actually in concern. And Alexa thought miracles didn't exist.

"Okay, thank you, Ashley." She slowly walked to Dom's office and knocked slightly.

"Come in!" the deep voice barked from the other side of the door.

She stood there for a moment her hand on the knob, he sounded so angry, and she knew what happened when men were mad. She couldn't go in there. She stepped back from the door.

"Alexa? I'm sorry, come in." A hand reached for hers as the door opened.

She pulled back from him. "You're angry."

"Yes, but not at you. Please come in, Alexa, I need to talk to you."

She still hesitated.

Dom frowned at her. "Either you come in here, or I'm throwing you over my shoulder and taking you home so we can talk."

She scurried in through the door, and Dom shut the door but pinned her against it, gently. "What's the matter?"

"Nothing."

"Alexa, don't lie to me," he whispered, his nose nuzzling against her neck a little. "What happened to your top button?"

"I-I don't know."

"Alexa, do not lie to me," he said a little more sternly and brushed his nose against her neck a little harder. "I will not tolerate you lying to me, there will be consequences for lying." She jerked her head away from him. "Alexa, talk to me, where did you go?" He sighed in defeat, knowing there were a lot of things they were going to have to hash out between them, but he could wait for now.

"The rock oasis out back," she answered calmly, staring anywhere but at him.

"And why do you have red marks on both sides of your mouth?" He leaned forward and pressed his lips to one, then the other.

She sucked in a deep breath. "I had my fingers against my mouth for a long time."

"I'm sorry for what happened with Patrick, I believe you though."

Her head jerked up, and hazel blue met hazel green. "You believe me?" she whispered.

"Yes, I do, something is going on with Patrick and Carla. I am sure they are up to something, I just can't prove what."

"I see." She looked back down at the ground.

"Alexa?" he whispered her name.

She looked up at him.

"You did well standing up for yourself, and I am very proud of you. You could have let Patrick steal everything from you today, but you did not. I know you keep saying we are no good for each other, but I have to know something, can I find out?"

Her gaze searched his, what was he talking about? Her breath caught in her lungs as he moved even closer to her, but she didn't feel scared of him.

---

It was her spitfire attitude that turned him on so much. She was so passionate he could only imagine finding out what else she could be passionate about. He had been trying for three weeks to fight it, and he finally needed to know what she tasted like and how she would kiss him.

He dipped his head and claimed her mouth as she let out a startled gasp.

But her reaction was instant, she laid her hands against his chest, but she didn't push him away. He pressed closer to her as his hands rested against the small of her back. He grew hard against her, and his hands went down to her ass, squeezing it harder.

God, he wanted this woman, she tasted so sweet and delicious. He slid his tongue to her bottom lip, begging for access to her warm wetness, and she opened. His tongue dove in claiming her tongue, entwining them together in an erotic dance. He could bend her over his desk right now and not think twice about it if she'd let him.

Her hands slid up his chest and around his neck, her fingers laced in his hair. He groaned into her mouth as she pulled on his hair a little. He pulled her harder against his body then lifted her pressing her against the door, wrapping her legs around him, making her skirt ride up around her creamy thighs.

She let out a moan when he nipped at her bottom lip. He ran his nose against her jawline, then his mouth found her neck and began to suck and nibble at it, brushing his tongue against every nip soothing the skin.

She was moaning and brushing her soft body against his hard one. Desire clutched him like a fire, making him so hot. He made his way down her neck and across her cleavage, he had access now due to her top button missing.

---

Alexa had never done any of this before, she clutched her fingers tighter in his soft black hair, and she moved against him. How did trying a kiss turn into this hot erotic pleasure fest? She was probably doing everything wrong. She let out a moan at each touch of his lips against her heated skin.

She leaned her head back as he began to unbutton her blouse slowly. "Dom," she gasped as he pushed her shirt away from her burning skin. She gripped his hair tighter as she squirmed against him. One of his hands ran up against her exposed thigh while his other hand dipped between them, brushing against her folds. She jerked away but wasn't able to go far with the door in the way.

His lips crashed onto hers, making her forget everything she was stressing about. She arched her back against the door pushing his fingers against her more.

She felt his fingers move under her lacy thong and slip into her already soaking wetness. She pulled back from his lips, and their eyes locked as she moved her hands to his suit jacket. "Dom," she whispered, feeling the pressure build as he moved his thumb to twirl around her sensitive spot.

---

Dom smiled at her as he toyed with her swollen little jewel, and his fingers drove into her slowly. She was coming alive for him. He loved the way her body moved against him.

He bent his head and took her delicate ear between his teeth and nibbled and sucked. "Oh, Alexa, you're so tight," he whispered. "So wet for me, too, how can you say we'd be bad together?"

She whimpered as her thighs tightened around his hand that was playing with her. He smiled and began to suck on her neck again. She couldn't be anyone's but his. This was crazy thinking. He never dreamed he could settle down, but she might well be the one.

"Dom, please," she begged as he curled his fingers inside her, hitting her sensitive spot. "Dom," she almost screamed out.

He pushed his lips down on hers, trying to quiet her some. He wanted to feel her come around his fingers so bad, and he didn't want to stop. He felt her body tense, and his other hand raked up her stomach, and cupped her breast in his hand as he continued the torture under her thong. He pulled back a little. "Come for me, Alexa, just let go I want to feel you." He went back to her neck as she writhed against him and clung to his jacket.

"Dom." She arched her back even more as he took her nipple into his mouth through her bra and grazed it with his teeth.

He smiled when she jerked, and clamped down on his fingers. He slowly removed his fingers. He looked down at her as he set her feet on the floor, fixing her skirt. "You okay?"

She was bright red as she looked down at the ground, but she nodded her head.

He cleaned his fingers by placing them into his mouth, and sucking off her juices. He moved his other hand to cup her chin gently and tilted her head up. "I'm sorry," he whispered, as he ran his thumb against her chin a little.

"It's okay." Her voice was laced from the passion they just shared. "What about you?"

"What about me?"

"Um, don't you want something in return?" she asked, her eyes wide as she looked at him.

He shook his head. "No, I'm good, maybe later." He smiled at her and bent his head down to kiss her softly.

"Did I do something wrong?"

"No of course not, you were wonderful, now come talk to me for a little bit, I'll try to behave." He smiled wickedly at her. He didn't need her thinking the only reason he did anything to her was to get her to do anything to him. He took her hand and pulled her over to the table in his office.

He sat down in the chair and pulled her down into his lap. "How's your ankle?"

"It's okay," she whispered as she curled up into him and hid her face.

"What's the matter, Lex?" Dom asked as he tilted her head up.

"I've never done any of that before," she admitted and looked away from him again.

"Fuck." He looked at her. "Really?"

She buried her head against his chest.

He wrapped his arms around her and rubbed her back slowly. "I'm so sorry," he whispered against her ear. "God, I'm a fucking ass." If he had known she was innocent he never would have tried this in his office right under everyone's nose. "Why didn't you stop me?"

"I didn't want to stop," she whispered.

He began to button her blouse back up. "So you do want me?"

She nodded a little. "I just don't know how to do any of this. And if things don't work between us I'd have to leave here, I won't be able to look at you without feeling completely embarrassed."

"There's nothing to be embarrassed about, you have needs, and I want to meet those needs in more ways than one." He kissed her cheek gently.

"I have to get back to work, are you really not angry with me?" She looked up at him meeting his eyes with scared ones.

"No, I am not mad at you over anything, I could never be mad at you, there are a few things we need to correct and we will get there, slowly." He caught her lips beneath his. "Go on a date with me tonight?"

"Maybe." She slowly got up from his lap, but he pulled her back between his legs and kissed her once more before letting her go.

He wanted her back as soon as she walked out of his office and shut the door softly. Damn, what did he do?

## Chapter 8

Alexa headed to her office quickly, what if everyone knew what they had just done? She glanced around when she saw Carla walking over to her. She groaned a little as she watched Carla come even closer.

"Ms. Mills, I need to talk to you in my office now." Carla walked past Alexa to her office.

Alexa glanced around again, then followed Carla to the HR office. She took a deep breath as Carla sat behind her light wooden desk.

Carla folded her hands and placed them on top of the desk. "Patrick told me what happened today with Mr. Benson. We don't tolerate insubordination around here, and Nicky and Patrick are furious about what happened in the meeting. We discussed it and regret to inform you that we are going to have to terminate your employment with us. I'm sure you understand, dear." A smile touched her lips. "Please remove your personal belongings from your office, return the tablet within ten minutes and vacate the premises."

"Dom decided this also?" Alexa managed to get out. She

couldn't believe it after what they had just done in his office and the conversation they had afterwards. Did he lie to her?

"Yes, I'm afraid so. It was nice to have you here, even for the short time, but with that attitude, Nicky's realized his mistake." Her dim green eyes showed no remorse in her words.

Alexa nodded her head and walked out of the office. She'd believed him. He said he wasn't angry with her. He'd done things to her no one else had. She went to her office, grabbed her stuff, and left, fighting the tears. She didn't even drop her tablet off to Carla. She just left it on her desk.

She glanced around for a moment, then left the building. What was she going to do now? She couldn't run back to Brandon, she'd tell him everything that had happened, and he'd be so disappointed in her, and she was already embarrassed enough as it was.

She darted around people who were walking toward her in a rush. As she passed the strip of restaurants, she saw a few with help-wanted signs. She stopped at each one and applied. She couldn't look for other publishing companies because they were so far away, and she couldn't get to them without a car.

She continued to look for more help-wanted signs, fighting the pain she was feeling. He used her, but why? He got nothing in return unless he'd thought more was going to happen.

She found a bench and sat down for a minute. Her ankle was throbbing. She pulled her foot across her other knee and rubbed it. She wasn't having much luck. She was going to have to call Brandon.

Alexa ran a hand over her face, she was scared. If she didn't get a job, she'd lose everything she had, and Tate would become so angry because she couldn't give him money. Now she'd be vulnerable because she would no longer have the bodyguard who was provided by Dominick Mackenzie.

Dom finally finished everything for the day and headed to Alexa's office, hoping she was done. "Babe, are you ready to go home?" He stopped when he saw it was empty, none of her stuff was on the desk, and the company tablet was sitting neatly in the middle of it. Had he made her that upset? He pulled his phone from his suit jacket and called her. It rang twice, then went to voicemail. She ignored him. He dialed his head bodyguard. "Find Alexa Mills, now!" he barked into the phone loudly. "I don't care how long it takes, or the cost, get everyone on it now."

Dom cut the call and saw Carla getting ready to leave. "Where's Alexa, Carla?" he demanded as he walked over to her.

"Oh, I'm so sorry, Nicky." She turned around to look at him and moved closer to him, placing her hands on his chest. "She quit right after she came out of your office earlier, I tried to talk her out of it, but I must say she seemed very distraught over something."

Dom pulled back from Carla. "Fuck." He rushed out the door, trying her number again, begging her to answer. He even sent a text apologizing to her and asking her to tell him where she was.

He got in his car and rushed to her house, 'Where could she be?' he wondered when he saw all the lights still off. Brandon. He pulled out his phone and dialed the number for BAP.

Brandon luckily answered the call. "Brandon Adams Publishing, this is Brandon."

"Brandon, have you seen Alexa?" Dom rushed out.

"Um, no I haven't. Why, what's up?"

"Carla told me Alexa quit today but she didn't say why. And she looked distraught over something."

"That doesn't sound like Lex at all. What happened,

Dom?" His tone was so suspicious, and Dom didn't blame him.

"Brandon, I was so stupid. I kissed her in my office today. I don't know where she would have gone," he admitted as he searched the sidewalks as he drove around.

"Did you only kiss her?" Brandon demanded.

"I didn't have sex with her." He wasn't lying, he just kissed her in so many spots on her body and touched her intimately, but Alexa didn't stop him. And when he wanted to bend her over his desk, he refrained from doing so.

"I don't think she would have quit just because of a kiss. She's got more pride than that, did you try her house?"

"Pitch black, Brandon. Tate's back and has come into contact with her twice, I'm worried about her."

"Fuck, try the park, the library is closed already. I'll call her mom and sisters and see if they've heard from her."

"Thanks, Brandon." Dom ended the call and kept looking for Alexa, praying his anger would simmer before he found her. He would never pull her over his knee in anger but he had to move sooner rather than later. She needed to learn what was and wasn't acceptable and this wasn't acceptable, along with her attitude with him, he had been patient long enough.

---

Alexa glared at her phone when she read the text from Dom. She shoved her phone back into her purse. He apologized for firing her? Not for what he had done in his office and then firing her, just for firing her. What a jerk.

She wanted nothing to do with him ever again. She would show him, she made it before he brought her on at MAEP and she could make it again.

She got up from the bench when her phone began to ring.

She pulled it out and saw her oldest sister's name on the ID. She let out a deep breath and answered, "Hello, Noelle."

"Alexandra, where are you?" Noelle asked. "Brandon is worried sick about you. He said something about you quitting, what's going on?"

"I quit BAP like three weeks ago, I got a new job at MAEP, but I didn't quit, they fired me today."

"What, why? Are you okay?"

"Fine, just out trying to find a new job." Alexa took another deep breath. "And because I yelled at a couple of my bosses today because one was stealing all of my work."

"Oh, Alexandra, Daddy always said that attitude of yours was going to get you in a lot of trouble."

Alexa bit back a sob. "Yeah, because letting people do whatever they wanted to me has worked over the past fifteen years. I'm fine, Elle, I can handle myself, just tell Brandon I'm fine, I'll have a new job soon."

"Just go back to Brandon."

"I'll never be able to show myself at BAP again, everyone will know what a failure I am. Brandon will never be able to look at me again knowing I failed, I can't bear the disappointment he will have in me. I'm okay, so I'm going to go now, bye." She ended the call. She scanned the businesses and noticed a lit-up help wanted sign was posted on a bar.

She could waitress. She'd done it before Brandon came into her life. Her father always made her work at the family restaurant he owned while Noelle and Delilah got to be actual kids and teenagers.

She walked into the bar, it was so loud and crowded, but it would mean good tips. Hopefully. As she headed up to the bar counter, she was grabbed on the ass, and she turned around quickly, startled. "Can I get some fries with that shake, it's super nice," a rude burly man asked as she turned.

Alexa stepped back from the huge scary man quickly when

she caught the sight of the tattoos on his arms. His arms made up at least both of her legs. She scrambled further away. "I'm sorry, sir, you're not my type," she barely got the words out, fear taking over.

"Oh, baby, for you, I could be any type you are looking for."

"Honestly, no, I'm okay."

"Too good for me, huh?" He stepped closer.

Alexa felt the tears start to spring, threatening to spill over. She stepped around the man. This was a bad idea. She was going to have to go back to Brandon, hopefully, he wouldn't think any less of her.

She practically ran to the door forgetting about her ankle.

---

Dom pulled up in front of the bar. He needed a stiff drink. He couldn't understand what was going on. Alexa still hadn't texted him, nor returned his phone call. And still, no word from anyone else about where Alexa might be.

He got out of his car and headed to the door. Right before he opened it, the door flew open quickly, and someone ran right into him at full force, making him topple over with them.

---

Alexa let out a scream as she ran into someone, and they both fell to the ground. She was sprawled over them, scared it was another jerk like the one in the bar she scrambled away, and the tears fell free.

"Lex, baby, hey, calm down." The deep male voice washed over her as the arms went to wrap around her.

"Don't touch me, just leave me alone." She backed up into the door, and it was thrown open slamming into her and pushing her forward, pivoting toward the ground when she tried to stop herself with her hurt ankle.

The arms went around her again. "Baby, come on, let's talk, please?"

"Just leave me alone, you fooled me enough for a lifetime. I thought you cared about me, so stupid of me to think you did." She glared at him, since when did he call her baby, she was not his, never would be, and he made sure of that.

"Alexandra, I do care, I wouldn't be out trying to find you if I didn't. Lex please, I don't want to hurt you." He tightened his arms around her.

"You tried to get what you wanted and decided it wasn't good enough. I think you've hurt me more than enough. Now let go of me, Mr. Mackenzie." She glared at him..

Dom looked at Alexa completely confused. "Honey, what are you talking about?" He didn't understand what was going on, she was more than good enough for him. "Sweetheart?"

His phone began to ring, he glanced at the ID, Brandon. "Hello?"

"Dom, she told her oldest sister she didn't quit."

"What?" Anger flew through him like a gust of powerful wind.

"She said you fired her for her attitude."

"That's rich, her attitude is what made me want her so badly." He meant both professionally and pleasurably. "That's why I hired her, Brandon. I got her now, though."

"Keep her safe, Dom, Noelle also told me Tate's looking for her again, and he sounded very upset to her."

"I see, okay, thank you, Brandon." He ended the call and pulled Alexa closer to him. "Come with me, baby girl. Tate's looking for you again. I'll get us some food, then we need to have a very, very long talk." He ushered her to his car, and she let out a yelp of pain as her ankle gave out on her a little.

Dom held her closer to him when she about fell, he put

her in his car and was glad she didn't try to get out when he went around to his side and got in.

He began to drive, he stopped to get a hot 'n' ready pizza, and some crazy bread from Little Caesars then made his way home.

"Just take me home, Mr. Mackenzie, I don't need anything from you," Alexa said, glaring at him.

"After this afternoon, I need plenty from you," he whispered, taking ahold of her hand.

She pulled it back from him. "Doesn't mean you'll be getting anything, I refuse to be your whore."

"Baby, you'll never be that to me." He pulled up to the vast black metal gate in front of his home and pressed a few buttons, the gate swung open. "You mean something to me."

"Yeah, I'll bet." She froze when her gaze landed on his home. He glanced over at her and smiled a little.

---

Alexa had no clue what she was looking at, the house was enormous and made her apartment look like a run-down shack.

It was beautiful and made her speechless. The house was made of tan stones, different sections of the roof came up to very steep points, and the windows, which were lit up, took up most of the house.

She glanced at Dom then back to his home. There were at least three different chimneys, one on the left, in the middle, and to the right. She wondered if they were actually working fireplaces.

Each window was trimmed in black. She couldn't catch her breath from the sight and shock. Why would he bring her here? She would never have imagined this place in her wildest dreams.

There was at least a twelve-foot-tall wall all around the property. She supposed she could be safe here, but that didn't mean she'd get to stay or even wanted to stay.

She watched as he pulled into a garage that was the size of an average house. As he pulled in and shut his car off, she glanced around, seeing a couple of older Camaros, a couple of black SUVs but nothing else.

He got out of the car and went around to her side. He held his hand out to her as he opened her door.

She placed her hand in his. He helped her out as he held onto the pizza and crazy bread in the opposite hand. He led her to the white side door, then took her through a breezeway before entering the house. She gasped as she looked around her, everything was light in color, nothing compared to the office. The flooring was a cream tile, the walls a sky blue.

Every light fixture her gaze landed on was a crystal chandelier.

He led her toward another room, which she discovered was the kitchen, it made up two of her apartments alone.

There was dark bamboo flooring. The countertop was a sparkling white granite. All the appliances were stainless steel, the cabinets a light oak. He dropped her hand, slowly brushing his fingertips against hers as he let go sending tingles through her body, remembering where that hand was earlier. He went to the fridge, pulled out a glass bottle, and then the cabinets to get two long-stemmed glasses and two plates.

He headed to another room off of the kitchen, and she followed him. They came to a table that could easily fit twenty people. He set down the glasses, the bottle and the pills.

He then motioned for her to sit. She did as she laid the pizza box on the table. He opened the bottle making a pop sound that echoed throughout the room. He began to pour her a glass of the light red liquid. She glanced at him.

"Dig in, baby. We eat first, then we talk," he whispered

gruffly and kissed her temple gently then sat down beside her.

She glanced at him then stared at the dark wooden table that matched the kitchen floor and the dining room floor as well. She bit her bottom lip, feeling awkward, but grabbed a couple of slices of pizza after Dom opened the box.

She ate slowly, she glanced at the glass filled with the delicious looking drink but darted her eyes up to him.

"Go ahead, sweetheart." He smiled at her. The smile that made her go weak at the knees.

Alexa reached out a trembling hand and took the glass. She put the glass to her mouth and took a sip.

She gasped at the flavor as it rolled against her tongue and down her throat. She had never tasted anything so delicious. The flavor of strawberries sent tingles through her mouth. She took another small sip then placed it back on the dark table. "Why did you bring me here, Mr. Mackenzie?"

"Eat first," he ordered.

She shot him a glare and finished her food in silence.

---

After they finished, Dom took the plates and box to the kitchen. He placed the dishes in the dishwasher but left the box on the counter.

Alexa was speechless at the sight of his home, but that wasn't why he brought her here. He threw the bag for the crazy bread away. She seemed more into that than the actual pizza. He smirked a little.

He headed back to the dining room. He smiled, she stood at the huge window that faced out back to the in-ground pool. She had the glass in her hand as she stared at it.

He went up behind her slowly and wrapped his arm around her waist and pulled her back into his chest. "What are you thinking?" he whispered against her ear.

"That I shouldn't be here, I don't belong here, Mr. Mackenzie. I want to go home and be alone."

"But you're not alone, not anymore, come with me." He moved from her, took her hand and led her to his living room. They walked to a seating area he had built in the floor in a circle, down the steps into it and they sat down on the dark cushions. He pulled her back against him and just held her while she finished her strawberry wine. Her body began to relax into his. He began to rub her shoulders as she relaxed, even more, her hand becoming loose around the glass.

He took it from her hand and placed it on the table behind the circular sitting area.

"Hey, I wasn't done with that." She frowned at him.

"I know, I didn't take it very far, just relax for me right now." He kissed along her neck gently, and she let out a little moan. He smiled. He got such a reaction out of her, which made him burn and ache for more. He nuzzled her neck with his nose a little as she seemed to relax again beneath his hands and lips.

"We're supposed to talk," she whispered.

"I know, baby, I know, soon." He continued to knead her shoulders. "Want me to rub that sore ankle for you too?"

"No, it's fine." She glanced back at him.

He replaced his body with a pillow and she leaned back against it, as he went to her feet and began to massage her ankle gently. She let out another moan leaning her head back. He was going to be in some major trouble if she didn't stop making noises like that, but then again, they were just so fucking sexy it's precisely what he wanted to make her do, preferably while she was beneath him, instead of lying next to him with her feet in his lap.

What was he going to do? He couldn't fight it anymore, and yet something happened in the office, and he had to get to the bottom of things. Fast.

## Chapter 9

"I did it. I got rid of her, ha!" she screeched, sitting across the table from him.

"How are you so sure?" he asked, still feeling unsure.

"Oh, I just know, I told the bitch it was as much Nicky's idea as ours, that he didn't appreciate the embarrassment she had caused with Claude. She was so hurt by what I said she will not answer his calls or texts. Hell, she probably wouldn't even open her door to him now," Carla explained, then took a long drink of her white wine.

"Wow, so you really think they were involved?" Patrick raised his eyebrows high.

"Yeah, I do. If not, it was only a matter of time, but now that chance is gone. Come on, Patrick, you know she was going to ruin our plan, it needed to be done."

"And what happens if he gets her to talk to him and he brings her back?" he growled out.

"Already taken care of, you remember Sandra Carpenter? I called her after I fired Alexandra, she was more than willing to take the job, and starts tomorrow, there's no spot to give back to Alexandra Mills." She was grinning from ear to ear.

Patrick sighed. "I don't know, Carla. He goes and does what he wants, when he wants, it's a never-ending circle with him."

"Then we strike if he does, take him down before he does, we can get this company away from him in a heartbeat. Honestly, if you talked to your father and Cal, they might strip the company from him."

"You do realize you are talking about the man who has made millions for **MAEP** since he took over for his father, right?"

"Yes, but how screwed up is he going to be without his precious little woman in the picture?"

Patrick took a deep breath. "We'll just have to see how it goes, I guess." He swigged half of his beer down. This was going to be interesting or disastrous, and he was leaning more toward catastrophic.

## Chapter 10

Dom smiled at Alexa as she closed her eyes and let out a little moan. He moved from her ankle and slowly up her body, pressing gentle kisses against the exposed skin of her legs. When he reached and kissed her neck, he held his weight off of her with his hands on either side of her head. "Honey, what happened today after you left my office?" he asked, in between the kisses on her neck.

She opened her eyes just as he leaned back a little. "Carla, Patrick, and you fired me." She wiggled out from underneath him and moved as far as she could from him.

He looked at her completely baffled. "What did you mean when you added me? I told you I wasn't going to fire you and that I wasn't angry with you. Why would you think I'd fire you after I told you I wasn't?"

"You also didn't finish in the office, you just stopped." She stared at her hands on her knees. "And what else am I supposed to believe after..." She stopped and stood up from the in-ground couch.

Dom stood up and walked up to her, touching her shoulder. "After what?"

"Nothing. Carla told me you, Patrick, and she talked about it and all decided it was best if my employment was ended." Alexa pulled away from him and went up the steps to another window and stared outside.

He sighed as he watched her wrap her arms around herself tightly. He slowly walked up to her laying his hands on her shoulders. "Why didn't you come talk to me?"

"I don't know, I didn't want to look like a fool if she was right. She does hate me after all, and if she saw that you really turned me away she would have eaten it up, loved it, and I wouldn't have been able to handle that too well."

Dom made her turn around toward him. "Baby, you should have come to me right away. I've told you many times you have a place in my company, you always will, too, not just because I want you but because I know what that brain of yours can do for the company. It's flourishing even more because of you and your ideas, because of the people you've worked with and have chosen, I'm never letting you go." He pulled her against him and kissed the top of her head. "I understand your lack of trust in men, but, baby, you can trust me to need you at MAEP, I want you there too, and I'm going to keep you safe."

She tilted her head up to look at him. "Really?"

"Yes." He dipped his head to claim her lips. "May I?" he asked instead of just doing it.

She bit her bottom lip hard then nodded her head.

He finished the move and caught her soft full lips, moving his hands up to cradle her face as he deepened the kiss when she let out a whimper.

His tongue slid between her lips, and all he tasted was the strawberry wine. He massaged her tongue with his as she gripped the sides of his jacket. He pulled back slowly and rubbed her cheeks with his thumbs. "You're so beautiful and talented, you ever leaving MAEP will be of your own accord, when *you* are ready to move on, I will let you."

She nodded to show she understood. "Thank you. I'm sorry I ignored your texts and calls, and I'm sorry I didn't talk to you before I left."

"It's okay, just don't do it again, are we clear?" His tone changed to demanding.

"Y-yes."

"Good." He clasped her hand in his and pulled her back to the couch. "How about you finish your wine now." He let her sit down and grabbed her glass, handing it to her.

"Then I can go home?" She looked at him with soft, pleading eyes.

"Actually, I think you should just stay here with me tonight, Brandon talked to your oldest sister, she told him Tate was looking for you and he didn't sound too happy. I don't feel comfortable taking you home, plus it'll give the bodyguard a break. Fuck!" He shouted a little.

Alexa jumped when he shouted, spilling her wine all over her shirt. "What, what's wrong? What'd I do?"

Dom looked at her and saw how badly he had scared her. "No, baby, I'm sorry, it wasn't you, I forgot to call my body-guard to tell him I found you." He pulled out his phone and made a call. "Angelo, I'm sorry. I found Alexa about an hour ago, you can call off the search, she'll be staying here at the house tonight also, so you don't need to post anyone outside of her house." He ended the call and looked over at Alexa.

His eyes widened when he saw her take her shirt off. "Lex, what are you doing?"

"Well, you've already seen me with my shirt off," she whispered. "And I spilled my wine. It was a little cold." She looked down at the floor. "I- I can put it back on." She went to slip back into it.

Dom stopped her, pulled the shirt out of her hand and threw it behind the couch. "No, I kind of like the view." He pulled her into his lap. She let out a gasp when his arousal pressed up against her. "Okay, I really like the view, you're so beautiful."

He smiled when she blushed.

---

Alexa couldn't believe she was in his home, sitting in his lap, shirtless. She closed her eyes when she felt his hands brush against her back then around to her stomach, his thumbs grazed her skin right below her bra-covered breasts. "Dom," she moaned.

His hands moved further up and cupped her perky, bra-restricted breasts. She moaned, leaning her head back as her nipples beaded against his hands.

"Dominick!" She moaned loudly, aching to feel his hands against her with no clothes to reduce the feeling. She let go of his jacket to unhook her bra, causing her to fall back a little.

He acted fast and grabbed her ass, yanking her forward into him, crushing his chest to hers. "Be careful, little one," he whispered. "What were you trying to do?"

Their eyes locked, and her hands reached behind her the rest of the way, and she unclasped her bra, letting her plump breasts free.

"Alexandra," he moaned as he gazed down at the exposed flesh.

"Dominick, please," she begged him as she reached between them and pulled his shirt from his black dress pants.

"God, I love hearing you say my full name." He crushed her body to his, halting her hands, as he fiercely captured her mouth with an urgency that she returned.

She moaned, grinding her aching need against his as they sipped each other. She almost let out a scream when he pulled her bottom lip between his teeth and nipped at it. She gasped, enabling him to plunge his tongue into her mouth and mate with her tongue.

She pulled back as they both gasped for air. "Dominick," she gasped.

He pulled her against him making her rest her head on his shoulder. "I know, Lex. God, don't I know," he said gruffly. His hands cupped her full breasts, grazing his thumbs against their rock-hard tips.

"Dom," she cried out, arching her back.

"Use my full name, baby, please?" he begged as he adjusted them so she was lying on her back on the couch. He dipped his head, replacing one of his thumbs with his mouth, flicking the tip with his tongue and then catching it between his teeth, tugging a little.

"Dominick!" she screamed, digging her fingers into his hair.

He shoved her skirt up around her waist and tugged down her thong. His fingers stroked against her folds gently, then he pressed between them finding her soaking wet.

"Dominick, please!" she begged, wanting the release he had given her earlier. She arched her back as he filled her with one finger and thrust it into her warm, soaked entrance.

He moved from her breast and kissed down her stomach slowly. "Baby, don't move." His voice was laced with desire as he continued to move down. He encouraged her thighs to open more and for her to raise her legs up at the knees. "Just relax, okay?" He looked up at her.

She looked at him, and their eyes locked. "What are you going to do?" She could hear the fear in her voice.

"Trust me, baby girl, trust me," He answered with shallow breaths. "Can you do that for me, baby?"

She let out a shuddering breath as she nodded her head.

"Okay, stay like this." He, more or less, commanded as his middle finger joined his forefinger.

She arched up from the couch, but his other hand pressed her back down. She tried hard not to squirm as he pushed his fingers deeper into her aching center.

She closed her eyes tightly as his face came close to where his fingers were. "Dom," she whimpered in fear.

"Shh, baby, it's okay," He reassured right before his tongue found her sensitive, sweet spot he had played with his thumb earlier.

"Dominick!" she screamed and tried to pull away from him, but then the pressure began to build inside her more as he thrust his fingers faster and swirled his tongue around her swollen jewel. He flicked his tongue back and forth repeatedly and pushed his fingers into her even more quickly.

She screamed again as she pushed her hips up from the couch. Dom pushed her back down as her breathing became even more ragged.

"Let go, baby, just let go," he encouraged as his tongue dove back to her over sensitive bud.

She felt herself climbing higher and higher, plunging into the pulsating waves of pleasure, and she screamed his name so loud it echoed through the vast house.

---

Dom pulled his mouth and fingers from her, cleaning his fingers by licking them. He moved beside her and wrapped his arms around her gently. He kissed her forehead as she tried to hide her face from him. "Baby, don't, I love seeing you glow from the pleasure," he whispered, tilting her face up, "you look so beautiful."

She dug her head into his chest. "I'm so sorry," she mumbled.

"We've been through this before, you never have to say sorry to me, even in my house, just like yours." He rubbed her back soothingly.

"But I was so loud," she mumbled.

Dom rolled on top of her, tilting her head up with a finger locking eyes with her. "And I loved it, do you want me to do it again?" he teased. "Because I will make you that loud any time of the day." His lips brushed hers. "Come on, let's get you cleaned up then to bed, you'll stay here tomorrow, but I'll expect you at the office the day after, bright and early," He teased as he scooped her up in his arms and headed to the right side of the house to his room.

He knew she could have so much passion and be a spirited partner if she'd just let loose and didn't think. There was so much more he couldn't wait to teach her.

He took her into the bathroom and started the shower. "Use anything you need to tonight, and I will find you something to sleep in."

***

Alexa felt like she was in a daze as she began to get out of the only piece of clothing she had left on, her skirt, and got in the shower. She began to wet her hair and then washed it and cleaned herself up. She shut the water off and got out, grabbing the towel Dom had laid out for her. She smiled a little and began to dry off.

She jumped when he opened the door. "What are you doing?"

"Giving you a shirt to wear to bed, I'm afraid that's all I have."

"But I'm in here with no clothes on now." She tried to cover herself with the towel.

Dom chuckled as he moved closer to her and pulled the

towel from her wet body. "I've already seen a lot of you tonight, I think I can handle seeing a little more fully what I just enjoyed."

She turned red as he walked closer to her and kissed her gently, he then wrapped the towel around her and helped her dry. She moaned when his fingers brushed against her folds, and her knees went a little weak.

He scooped her up after he grabbed the shirt he'd picked for her and headed out of his room.

"Where are we going now?" she asked.

"That's my room. I'll give you your own space for tonight. You'll be right next to me in this room, if you need me just come get me."

"O-okay," she stuttered a little.

"Are you going to be okay in here?"

"Sure, do you have a brush I can use?" she asked, gesturing toward her wet hair.

"Um, a comb."

"That'll work, thank you."

He smiled at her as he slid the shirt over her arms and slowly buttoned it up, he had her sit on the bed. "I'll be right back, baby."

She nodded her head and waited for him to come back. He handed her the comb as soon as he came back into the room. She sat on the bed as she combed out her hair. He ran the back of his knuckles against her cheek slowly and softly.

She handed him back the comb and slowly stood up to fold the blanket down on the big king-sized bed. She hugged her waist tightly, a little afraid of the enormous bed.

Dom pulled her toward him. "You okay?"

"Yeah, I'm fine," she whispered as she glanced at the bed again.

"Okay, why don't you get some sleep. I'll see you in the morning, okay?" He picked her up to lay her down. "Just remember I am right next door if you need me." He covered her with the blanket and kissed her goodnight. He headed out the door and went to shut the light off.

"Can I have that on?" she asked.

"Sure, goodnight, baby."

"Thank you, goodnight, Dom." She watched him close the door to just a crack, and she rolled onto her side, curling up into a ball and slowly began to fall asleep.

## Chapter 11

Dom got out of the shower and dried off. As his head hit the pillow, a scream ripped through the silent house.

He was up in a flash and running to Alexa's room. He pushed the door open as another scream came from her. Then he heard the sobs. He slowly climbed on the bed. "Alexa, baby, wake up." He gently shook her shoulder.

Her eyes flew open, and she was across the bed in a flash, almost toppling off of it.

Dom grabbed her arm and pulled her to him. "It's okay, Lex, I'm right here," he whispered against her ear. He rubbed her back gently. "It was just a dream, baby, just a dream."

He smiled when she climbed in his lap, wrapping her arms around him. Her small body trembled against his. "You have bad dreams often?"

"No, just sometimes when something doesn't go the way I planned or when I screw something up, and when I'm really stressed out or failing at something." She rubbed her cheek against his bare shoulder.

"And what's the problem tonight, little one?"

"All of the above."

"Well, everything will be fixed the day after tomorrow. I'm making you my assistant, so no one will touch you or your job, you'll be my consultant," he explained, hoping to ease her mind.

She leaned back away from him. "Are you sure you want to do that?"

"Yes, you'll have the security you need, are you okay now?" He brushed his knuckles against her cheeks.

"I guess so," she whispered and went to move from his lap.

Dom stopped her quickly. "If you're not okay, just tell me, little one, I'll understand."

"I think I'm okay."

"What were you dreaming?"

She shook her head and hid her face against his shoulder.

"Okay, okay, little steps, you going to be okay by yourself?" What the hell was he asking? If she said no, he'd end up taking her to his bedroom, which would end badly because he'd end up putting the moves on her again or she'd get so attached and would want it every night.

"I'll be fine," she whispered, which was not very convincing.

"Come on." He pulled her up into his arms and headed to his bedroom. He laid her down gently. He moved to turn the light off.

"Dom, can you leave it on?" she squeaked out.

"How about we turn on the bedside lamp, will that be okay?" he asked gently. She nodded her head a little. "Okay, you turn that on first, and then I'll shut the overhead light off."

She did as he told her, and he turned off the overhead light, the whole room was cascaded with a soft glow.

"Is that okay for you, Lex?"

"Should be," she answered softly.

He walked over to the bed. "Are you sure?" He watched her nod her head. "Okay, baby, scooch over a little." She did as he asked, and he lay down on the bed and faced her. "What makes you so afraid of the dark?"

She closed her eyes and let out a sigh. "He'd get really drunk at night, that's when he'd come in and start beating me."

"For no reason?" Dom tried to keep his anger at bay. "I mean, I know no parent should do what he did, but nothing would set him off?"

"Just the alcohol, the fact I wasn't a boy, and I wasn't even supposed to happen at all. He hated me," Alexa whispered.

He reached out for her and pulled her up against him. "Well, for the record, I don't get completely wasted, I am thrilled you aren't a guy, and I definitely don't hate you." He pressed a kiss against her cheek.

"Dom, can I ask you something? It's been bothering me since you've mentioned it a few times." She hid her face in his chest a little.

"Of course. What's up?" His tone was soothing as he tried to encourage her to ask what was on her mind.

"You mentioned consequences, what kind of consequences?" she asked in a hushed voice.

Dom let out a sigh. How was he going to explain this to someone so sensitive? "Babe, I am not like most men, I am very discipline oriented. I prefer my women to act a certain way, please me a certain way, and to not give me the attitude you have given me a few times, or to disrespect me by rolling their eyes."

"So, discipline, like spanking?" she asked quietly as her eyes widened as their gazes locked.

"Amongst other things, yes. This is why I tried to stay away from you, I know what your past is and I don't want you to feel as if you are being abused again. You must know, though,

I will never raise a hand to you in anger, but there are certain rules I need you to follow if we continue, well, whatever this is that is going on between us. Do you understand?"

Alexa's eyes were still round but there seemed to be less fear in them this time. "I think so, I just, I don't know. What other things?"

Dom smiled at her faintly, shaking his head. "We can discuss everything else once you aren't so tired or shaken up. Try to get some more sleep, baby girl." He looked down at her and kissed her cheek gently. When he pulled back he saw her eyes were already closed.

He couldn't help but smile as she snuggled closer to him and laid a hand against his somewhat hairy chest. She didn't run screaming from his bed or arms, so that was a plus, maybe she could be what he needed and wanted after all. Who would have thought?

*Slow down, Dom, you still haven't told her everything, things are just going to have to go slow with this one and if you screw up too much then you will lose her. Forever*, he told himself.

He let out a sigh as he cuddled her fragile, small body to his. And who was going to get attached?

---

Dom groaned when he heard his alarm go off. He went to roll over to shut it off, but something was stopping him. He looked down to see Alexa snuggled up into him, one of her skinny legs was thrown over both of his, her arm was over his stomach, and her head was on his chest.

She looked so adorable, and he didn't want to disturb her. He tried to reach for his clock but ended up knocking it to the ground.

"Fuck," he grumbled loudly as it clattered to the floor.

He felt Alexa jerk away from him, and he leaned down to

get the clock. He shut the loud buzzing off, then turned back to Alexa, who was now cowering on the other side of the bed.

Dom moved closer to Alexa and wrapped his arm around her and pulled her into him. "Sorry, baby, I really need to watch my temper around you." He ran his hand up and down her arm lightly.

"No, it's okay, I shouldn't be so jumpy."

"Are you okay?" He kissed her temple gently.

"Yeah I'm fine, are you sure you don't want me to come to the office today?"

"Yes, I want to see how they react without you there today, make them think they've won."

She nodded a little. "Can you drop me off at home before you go in? If it's too much of a burden I can walk."

Dom pulled Alexa into his lap and then rolled her onto her back and leaned over her. "No more walking places, not until I get rid of Tate for good, and I'd rather you stayed here for a little bit." He leaned down to nuzzle her nose gently.

"But, I need my stuff, Dom."

"Give me your key, and I'll have Angelo pick some things up for you. He can take his girlfriend with him to get the more delicate things, although I really like you in just my shirt."

"You're terrible, but I'll need things for tomorrow, and only I know what I will want to wear."

"Then, I'll have Angelo bring everything, or you could quit being stubborn and just write everything down."

"Or you could just let me go home. I'll be careful."

Dom shook his head and dropped his forehead against hers. "Stubborn, so freaking stubborn."

"We both know this is only a temporary thing, so I just need a few things, so either let me go get them, or I'll just find some way to get home."

Temporary thing. That hurt a little as strange as it was, he kissed her lips gently. "Fine, take the car to get your few things,

I'll take one of the others but if you need anything or something happens while you're there you call me, okay?" He
watched her bite her bottom lip. He reached out to pluck it
from between her teeth. "Promise me."

"I promise."

"Now, I'm going to go take a shower and head in." He
kissed her gently, then headed to the bathroom.

---

Alexa watched him walk away, her mouth literally watered as
she watched his muscles work along his back as he moved.

Once he was out of sight, she rolled from the bed. She
looked at the clock, 4 a.m. She slowly looked around the tan
room. It was pretty empty besides a large chair that was tan,
along with the California king bed, which had white silk
sheets, and a dark blue comforter.

The frame was black metal and had many circular designs
along it. She took a deep breath and slid from the bed and
made her way to the kitchen. She wondered what a man like
him would eat for breakfast.

She began to go through the cabinets and managed to find
bread, vanilla and sugar. She pursed her lips and went to the
fridge and grabbed the milk and some eggs. She grabbed a
skillet out of another cabinet.

She cracked three eggs into a bowl and began to beat
them with a fork. She mixed the rest of the ingredients and
began to fix some French toast.

She was starting to flip the first four when a pair of arms
wrapped around her from behind. She let out a scream.

"Easy, honey, just me." Dom's deep voice whispered
against her ear. "I keep forgetting you are delicate." He
pressed soft kisses against her neck making her squirm against
him. "What are you doing?"

"Well, you've brought me breakfast and coffee for the last few weeks, and since you've banned me from MAEP today and let me stay last night, I thought I could make you breakfast in return. Even though I owe you way more than breakfast."

His nose nuzzled her neck. "Just be wearing this when I come home, and that'll be repayment enough."

"No promises," she whispered, nudged him away from her and finished making his food.

She went to get a plate for him. She handed the plate to Dom once she filled it up with the four slices. "Enjoy."

"What about you?"

"Fixing mine right now, you can eat, Dom." She began to make herself two pieces.

She headed into the dining room slowly, she grabbed the bottle of syrup from the table and went to sit across from Dom.

He grabbed her hand. "Where do you think you're going?" he asked, his eyebrows raised high.

"To go sit down," she answered meekly.

"I'd rather have you beside me." He pulled her close to him.

She shook her head, but sat down in the chair beside him, he didn't let go of her hand. She glanced at him as he began to eat. She shook her head again then began to try to use her left hand to eat since Dom had ahold of her right one, which was her dominant hand, of course.

Alexa struggled a little but managed.

When she heard Dom clear his throat, she looked over at him slowly as he stood up.

"I better be going, Lex." He paused as he looked down at her. "Thank you for breakfast, it was delicious." He bent down and kissed her lips softly. "Be careful today, and don't hesitate to call me if you need me either."

He was probably tired of telling her that but seemed to need to. "Dom," she called out as he turned away from her and began to walk toward the doorway from the dining room to the kitchen. He turned back to look at her, her breath was stolen as she finally got a good look at him, his suit was all black today, and the crisp white shirt beneath his jacket made his tan pop out even more. He looked like some kind of god, honestly.

"What'd you want, Lex?" he prompted as she just stared at him.

She licked her lips trying to ignore the flip her stomach kept doing. "I'm, I'm sorry, can I use one of the SUVs instead of your car, I'll be a nervous wreck driving it."

He opened a drawer of the table he was standing beside, against the wall of the walkway from the dining room to the kitchen. He pulled out a set of keys, the metal ring hanging by his forefinger palm up. "Here you go."

She slowly got up and went to get them. "Thank you, and you're sure about this?"

She felt him tilt her head up by her chin with the same finger she had just taken the key ring from. "Very, I want you safe." He leaned down and plundered her lips slowly with his.

He pulled back when she let out a moan. "Just keep your promise. Call me if you need me."

She nodded her head, and he began to leave again. She let out a shaky breath. She was glad someone was sure about this because she sure as hell wasn't. Especially after both incidents last night. She felt her face heat up as she remembered the act on the couch. That was more embarrassing than having the nightmare.

She began to clean up her mess, putting the dishes in the dishwasher. She went to the living room and grabbed her discarded bra and blouse from the night before and her purse.

She went to his room and then into the bathroom. She

started the water for a shower after tossing his shirt onto the long vanity top that took up the long wall's length. The other side was the toilet. Along the shorter wall was a tub and walk-in shower. She couldn't believe he had both in here, and yet nothing was cramped. Everything in this house was so spacious.

She didn't belong in a place like this. This wasn't what her future had held, so she shouldn't get used to it. *He'll drop you as soon as Tate is either out of the picture or when he gets completely bored with you when he realizes how much you can't do and don't know how to do,* she scolded herself.

She straightened her clothes on the vanity top and got into the hot water letting out a moan as the water cascaded down her body. She wished he were in there with her. But she had to stop such foolish thoughts. He would tire of her within a week. Guaranteed.

---

Dom pulled up into his usual parking spot. Thoughts of leaving Alexa alone were nerve-racking. He didn't want to leave her alone. He suddenly had such an intense ache to be beside her all the time. He about flipped when she went to sit across from him instead of beside him.

She was so strong yet shy, and she was making a place inside of him, that he wanted to be filled again, feel empty the minute he walked out of the dining room. He should have stayed with her.

He let out an irritated huff as he opened his car door and shut it with more force than necessary. *She handled things before you came into her life, she will be okay.* The only difference now was he was in her life, and he wanted to be. He didn't understand what was going on with him.

He'd get around Alexa, and he would lose every standard

he ever had: don't hold them, don't be sweet to them, get what you want and leave. But with her he was giving her what she needed and was forgetting about himself. And what happened when he did think about himself and get what he wanted, would he end up hurting her and dropping her like a sack of potatoes? He was so frustrated with himself.

He unlocked the building and headed in to his office when his phone began to ring. Oh great. "Dad," he answered shortly.

"Dom, we need to talk. Have your secretary clear at least two hours today and have her let me know what time and I will be there," Calvin Mackenzie demanded in his authoritative tone that no one questioned, except Dom.

"Why?" he asked lazily.

"Because I have heard a few things that I assure you I am not happy with."

"Like what?"

"Don't you question me, boy, do as you are told," Calvin practically yelled.

Gee and Dom wondered where he got his attitude issues from. "Yes, Father." He hung up the phone, throwing it on his desk, and sat in his chair brooding. What could this unloving figure in his life possibly want? Then again, it hadn't been until his mother had run around on Cal that he became this cold. And it definitely had affected Dom, he was always so unfeeling, didn't give a shit about anyone or anything except himself until a certain someone tumbled into his office and spouted off.

He was already in a foul mood because his little spitfire wasn't going to be around him today, thanks to Carla and now this. Just great. Just fucking great.

Alexa got out of the shower and dried off. She decided instead of getting dressed in her clothes right away, she'd slip back into the dress shirt Dom had given her the night before. She found the comb he had let her use and untangled her knotted wet hair. She ran her tongue over her teeth, they felt sticky from the syrup she had earlier. She opened the medicine cabinet and found a toothbrush. She thought twice about using it, but she wanted her teeth clean.

When she was done, she climbed into the huge bed, lying down and covering herself with the comforter. She snuggled into it and began to make a mental list of things she needed.

As she began to think, she began to doze off. This was accomplishing nothing at the moment but felt good. She wasn't worried about anything right then. Even though things would probably end badly, she felt okay for once in her life.

## Chapter 12

Alexa let out a sigh as she began to wake up from her nap, she stretched a little and slowly sat up. She could get used to waking up to this comfortable bed every day, but that was a bad idea. Soon she would be back in her shack with the lumpy mattress and worn-down couch. *Yeah, don't get used to this,* she thought.

She would never be right for Dom, she refused to give up so much to a man. She would never willingly bend over his knees and let him spank her. It was not her cup of tea, she had read a couple of books that involved the spanking lifestyle and they did nothing for her.

Hell, not much of anything did much for her, that was until she met the young, jaw dropping Dominick Mackenzie. Man, did he do quite a bit for her. She shoved the thoughts away quickly and slowly got out of bed and changed into her clothes from the day before. She grabbed her purse and headed out of the bedroom, down to the kitchen. She plucked up the keys and made her way along the breezeway and out to the garage.

She pushed the unlock button on the key fob and headed

over to the SUV that created the beep noise. *Well, here goes nothing.* She climbed into the SUV, pushed the garage door opener, and headed out toward the gate. '*Oh, great.* Dom forgot to tell her how to open the gate. Shit. She looked around the SUV and saw a remote in the cup holder. She picked it up, hit the green button on the small remote, and the gate opened.

She'd have to call him later to find out the code to get back inside. She made sure the gate closed behind her and she headed to her place. She began to make mental notes again of what she needed or wanted to get as she made her way through the traffic.

---

Dom glanced at the clock on his desk. His dad should be there soon. He checked his phone to make sure Alexa hadn't texted him. Well, that was a good sign even though it didn't settle his nerves.

His dad walked in, and Dom hurriedly placed his phone into his front pocket where he could feel the vibration go off if she needed him. "Dad."

"Dominick." Cal's dark gaze was hard as he sat down in the chair across from him.

"Care to explain the need to have this meeting today? I had to clear my schedule of Angela Lane and Claude Benson, so this better be good, dear father." He narrowed his gaze at the much older version of himself. His dad had grayed some time ago and became very wrinkly over the last couple of years.

"Patrick called me. He told me about your new hire. He said she is disrespectful, has a mouth on her, oh, and you're sleeping with her, which is why you gave her the job to begin with." His gaze hardened even more.

Dom let out a round of laughter as he stood up. "I had

never laid eyes on that woman until the day of her interview. Did he also tell you he tried to steal the work she had done with Benson, or that Benson loved her ideas and that's the reason he's staying with us, and she used to work for Brandon at BAP?"

Cal's face paled a little. "You got this woman from BAP?"

"Yes I did, she's perfect, Dad. The only reason she was disrespectful toward Patrick was because he tried to take credit for all her hard work, trying to tell Benson he helped her come up with everything. She wouldn't stand for it, unlike others who work here and hand over their work to Patrick without blinking an eye." Dom paced the office as he talked to his dad.

"So, you're telling me Patrick doesn't do his own work?" Cal raised a gray eyebrow.

"He does some, but if it interferes with his plans, he shoves it off onto someone else, which is what he did with Benson and my new hire. Others let him do it, she did not, and I wasn't angry about it either."

Cal pursed his lips, and said, "I'd like to meet her. I'd also like to see the finances."

"Well, unfortunately, I can only get you the finances, she's not here right now."

"If she's so great, then why isn't she here? Are you sleeping with her, Dominick? Letting her get away with whatever she wants when she wants?" He glared at his son, obviously upset he wasn't producing the woman.

Dom let out a harsh breath as he glared back at his father. He crossed his arms over his chest tightly, angry his father didn't trust him or his decisions all of a sudden.

---

Alexa let out a sigh as she pulled up in front of her run-down gray home. It really looked dilapidated. But was that because of the world she was introduced to all of a sudden or because it really was that way?

Her eyes darted around quickly before getting out of the black SUV. No sign of her father anywhere, but that's when he tended to strike. When her guard was down, and she wasn't expecting anything. Only this time, she would expect it.

She checked the side mirror, seeing it was clear, she opened the door and slid from the tan leather seat. She grabbed her key to the door as she dropped the SUV key into her purse. She rushed up the steps and slid the key into the door.

As soon as she unlocked it, she opened the door just enough to squeeze into the house and shut it fast, locking every lock she had. She let out a breath. Maybe this had been a terrible idea. She wrapped her arms around her chest, her hands clinging to her shoulders.

She wanted Dom badly. He was the only one who really made her feel safe. But why? He could break her heart in an instant and not think twice about it. And he had a lifestyle she could never imagine having..

Her breathing finally became normal, and she headed to her room slowly. She glanced around and let out a sigh. Why had she ever gone with the shade of purple that was surrounding her now? It was the shade of purple her dad used to leave on her body all the time.

*So you always remember your place and remember it could happen at any time.* She shook herself from the thought and began to get her things gathered up. Why was she doing such a stupid thing?

---

"I asked you, are you sleeping with her?" Cal's gaze turned even harder as Dom looked back at him.

Dom glared back, crossing his arms over his chest. "I don't see why that matters, what I do in my personal life is exactly that, personal and private."

"It's obviously affecting both of your work performances, I mean she's not here." Cal gestured with his arms. "Why isn't she here, Dominick?"

"It's called a personal day." Dom went back to his desk and pulled out a couple of folders and threw them toward his dad. "Look at those ratings for both Ms. Lang and Mr. Benson. Also, the sales have skyrocketed for those two since they have implemented her ideas. I have even considered her advertising ideas."

He watched Cal's brown gaze flick along the pages studying them intently. Dom sat there brooding as Cal went over the papers.

"This is after three weeks?" Cal demanded.

"Yes," Dom answered calmly.

"Wow." His dad was actually speechless for once.

---

Alexa made a mental note of everything she packed and thought it was going to be enough. Two boxes worth of stuff should be more than plenty. She grabbed the first box, stuffing the keys into the pocket of her sweatpants that she had changed into earlier before starting to pack. She headed toward the door and managed to get it open and closed it behind her just enough so it stayed ajar.

She went down the steps trying to look around at the same time. She was pushed roughly on her back and tripped over her feet. The box tumbled to its side, letting everything fall out on the sidewalk. Her arm hit the concrete hard, making her scrape it up pretty bad.

She let out a little scream when she was shoved onto her

back. Hazel eyes met hard brown. She tried to scramble away from him. Why had she been so careless?

She screamed louder when Tate reached down, snatching her up by her hair. "Shacking up with the man, huh, how much do you think he'd pay to get you back?"

"Nothing, it's not like that!" Alexa yelled at him, trying to get out of his grip.

He yanked harder on her hair. "Oh, I think it is like that," he snarled at her.

She tried to pull away again, and he shoved her toward the house. She fell against the steps scraping her hand and other arm. She felt her skin begin to sting as she was pulled up. She took advantage of his hands being occupied and swung, managing to punch him in the face, surprisingly hard.

He stumbled back from her, she scrambled up the steps and into her house. Her ankle was grabbed, and she fell just inside the door hitting her face against the floor, the pain brought tears to her eyes, and she screamed as she was dragged back out of the house.

She grabbed the keys out of her pocket. She managed to place them between her fingers, and as her father pulled her around toward him, she punched him in the face again, making the keys dig into his cheek a little.

He jerked back, yelling profanities at her. "You stupid bitch!"

She got her leg up and shoved it into his stomach, making him fall down the steps. She ran into her house, slamming the door shut. She locked the door but jumped back yelping when she heard the loud bang against the door. She rushed forward to lock the deadbolt and chain.

Where'd she put her phone? She tried to rack her brain as the door seemed to be caving in against the force Tate was slamming it with. Her heart was pounding so fast and hard.

She went to her room where her phone was lying on the

bed. She snatched it up quickly and began to call Dom. It rang five times and went to voicemail. She cursed and hung up, then tried again. The same result. She texted him quickly. *Tate here, need help.* She let out a breath as the door kept taking the onslaught Tate was delivering to it.

She heard the wood splinter a little. She ran to the kitchen and grabbed a sharp knife. He wasn't getting to her this time. She scrolled to Brandon's number and called him, and he didn't answer either. *No, no, no.*

She crouched down behind the island in the kitchen. She kept looking at her phone, still nothing.

She began to call MAEP and Ashley answered on the second ring. "Ashley, Ashley, I need Dom, like right now, I tried to call and text him, please, Ashley."

"Alexa? I'm sorry he's in a meeting that I was told no one was to disturb."

"No, no, no, he told me to call him if I needed him, and I need him please, just tell him," Alexa begged as the door crashed in more, she let a sob escape as she curled up more in to herself clutching the knife handle so tight her hand was cramping.

"Oh, Alexa, I'll try, no guarantees, but I promise I'll try." Ashley ended the phone call.

Alexa dialed 911 next. There was no way Dom would get there in time, and she didn't think the cops would either, but she had to try. She told the dispatcher where she was, what was going on. She let out another sob as she heard the door splinter more.

She was going to die. No one was going to get there in time.

---

Ashley stared at the phone for a minute and got up from her desk. She stared at the dark wooden door, and with a deep breath, she knocked lightly. Hoping she wouldn't lose her job for this.

"Yeah!" Dom scolded at the interruption between him and his father. His gaze darted to his door. He was surprised to see Ashley standing there in his doorway. "What, Ashley?" he demanded, frowning at her.

"I'm so sorry, sir, but Alexa just called me at the desk. She sounded upset, and like she was in some sort of trouble, she told me you told her to call you if she needed you?" she said, with so much questioning in her tone.

"Why didn't she call me?"

"She said she tried to, sir, and a text also."

He pulled his phone out of his pocket and made the screen light up. Two missed calls from her and a text that read *Tate here, need help*. He cursed under his breath and headed toward the door.

"Where do you think you are going?" Cal demanded.

"Sorry, I have to go, Dad." Dom rushed out the door leaving his dad behind.

He rushed out to his Camaro and headed to Alexa's. Twenty minutes since he had gotten that text, twenty fucking minutes, and he was sitting on his ass in his office. He didn't understand how he didn't get her phone calls or text.

He didn't care that it was dangerous, he kept going around people who were slowing him down.

---

Alexa was trying so hard to fight the tears as the wood kept breaking. Where were the police or Dom? She finally heard the loud crack and bang as the door gave way.

She covered her mouth, trying to stifle the sobs coming from her.

"Oh come on, Alexandra, you can have me out of your life forever. Just come with me right now, and we'll have a little chat with your boyfriend. Come out, come out, wherever you are." She heard his boots getting closer to the kitchen. "We're going to play your favorite game, huh? Don't think I don't remember you used to love to play hide and seek."

She closed her eyes tightly, trying to keep from vomiting. When she got a little older, she used to hide from him, and when she did, it only made it worse for her when he found her. She heard the sirens off in the distance, and they sounded too far away yet. She felt the island move closer to her back then suddenly it was tipping over on to her.

She scrambled away quickly, and she was face to face with Tate. Fear gripped her like a vice grip that was tightened as far as it would go and wasn't letting go any time soon. She held the knife out in front of her.

His cheek was smeared with his blood from the two marks she made with the keys. His hair was disheveled along with his black jeans and white t-shirt. She backed up as he moved closer to her.

"Not so brave, no matter how much you pretend, are you?" He grabbed her wrist tightly, slamming her body and wrist into the wall, causing her to drop the knife and scream in pain.

"He won't pay anything for me. We're nothing to each other, please. I'll get you the money somehow, just let me go, please stop," Alexa pleaded but was met with a harsh slap. She grimaced in pain and felt the trickle of blood flow down her chin.

The sirens were getting closer, and her throat was gripped hard. "You called the cops?" Tate demanded.

She shook her head, trying to reassure him she didn't. He

pulled his hand from her throat, then his fist slammed into her cheek, the force knocking her to the ground.

"You are a lying bitch. You better watch your back from now on, tell your lover boy to watch his too. I'll be coming for you and his money, I will get what I want." He left the duplex quickly as the sirens got even closer.

She held her cheek as she let the tears fall. Her heart was beating so fast, along with her body trembling. She could barely catch her breath.

She heard the rough, deep voice yell, "Go after that asshole!"

She couldn't move, all she could do was lie there and cry. She had been so stupid, and everything hurt.

---

The minute Dom pulled up behind his SUV, he took in the scene quickly. The box was tipped over, clothes were all over the sidewalk, he saw her door was literally broken in two. He then saw the guy he couldn't mistake running down the sidewalk.

He saw the squad car pull up and he shouted for them to go after the ass who was running down the sidewalk. He rushed into the duplex. He had to climb over the door that was halfway hanging on the opposite side of the hinges, and the other half was on the floor. He groaned at the sight. This wasn't good. "Alexa?" he called out as he managed to get over the broken door. "Lex?" he called out again but still nothing. Fear gripped him tightly when she still hadn't come out or yelled for him.

He scanned the area, the living room looked untouched, his gaze jerked to the kitchen, he saw the island tipped over, and then he saw her. "Lex!" She was curled up into herself, trembling and covering her face with her hand. She wasn't moving. He rushed to her and knelt in front of her. "Honey, can you move for me, please?" he coaxed as he laid a hand against her side that was heaving way too fast.

He didn't know what to do, he slowly moved her hand from her face. "Baby, look at me, come on, look at me, please?"

She opened her eyes a little and glanced at him, but curled further into herself. "Just go away," she sobbed out.

"I'm not going anywhere, baby. I am right here for you, I am right here, I am so sorry I didn't get here in time, come here, little one." He helped her sit up, and his blood rushed to a boiling point the minute he saw her. She was bruised on her cheek, her lip was cracked and bleeding. He raked his gaze over the rest of her body. She had scrapes along her arms and her other cheek. "Goddamn it," he breathed out and pulled her into him. "God, fucking damn it, I'm so sorry, Alexa, so sorry." He wrapped his arms around her gently, but she clung to his suit jacket, moving even closer to him as she began to cry uncontrollably. "I'm here now, baby. I'm here, never again, I wish you would have listened to me," he whispered against her ear, and she trembled in his arms even more.

He let out a huff, she needed a red ass after this, she made him give in to her and go against his better judgement and that sure as hell wasn't going to happen again. His word was final in his house, and she wouldn't continue to bat those pretty eyes of hers, and get her way, especially when it came to a dangerous decision like this. But all of that could wait. Right now, she needed his comfort and care. When she was feeling better, they would be having a long discussion and his rules and consequences would be laid out clearly and he wasn't taking no for an answer.

He looked up as the cops came in through the door. "Did you get him?"

One of the officers looked at the mess throughout the

kitchen, and the woman he held close to him. "No, we lost him in the crowd. We'll keep searching, though, what is his name?"

"Tate Mills, her father, he attacked her."

"I suggest you take her somewhere safe until we find this guy."

"That was the plan, she was going to stay with me until we found him. I've had my team searching for him too, she came here to get some of her things to move into my house."

"You're Dominick Mackenzie, aren't you?"

"Yes, she'll be protected at my home, can I get her out of here?" he asked while almost glaring at the officers who failed to grab Tate.

"Yeah, I think we got the gist of what happened here today if we have any questions we will call you."

Dom picked Alexa up and headed out to his car.

## Chapter 13

Alexa felt pain every time Dom took a step, she tried to get him to put her down. "I'm going to get blood all over you," she croaked out between sobs.

"I don't care," he answered calmly. He managed to keep a hold of her and open his car door. He crouched down to place her in the seat. He yanked off his suit jacket and put it over her shoulders then snapped her seatbelt. "I knew I should have come with you or sent Angelo. I'm sorry I didn't insist." He shut the door softly, but she still jumped.

She stared at her hands. They were damaged and one was bleeding too. Then she felt stinging on her leg. She managed to roll the leg up on her sweatpants and saw she was bleeding there also. She let out a shaky sob.

Dom started the Camaro and whipped it around as he made a call. "Yeah, I want everything moved by the time I get home tonight, no not the furniture just personal items, clothes,, soaps, anything she will need, she's staying with me indefinitely."

Alexa jumped when her phone began to ring, Brandon. "Hello?" Her voice sounded raspy as she answered.

"What's wrong? I'm sorry I missed your call. I was in a meeting."

"N-nothing, I'm fine, Brandon. I'm, I'm s-sorry I called," she sobbed into the phone.

Dom pulled the phone away from her swiftly but gently. "Brandon? Yeah, I'm with her now, she looks pretty roughed up, she was at her house getting some things she needed since she'll be staying with me. I don't know what all happened, I'm taking her with me to MAEP. I don't have a choice, my dad's there at the moment."

Alexa darted her tear-filled eyes at Dom at the news that Calvin Mackenzie was there. She looked back at her scraped up hand. She moved her other wrist, at least the pain was mild. She didn't want to go to MAEP. She was going to cause Dom so much embarrassment, between her old black sweatpants and low cut, thin-strapped tank top. This was a mistake. Maybe she could get Brandon to come get her.

She reached for the visor and looked at herself in the mirror. Blood was caked against her chin, a dark red now that it had somewhat dried. She had a bruise near her mouth, around her neck also. Her face was scraped up pretty bad too from the fall, bruises on both of her cheeks.

She began to cry all over again as she slammed the visor up and hung her head in her hands.

"Look, Brandon, I don't care if you come or not, she may need you though, but I'll keep business out of this. This is a personal matter that involves a woman we both care about." Dom's deep voice flowed over Alexa. She glanced at him. Now he was telling Brandon he cared about her? Was it true? He did leave a meeting with his father to come to her, but that didn't mean he cared so deeply for her that he'd never break her heart. Or did it?

She felt her phone being laid down next to her. Then a hand on her thigh gently. "Baby, are you okay?"

Really? Was she okay? Of course not, but all she did was nod her head in response.

"I mean, you can move, okay? I know it hurts, but there's nothing that can't move, right? Do we need to take you to the doctor?"

"I'm fine. No doctor," she croaked out.

------

Dom shook his head as he ran circles with his fingertips against her thigh. He wished she wouldn't try to be so strong, but she was proud. He pulled into the parking lot, and before he got out, Alexa opened her door slowly and started to get out. She groaned in pain as she swung her legs out of the car.

He rushed around the car and picked her up carefully, closing the door with his foot. He headed into the building, where he ran into Carla.

She shot him a glare as he carried Alexa close to his body. "She's not supposed to be here, she quit yesterday, and I don't want her on this property anymore."

"Yeah, not happening, she's back on at MAEP. You're never interfering with her again. Sorry, Carla, but she's my personal consultant, you lose." He glared at the redhead, and she backed down immediately.

He stormed past her. "Get me some towels, wet and dry!" he barked at her, causing Alexa to jump. "Sorry, Lex, you're okay, I've got you." He walked into his office and laid her down on the couch gently, but she still let out a scream of pain.

"Dom?" His father's voice broke through his thoughts.

"Dad." He looked at Alexa again then turned to Cal.

"This is where you went?"

"Yeah, she was in trouble."

"Is that Alexandra Mills?" Cal's voice was just above a whisper.

"Yeah."

"What happened?"

Before Dom could answer, Brandon came rushing into the office. "Lex, sweetheart?" He rushed up to the couch. "God, honey, are you okay?"

"I guess so, at least nothing will hopefully scar this time," she mumbled.

Brandon sat on the edge of the couch and rubbed her head gently.

"What's he doing here, Dominick?"

Both men turned to look at Cal. "He's pretty much her dad," Dom answered easily.

"Stepdad," Brandon answered as he turned back to Alexa.

Dom stared at them both. Well, this was new information.

"What?" Cal yelled, making Alexa jump up from the couch, and push herself into the corner beside the sofa.

Dom glared at Cal. "Dad, stop it. If you're not going to control yourself, then you can leave." He went up to Alexa slowly. "Babe, you're safe here, no one's going to hurt you here." She pushed him away from her.

"Don't touch me, just leave me alone." She moved further away.

Dom tried again. "Alexa."

"Don't!" she yelled.

Brandon got between him and Alexa and moved closer to her. "Lex, stop. Nothing's going to happen here."

Dom could only watch as Alexa moved away from Brandon and told him to leave her alone also.

"Alexa, stop, not now, stop it," Brandon said.

"No, just let me be." She went to step around Brandon, but he grabbed hold of her tightly. She began to struggle

122

against him until the tears took over, and they both sunk to the ground.

Brandon knelt beside her as she sat on her butt. "I know, sweetheart, I know, just stop, I know," he said softly.

"I fought back this time, and it still didn't stop him," she cried out, clutching her head in her hands. "Nothing ever stops him or any other man, they just do whatever they want."

Dom's chest ached at seeing her so destroyed. He watched as Brandon rocked her back and forth.

"No, sweetheart, not every man, you've got me, and Dominick, we're not like that."

"It's his fault, he told Tate I was his girlfriend, and that's why he was trying to kidnap me. Tate was convinced me and Dom really are a thing and that he'd pay to get me back. I begged, pleaded with him, I told Tate me and Dom were nothing, he didn't believe me."

Brandon glanced at Dom.

Dom took a step forward. He felt like he'd been sucker-punched. In a roundabout way, he'd done this to Alexa. He looked at Brandon, not knowing what to do.

"Lex, he was only trying to help, he would have given a lot, has given a lot already to keep Tate away from you. Tate is an asshole. Dominick is trying to protect you, you shouldn't have gone alone, and you know that," Brandon told her calmly.

Alexa looked up at Brandon and Dom. "Dom," she whispered, seeing the pain she had caused him on his face.

Brandon backed away and stood up, helping her up.

She stared at Dom, he dropped everything to come for her, he tried to protect her, and she'd been stupid. "Dom," she sobbed out, stepping toward him.

He didn't hesitate. He walked over to her and wrapped his arms around her, lifting her from her feet.

"Dominick!" Cal yelled, making Alexa jump and cling tighter to the man holding her so close.

Dom turned to his dad still holding her in his arms. "I think we're done here, Dad, you saw the paperwork. I'm not sleeping with her, and she's vital to this company, she's staying on. And since Carla thinks she can touch her job Alexa is now my personal consultant, no one will touch her ever again, end of discussion."

She glanced at Dom then to Calvin Mackenzie. The only difference was Calvin was older, gray, and wrinkly. She hid her face against Dom's broad, muscular, and warm chest.

"She's our competitor's step-daughter, you really think this is a wise choice?"

"Yes, I do. Brandon helped her grow in his company, now I'm going to help her grow in this one, he gave her his blessing to be here, and I'm keeping her."

His voice was a deep rumble beneath her ear. She looked up at him. "If it's that much of a problem, I can leave," she whispered.

"Not happening, I want you, Lex and no one is changing my mind," he said just as Carla came into the room.

"Fine, Dom, but if she ruins us, it'll be your ass."

"Fine by me, Dad."

"Here are the towels you asked for," Carla announced and handed the towels to Dom. Alexa could see the glare on Carla's face.

She jumped a little as Dom snatched the towels from Carla. "Now everyone out!" he ordered.

She clutched his neck tighter with her arms, but she didn't jump this time. She watched as everyone started to leave the room.

Brandon kissed her temple. "You need your mother or me just call us, we'll put resources into finding him. I'm sorry, I thought he was out of your hair, he hasn't shown himself until recently." He shut and locked the door behind him as he left.

Dom set her back down on her feet. "Okay, baby, get undressed," he said gently.

She managed to shrug out of his jacket that was smothered in his Axe Essence scent. She managed to get her sweatpants down but struggled with the tank top.

Dom stepped forward and managed to get her out of the tank top. He began running the cold, wet towel against her body where there was dried blood.

He examined her wounds closer. "We can clean the rest of you up when we get home, baby girl. I'm so sorry, little one, I don't know why I didn't get your calls. I would have been there the minute you called me. Can you stay in here for a little bit? I have one more meeting to go to and then I will take you home."

"O-okay," she rasped out.

He leaned forward and kissed her lips gently. He helped her get redressed and put his jacket around her again. "That's my girl."

"Dom, your shirt," she croaked out.

"It's okay, got it covered." He stripped the blood-covered, white shirt off, making his forearms, and biceps ripple along with his abs and pecs.

She took in a deep breath seeing him without his shirt on. She couldn't fight what it did to her. She watched as he laid the shirt on his desk and went to his closet, pulling out a very light blue dress shirt.

He walked back over to her and kissed her again. "You can get some rest if you want to, I'll lock the door. I'll also have one of the security guys outside of it, nothing is going to happen to you here."

She nodded her head. She felt his knuckles gently stroke her cheek.

Then out the door, he went. She felt so empty without him already. She pulled the jacket around her tighter, her body protesting. She lay down on the couch, and her eyes began to close. Sleep overtook her quickly.

## Chapter 14

Dom made his way to the conference room where he'd just yelled at every staff member when he had to go. His body was tense, his gaze intent as he looked around at everyone.

As soon as he'd walked in, everyone grew quiet. He shut the door hard. Anger swirled through him when he saw the blonde bimbo from the interview before Alexa's. His gaze hardened even more as he glared at Carla, the other dumb bimbo.

His mood became even fouler. "I'm sure most of you have now heard about some of what has happened to Ms. Mills. Some of you may think what was acceptable before, which wasn't, is still okay. Well it's not, she's my personal consultant now. After today, anyone who looks at her wrong, snickers at her, gives her any kind of hell whatsoever will find themselves answering to me which may include winding up on their asses and out the door. If you mess with her in any way you're going to deal with me, am I understood?" His gaze flew to everyone in the room.

He watched as everyone only nodded their heads. He dared one of them to ask any questions. And no one did.

After one last glare at everyone, he made his way for the door. "If anyone needs me, call my cell. I'm taking her home and will be gone the rest of the day." He opened the door and headed back to his office, not hearing one word come from the conference room.

He got back to his office and stopped, looking at his head of security, Angelo, he was stocky, shorter than himself, black hair that was on the longer side, and was always slicked back. "Everything moved as I asked?"

"Yes, sir, the door is replaced, too, got the SUV home also."

"Good." Dom pushed the key into the lock and turned it. His eyes landed on Alexa right as he opened the door. She looked so small and fragile in his big suit jacket. He smiled at her and scooped her up into his arms gently.

She let out a startled gasp, and her eyes flew open.

He pulled her closer to him. "Easy, babe, just me, time to go."

She relaxed in his arms and snuggled into him, making his body clench a little.

He kissed her forehead gently and headed to his car. "You want anything to eat? I haven't eaten since breakfast, and I'm sure you haven't either."

She grumbled a little as she managed to open the door to the car for him. "I don't want anything."

"We won't go in, baby. We'll get it and take it home." He tried to persuade her.

"Fine, maybe chicken, mashed potatoes and gravy," she whispered.

"No problem." He sat her down on the seat softly and snapped her seatbelt on her. He went to the other side of the car and headed to the restaurant.

He ordered, they got their food, then headed to his house. He pulled up to the gate, entered the code, and drove to the garage.

He put the door down and made his way over to the passenger side and helped Alexa out of the car. "You okay, baby?"

She nodded her head as she leaned into him with the bag of food in her hands. He put his arm around her and took the bag from her.

He took her into the kitchen, then to the dining room. "You sit here, baby, I'll get everything we need, we'll eat then get you cleaned up better." He helped her sit in a chair then headed back to the kitchen.

He would have her eat and relax some, then the conversation would turn serious and they would get on the same page.

He grabbed plates, forks and spoons. He headed back to Alexa. He placed one plate in front of her while the other he put in front of the empty seat next to her. He watched her get her food first. Then he helped himself.

"What do you want to drink, honey?" He could have slapped himself in the head for forgetting drinks.

"Whatever," she whispered, her face looked so blank.

He sighed as he stood back up to go to the fridge, he scanned the contents. Damn, he needed to go shopping. He grabbed the last two Mountain Dews then headed back to Alexa.

They ate in painful silence, once they were finished Dom cleaned up, he put the dishes in the dishwasher and threw away the trash.

He headed back to Alexa, but she wasn't in the chair he left her in. His eyes darted around the spacious room. His frantic gaze landed on her standing at the window looking out at the pool again.

He walked up to her slowly and wrapped his arms around

her stomach loosely, leaning down toward her ear. "When it gets warmer, I'll let you swim in there," he whispered.

"I won't be here by then, though," she whispered back.

Dom frowned. "What makes you say that?"

"Hopefully, Tate will be locked up by then," she whispered as she trembled in his arms.

"Maybe I'll just spoil you so much you won't want to go home," he whispered against her ear and placed a kiss right below it.

She turned in his arms and gazed up at him, her beautiful eyes met his. "Why would you want to do that?"

"Because you are just so spoilable." He nuzzled his nose into the crook of her neck. "Baby?" His tone turned questioning.

She looked up at him but didn't say a word.

"I'm sorry I gave him the motive to come after you today. I never thought that's what it would lead to, and for the record, I would have paid whatever he asked, to get you back."

She stared up at him looking so confused, she opened her mouth to say something but then snapped it shut. She looked down at the white with gray line patterned tile.

Dom pulled her close to him. "You go head up to the bedroom. I'll be there in a minute." He watched her head to the stairs and begin to go up the circular stairway. She went slowly, and he didn't blame her.

He pulled out his phone as he headed to the kitchen and began to call the person he had who did the shopping for him when it was last minute, or he had just plum forgot to do it. He rattled off items for her to get him and Alexa while he got two wine glasses and the strawberry wine from the night before.

He got done with the phone call and headed up his circular stairway. He went to his room but didn't see Alexa. He made his way to the bathroom. He leaned against the doorframe as she just stared at herself in the long mirror he had above his long vanity.

He watched intently as Alexa touched her bruises on her cheeks and mouth, she winced from the pain. Her fingers moved down to the bruise along her neck and pressed but didn't wince as bad.

She closed her eyes. "Could have been worse, could have been worse, no scars, no scars," she mumbled, opened her eyes again and just stared.

"Lex?" Dom whispered, and she turned to look at him. He stepped into the bathroom when he saw her eyes fill with tears. But she almost ran to him. She stepped into him close and wrapped her arms around him tightly. "I'm here, baby girl, right here," he whispered against her ear.

He managed to get her closer to the counter, where he set down the two glasses and the bottle of wine. One hand moved to her back while the other cradled her head gently. "Do you want to talk about it?"

"No." She shut the option down quickly.

"Okay, I'll listen if you change your mind, just so you know, how about a nice soak in the tub with a glass of wine this time?" He encouraged her.

"Okay," she whispered into his chest.

"Good girl, let me start the water." He kissed the top of her head and moved over to his Jacuzzi tub and turned the water on. He turned back to Alexa. "Jets or no jets?"

"Doesn't matter." She grumbled a little.

He sighed. "Baby girl, yes it does, it matters what you want."

"What I want? Really, what I want? I want to feel safe in my home, safe out on the streets, I want him to be stupid this time and get caught, I want him never to bother me again, I don't want to want you, because you scare me." Alexa broke down and began to cry. "I want to be able to look in the mirror and never see bruises again, and I want to never look at my scars again and be reminded of how I got every last one of them."

"Lex, I'm sorry," Dom started, he raked his gaze over her a little, the only scar he had seen on her was her wrist, but he never looked for any other ones. "Come here." He held his arms open for her. He was surprised when she walked into them. "I want to take all the pain away for you, little one, but a few things I will make sure of are: he gets caught, he'll never bother you again, you'll never look in the mirror again and see another bruise." He kissed the top of her head and swayed side to side with her a little. "Why are you scared of me?"

"Brandon warned me against you, about your reputation, I could lose myself to you and never find me again if I ended up being broken again."

"What if someone can change when they meet the right one?" Dom asked curiously as he continued to move them a little.

She just shrugged her shoulders a little bit.

*One step at a time, Dom Mackenzie, don't be such a brute.* He pulled Alexa with him as he stepped back to the tub. He shut the water off. He'd make her see he changed for her and only her. She had burrowed herself into his heart, and there was no getting her out, no matter what he had done before or had thought before. He wanted a new way of life only with Alexa.

He ran his hands up her sides slowly up to her shoulders and made his jacket fall off her. "Do you want me to do this?" he asked, motioning to the rest of her clothes.

She turned bright red but nodded her head. He rolled the tank top up her stomach, then got it over her head from the back and slid it down her arms. He pushed her sweatpants down her legs. He helped her step out of them, then stripped her of her bra and panties.

He helped her into the tub, he made sure she was comfortable and settled before he headed back to the vanity where he poured her a glass of wine then one for himself. He took them over to her and handed her the glass with a soft smile to go along with it.

---

Alexa tried hard not to tremble as she took the glass from Dom. She sipped it a little while leaning back against the wall of the tub, letting the strawberry flavor flow through her mouth.

She let out a sigh as she sunk lower into the hot water letting her beaten body soak. Could someone really change when they found the one? She didn't know. She never witnessed it before. Sounded possible.

Dom cleared his throat a little. She looked up at him. "I have to go downstairs for a minute, okay? I had groceries brought here for us. I'm going to have to go let them in."

She nodded her head as she went to set the glass of wine on the tile floor. She couldn't reach, and she let out a huff, then Dom reached for it and placed it on the floor for her.

"Thank you."

"You're welcome, my little shorty." He chuckled at her, as she stuck her tongue out at him.

She watched him leave while shaking her head.

She sunk lower into the tub, her feet didn't even reach the other side. Her eyes slowly closed, letting the hot water and the little bit of wine take her away, just for a moment. She wondered when they were going to talk about Brandon actually being her stepdad instead of like the father figure she never had like she had told Dom.

She was surprised he didn't throw her out of his life right then and there. Her life was so screwed up. She sunk lower, letting the water go up to her neck, and she still couldn't touch the other side of the tub. She huffed and just let herself forget everything.

---

Dom met the lady who did his shopping at her car. "Thanks, Lizzie, I know it was a long list on such short notice. I appreciate it."

"No problem, Mr. Mackenzie, Angelo told me a little bit about what was going on, is she going to be okay?"

Dom looked at Lizzie Jenkins, Angelo's girlfriend. "I can only hope so, I don't know what to do for her, except try to keep her safe," Dom answered as he began to grab bags out of her SUV.

"Well, Mr. Mackenzie, if anyone can keep her safe, it's you."

"She wants to go home so bad." He headed back to the door.

"Can you blame her?" Lizzie asked, looking up at him as they walked through the house to the kitchen.

She was about five-six, taller than Alexa but still petite with blonde hair. He let out a sigh as he placed bags on the counter. "I guess not."

"Sir, can I speak freely?"

"Eh, go ahead."

"All the years Angelo and I have been here with you, sir, we've never seen you so calm and caring toward an individual like you are with her, you really care for her, you love her, don't you?" Her soft brown eyes met his hazel ones.

"Lizzie, it's complicated, and I wouldn't say it's love, she just needs someone in her corner, one look at her and you can't help but want to be in her corner."

Lizzie smiled at him and shook her head a little. "Where is she right now?"

"Upstairs in the Jacuzzi tub."

"In your room, huh?"

"Yes, she needed to soak, she's pretty sore."

"Poor girl." Lizzie sighed.

They got everything put away, and Liz said, "If you need anything else, don't hesitate to call Angelo or me, Mr. Mackenzie."

"Thank you, Liz. I'm sure we'll be okay." He made sure she got in her SUV and then headed back upstairs.

He leaned against the wall of the bathroom, his eyes glued to Alexa. They needed to talk about Brandon, but he didn't know if it was the right time.

He watched as she relaxed in the tub and reached for her glass of wine. He walked over slowly, leaning down to get it for her. "Hey, little one," he whispered and found himself sitting on the floor next to the tub.

He tried to push everything away as he watched her drain the glass. He smiled and took the glass from her. "Is the water still hot?" He set the glass down on the counter above his head.

She shook her head, her expression a little blank.

He stood up and let the water out of the tub then helped her up. "Come on, sweetheart." He grabbed a towel from the closet and wrapped it around her. "I have your clothes in the other bedroom. You want me to help you dress?"

"No, I can do it, I think."

"Well, if you need me, I'll help." He rubbed her back gently.

"Thank you, Dom," she whispered, then left the bathroom.

Dom started the shower, while he waited for the water to warm he chugged down a glass of wine. How was he going to handle setting her right? He couldn't be too harsh with her but it needed to be taken care of. He huffed, he never had this problem before but he could be gentle with her but stern and very serious. He could do this.

He stripped down and got into the shower, he cleaned up, got out, and dried off. He put on a pair of gray sweatpants and headed to the bedroom next to his. He knocked on the door lightly before walking into the room.

She looked up, sitting on the edge of the bed, still only in the towel.

"Lex, what are you doing?"

"Nothing," she whispered.

"Lex." He walked into the bedroom. "Did you find your clothes?"

"Yeah."

"Why didn't you change, baby girl?"

"I don't know."

He took a deep breath and grabbed the clothes that consisted of pink sweatpants and a matching hoodie. He took her hand, guided her to his room, and sat her down on his bed.

He went to his bathroom and grabbed the peroxide and cotton balls. He headed back to her, and knelt in front of her. "This may sting a little, babe, but I want to clean up the scrapes."

She nodded her head.

He poured the peroxide onto the cotton ball. He started with her leg, then her arms, the side of her mouth, and her cheek. He smiled at her when she didn't flinch at all.

He helped her into her pants and hoodie. Then he went to get the comb from his bathroom. He climbed on the bed behind her and began to comb her hair gently.

Alexa felt so lost. Everything felt numb. She just couldn't bring herself to do anything or feel anything. Once she felt Dom stop combing her hair, she turned to look at him. Her eyes locked with his, they were looking at her with a soft, gentle look. "I'm sorry," she whispered.

"For what, little one?" He sat down on the bed, his legs folded Indian style right across from her. He reached out to cup her cheek softly.

"For not telling you about Brandon."

"It's okay, makes sense now that I'm thinking about it, and makes sense of how he had your sisters' phone numbers." He smiled at her.

"You still want me at MAEP?"

He reached out to her and scooped her up, placing her onto his lap. "Yes, I do, you had your reasons not to tell me about Brandon, I understand, and I still trust you."

She wrapped her arms around his neck and laid her head on his shoulder. She was glad he was there holding her and that he understood why she didn't tell him.

"How long has he been your actual stepdad?" he whispered against her ear, sending chills down her body.

"About four years, he hung around a lot at the house after he found out about Tate, my mom divorced him, and Brandon got a soft spot for me first but then also for my mom, he's always tried to help as much as he could, but Tate would always manage to disappear like he did today."

"Did he ever hurt your sisters at all?"

"No, Tate loved them, he didn't hurt my mom very often either, he just hates me, he never wanted another girl."

"Well now you have me also, and I hate him, too. He's hurt you for the last time, you're staying with me at least until he's caught, I've got you, baby." He laced his fingers of one hand through her hair while the other one pulled her closer to him, splayed against her back.

It touched her heart, hearing those words from him, more than Brandon's words ever did. She broke into uncontrollable tears as she tightened her arms around his neck.

He continued to rub her back, cradling her head against him. "I'm sorry, Lex, I didn't mean to make you cry more," he whispered.

She leaned back to look at him. "I'm sorry, it's like the knob on a faucet broke, and it's all I can do," she sobbed out.

He moved his hands to cup her cheeks and rubbed the tears away. "I know, it's okay, sweetheart, one day it'll turn back off, and I'll try to make it so it doesn't turn back on if you'll let me." He pressed his lips to hers. "I know small steps, one day at a time, and we have a while to get through this together."

She laid her hands on his cheeks and leaned into him, pressing her lips against his, moving frantically. She moved her hands into his hair, pulling gently. He surprised her when he got onto his knees, still holding her close to him.

He laid her down on the bed gently and continued to return her kisses. Sliding his tongue against hers making her moan, he slowly pulled back from her. She looked up at him, panting a little.

---

Dom slowly moved away from Alexa. "We still have to talk, Alexa." He turned his tone stern and very serious.

She slowly sat up a little. "What about?"

"From now on I will have the final say, you'll have a voice and an opinion but if I do not like it then what I say goes. I was against you going by yourself today and obviously I should have stuck with that instinct." He paused as their eyes locked.

"But-"

"No, no buts, I am in charge. Which means you will never have that attitude of yours with me, no more rolling those pretty eyes of yours at me either, and no matter how much you bat those eyes of yours I will not give in."

Alexa scoffed a little and rolled her eyes again.

"Did you just scoff at me and roll your eyes at me again?" Dom demanded.

Alexa swallowed hard but stayed silent.

"Answer me, Lex."

"Yes, sir, I did," she whispered.

Dom hung his head pushing away the anger, this was going to be hard work but he could do this. "What did we just get done talking about?"

"For me to not do those things and you are in charge."

"And what have I told you before?"

"That if I didn't stop there would be consequences, a sound spanking." She broke eye contact and stared at her hands in her lap.

"And you just broke some of those rules just shortly after our talk, didn't you?" He slowly moved to the side of the bed, taking her along with him, making her stand in front of him. "I'm not doing this to hurt you, babe. I'm doing this so you don't get too out of hand and you understand that everything I say and instruct you to do is to keep you safe."

She swallowed hard again and stepped back quickly.

Dom caught her hand and pulled her to him. "I'm not going to abuse you, Lex, I promise." He brushed his thumb against her hand gently. "You have to trust me for this to work, Lex."

"But, I don't think I trust you," she whispered. "I have never wanted this to be a part of my life, I am not that kind of person, Dominick. I can't be that. I gave up so much growing up, I will not give up my free will."

"Lex, you will have free will, as long as it does not involve something dangerous or disrespecting me. I have let this go on long enough, if you don't like this then I guess I will have to let you walk away, but I care, Lex, and this is the way I show I care."

Lex didn't say a word, she just stared into his eyes. He didn't want that determination to disappear from her eyes, she was a wonderful woman and he just needed to try to keep her safe and that was what he wanted to break, the irresponsibility she had shown today, and the disrespectfulness.

"Lex, lie over my lap," he instructed.

She shook her head quickly and pulled back, but he pulled her back to him and pulled her over his lap gently. As she tried to push away from him with her hands he grabbed them gently. "Alexandra, stop." He grasped her wrists carefully. "It'll only be worse if you fight me on this."

She froze at his stern voice and stopped struggling.

Dom smirked a little, she trusted him, as much as she hated to admit it, she trusted him. He slowly pushed her pants down over her round backside and rubbed his firm hand against each cheek gently.

"Now, why is this happening, Lex?"

"Because I rolled my eyes, because I got an attitude with you earlier, I put myself in danger when I went to the house by myself and every time I walked to and from your building." She gasped at the first whack of his hand on her cheek.

"And how are we going to change this?" Dom questioned as he smacked her other cheek and gently rubbed them both.

"I am going to listen to you, I am not going to go against what you want, and if you tell me something, it is for my own good," she explained to him as he cracked each cheek again then rubbed them soothing the slapped skin.

"Good girl, but I think you're missing something out of that equation." He smacked her slightly pink ass again.

"Sir, I'm missing sir. I'm sorry, I'll never forget, I'll mind you, please, Dom, stop," she sobbed out as she wiggled beneath his hand and tried to pull her hands free. She let out a cry when his hand slapped her turned up backside again. "Dom!" she cried out and went limp in his lap. "Sir, I'm sorry, really I am, I'll never do any of it again, please stop."

Dom slowly caressed the soft skin that was red now. He slowly let her off his lap, pulled her sweatpants back up, and pulled her into him hugging her gently. "Now, was that so bad?" he whispered.

She shook her head as she sniffled a little and went to rub her butt.

"I wouldn't do that if I were you, babe," he cautioned and she listened, laying her head against his shoulder.

He smiled slightly, she could be what he needed, she took the punishment well and actually listened to him when he said not to rub her tender backside, he slowly leaned back a little so he could look into her beautiful eyes. "You're so beautiful, why don't you try to get some sleep, sweetheart."

"You're not going to send me away are you? You'll let me stay with you, right?" she asked sounding embarrassed after their interaction.

Dom smiled at her and lay down on his back then pulled her close to him. "Of course, I'll never send you away, Lex. When the punishment is complete, you are forgiven and should feel free of any guilt and hopefully feel a little lighter. I will lie here and cuddle you, that's how it's supposed to be." He kissed her temple as her eyes slowly closed. She snuggled into him as sleep took her over.

## Chapter 15

Alexa woke up to soft kisses being pressed against her cheeks, lips, nose and forehead. She slowly opened her eyes, and a pair of hazel green eyes were looking at her softly.

"Hi, Dom," she rasped out. Her voice rough between the sleep and Tate's hand, squeezing her throat the day before.

"Hello, beautiful, how you feeling?"

She moaned a little bit as she moved to sit up. "Sore," she grumbled, a little surprised her bottom wasn't sorer than the rest of her. The spanks Dom had delivered the night before had been something else, something she had never experienced before and it wasn't all bad. It was nothing compared to what Tate had done to her, sure Dom spanked her but he stopped the minute she cried out and gave in. Tate would have just kept going, Dom was nothing like Tate.

Dom brushed her hair away from her face gently. "Do you want to stay home today?" He offered, sincerity written all over his face.

"I can't. One day was bad enough, and two is nonexistent for me."

"Alexa, if you need another day, I'll handle whatever you need me to so you're able to stay here."

She searched his eyes slowly. She wasn't a moocher. "No, I'll be okay, just let me stay in sweatpants and a hoodie, please? Just for today?"

He let out a chuckle. "Sure, why not, or you could work from here."

"I want to be near you, though, I feel safe," she admitted.

He smiled a crooked grin. "Oh, really?"

"Yes, you make me feel safe, Dom."

"Okay good, that's what I was hoping you'd feel, why don't you go shower then I will, then we'll go get your Starbucks." He kissed her softly and let her get out of bed.

She made her way to the bathroom but turned quickly. "Is in here okay?" she whispered.

"Yeah, I don't mind." He smiled at her. "You go get the water ready. I'll get your shampoo and stuff.

───────

He flipped back the covers and headed to the room he gave her. He grabbed the two bottles then headed back to his room.

He walked into the bathroom and shook his head when he saw her already in the shower. He grew aroused as he watched her perfect body move around through the foggy glass shower door.

He took a deep breath, shucked his sweatpants down with his free hand, and slowly opened the door. He placed the bottles on a shelf then closed the door behind him.

"Lex, I'm in here, don't freak out," he whispered, and she turned around to look at him. He smiled at her shocked look.

"What are you doing?"

"Well, I brought your things, and you looked so sexy, I wanted to join you. I can leave if you want me to." He began to turn toward the door, but he felt her latch on to his arm.

He turned to look at her. "You want me to stay?" he whispered as he searched her face looking for a no anywhere.

She pulled him closer to her and laid her hands on his shoulders. "Yes." She blushed.

He leaned down and kissed her gently.

She kissed him back, frantically as she tried to get closer to him. His hands went to her ass and pulled her up off the shower floor, wrapping her legs around his waist above his prominent desire for her.

She squirmed against him. He turned them away from the stream of water and pressed her back against the wall. He pulled his lips from hers and made his way down her neck, gently kissing the bruises that were there. He lifted her higher to capture her taut nipples, one then the other.

---

Alexa hated fighting the desire she had for Dom. She squirmed against him, letting out gasps as his tongue tortured her hard peaks.

She let out a scream when his hand slipped between them and dove into her aching center, making her toes curl. His thumb made circles around the sensitive jewel as his tongue did the same with her nipples.

"Dominick!" She grabbed his shoulders, digging her nails into them as she arched into his torturous tongue, thumb and fingers.

His thumb swirled around her faster as his fingers went a little harder and faster.

The pressure built and built, and she dug her nails deeper into his shoulders right as she was sent over the edge, letting out a glass-shattering scream.

He pulled away from her nipples as she rode out her ecstasy on his fingers and his lips caught hers. "See, this is what things will be like, you break the rules there are consequences, you follow the rules and behave and you get all the pleasure you could possibly want, and trust me you will never want for anything, I will see to that until the end of my days."

Alexa slowly searched his eyes and nodded her head meekly, he slowly set her down gently then grabbed her body wash.

He washed her body first and then her hair.

---

Dom got her rinsed off, fighting the urge to slam his desire for her into her wet tightness. It took so much control not to replace his fingers with his rock hardness. He kissed her gently one more time before he let her out of the shower.

Once she was out of the bathroom, he gripped his raging hard-on, her calling out his name replaying in his mind as he stroked himself with a firm hand. He couldn't wait to have her wrapped around him.

His ragged breath became even more intense as he felt himself reaching his temporary release of satisfaction. His body shook as he came down from his high of ecstasy. He let out a harsh breath wishing he'd just done it with her.

His imagination would never give her justice. He hurriedly cleaned himself up, then got out of the shower, dried off and went to get dressed.

---

Alexa was downstairs waiting for Dom wearing a pair of aqua sweatpants and a matching hoodie. Today she didn't even try to poke herself in the eyes to put her contacts in, she opted for her glasses. She had debated on putting some concealer on to hide the bruises, but she said forget that too. Everyone was sure to know what had happened to her.

She stared out the window in the living room at the pool. Today she finally noticed the two tan-colored stone stairways that descended from each side of the house. Would she be here long enough to enjoy that pool?

Oh well, time would tell. She heard a slight cough behind her, and she turned. She stopped halfway through the spin when her eyes landed on Dom.

He had chosen a navy-blue suit, the shirt beneath was a light gray buttoned down dress shirt, and a navy-blue tie matched his suit. Most women fell for men in uniforms, but she was falling for a devilish man in a suit.

She smiled as he came closer. "You look beautiful," he whispered and pulled her close to him. "I don't know how to share you with the world."

"Well the world is where I want to be, Dom, I can't stay cooped up forever," she whispered.

"I know, I'm sorry. Come on, let's get this day over with, I am ready for the weekend, two more days is pure torture." He put an arm around her gently and led her out to the garage.

He helped her into the seat then went around to the driver's side.

They went to Starbucks, where he got her a blueberry muffin and caramel Frappuccino while he just got a black coffee and a cinnamon raisin bagel.

He ate it on the way to the office, while she drank her Frappuccino with her muffin on her lap for later.

They headed into the building after he unlocked it, he grabbed her tablet from her old desk, and ushered her to his office. "For now this is where you'll work, I'll make arrangements to put another desk in here though."

"Dom, this is great and all but don't you want your own space, you'll tire of me eventually." She looked up at him, confusion on her face.

"No, you're fine, I don't want you away from me until we find that loser."

"Okay." She headed over to the table and set her things down and began to eat her muffin.

She watched him move to his desk beneath her eyelashes. How was she ever going to get any work done?

---

They were halfway through their day, and surprisingly she managed to connect with quite a few new prospects and with Mr. Benson and Ms. Lange.

She had just finished the conversation with Ms. Lange and hung up when her phone began to ring again.

"Hello?" She tried to sound chipper.

"Sissy, are you coming this weekend?" the high-pitched excited voice almost blew out her eardrum.

She yanked her phone away from her ear for a minute, once the voice stopped, she placed it back to her ear. "What are you talking about, Delilah?"

"Oh my God, you don't remember? The annual party that BAP and MAEP host for the Child Abuse Awareness Association."

"Oh." Alexa's voice fell, so did her happy spirits. "I don't know, Delilah."

"Oh come on, Lex, you know Brandon put a lot into that association, even managed to get MAEP involved, he did it so other children don't end up as you did. Even if you don't want to speak at the fundraiser, the least you can do is go."

"Delilah, it hurts a lot, brings back a lot of bad memories, and hits a very soft spot. Can we talk about this later?" She glanced over at Dom who was looking at her, a little worry on his face.

"Why don't you just move on, Alexa and help Brandon with this?" Delilah whined into the phone loudly.

"I wouldn't expect you or Noelle to understand. You've never gone through it, you witnessed it but never went through it, I'll never forget that Brandon started it because of me, but it's just not for me, Delilah."

"Alexa, you are such a party pooper!" Delilah groaned.

"Well, I'm sorry. I was never allowed to enjoy things like you and Noelle did, I worked in the diner while you two got to live your lives. Don't forget the only reason you two are in such a high-class society is because of Brandon. Still, I never wanted that. I just wanted to be loved, I appreciate him more than anyone in our family does. I'm not going, Delilah. End of story." She ended the call, and hung her head in her hands, refusing to look at Dom.

Her life was simple. She didn't need high-class parties or regular outings to make her happy. Her little shack made her happy.

---

Dom just watched Alexa sit there, her head in her hands. He sighed, went and locked his office door, and headed over to her. He placed a hand on her back. "Sweetheart, what's wrong?"

She glanced up at him and shook her head. "Nothing, Dom."

That wasn't the answer he was hoping for. He needed to be strong for her so she learned she could trust him with all things. He didn't want to, but he knew a punishment was needed. Luckily, his office was soundproof, as he felt it was better to address this right away.

"Alexa, did you just lie to me?"

She gasped, but answered, "Yes, sir."

"It seems a punishment is in order."

Alexa looked in his eyes and saw the emotion and feelings he had for her written all over his face. She felt terrible for lying. She needed to learn to trust him and this was the way, she felt it down deep in her soul. "Yes, sir."

He took her hand and helped her stand, and moved them both over to the couch in his office. He sat and stood her between his legs.

"How many do you think you deserve for this broken rule?" Dom questioned sternly, letting her make up her mind on how she was going to handle this punishment.

Alexa let out a breath and gazed at him for a moment. "As many as you feel I deserve, sir, I should have just told you what was wrong and I didn't, I'm sorry, sir," she choked out.

Dom pursed his lips slightly. "Well, we will go with ten, you are at least admitting when you are in the wrong, Alexa. I'm proud of you." He pressed his lips to her cheek and slowly slid her pants down letting him have a full view of her lovely, round ass. His body clenched and reacted instantly. He wanted to say forget the punishment and take her here and now but he couldn't let this go or it would just continue to snowball.

He put her over his knee and drew back his palm and the sound of skin hitting skin entered the office. She jerked a little and sucked in a sharp breath. "Count aloud, Alexandra."

She let out a sob but did as she was told. "One."

*Crack.* "Two." She wiggled her butt a little at the next slap of his hand. "Three."

He continued and she counted aloud until she reached

ten. He gently rubbed her bottom. He leaned forward a little and pressed his lips to each cheek. "That's my girl," he whispered as he continued to rub her ass and he spotted the somewhat wet fabric that barely covered where he desperately wanted to be. He smirked a little, she enjoyed what he did to her, no matter how hard she tried to fight it or seemed to shy away from it, she enjoyed it with him.

He slowly pulled her up from his lap and turned her towards him. "You're okay, babe." He leaned down and pulled her sweats back up, careful not to let the fabric graze her newly fiery ass.

He pulled her into his arms and placed her on his lap, holding her close. "Now, you can tell me what's going on." He rubbed her back gently, and waited.

She let out a sigh and laid her head on his shoulder. "That was my second oldest sister, she was reminding me of a charity event Brandon hosts every year."

"The CAA Association?"

"Yeah."

"That's this weekend, isn't it, hey, we can go if you want to, it's a good cause, we became a part of it as soon as Brandon set it up five years ago, oh…" Now, he understood. "Brandon set it up because of his involvement with you."

"Yes he did, I love him for it but–"

"You have never gone, I think I would have remembered seeing you there, and I never have."

"No, it hurts too much. Delilah, Noelle, my mom, and Brandon tried to get me to speak at it the first couple of years it was blooming, but I just couldn't, soon they stopped trying, but Delilah always tries to get me to go."

"Well I kind of have to go, baby girl, would you be okay if you went with me as my date?" He tilted her head up a little.

"As in a real date?"

"Of course, I'd never take you on a fake one."

"I don't have anything to wear." She turned away from him a little.

"My treat."

"Dom."

"Lex, seriously, I'd love to take you but if you really don't want to go I understand. But I'd be proud to have you on my arm at this function or any other formal I'd have to go to." He rubbed her back gently. He pressed a kiss against her cheek.

"Can I think about it?"

"Okay, sweetheart."

"I will let you know after work," she whispered.

He kissed her gently. "Just think, we could get your sisters to shut up."

She smiled as she shook her head.

"Now, let's get back to work."

"Yes, sir." She smiled even bigger and left his lap.

And he wanted her back right away, instead he headed over to unlock his door and then to his desk. He threw a glance over at her hoping she knew he had been earnest about being proud to have her.

He smiled as she curled her body up into the chair and began to get lost in her tablet. He chuckled and dove back into his own work.

---

Alexa let out a tiny hiss as she sat down on the cushioned chair a little harder than she should have, but she didn't react more than that. She gazed at Dom carefully; she couldn't believe she had just let him do that to her and she had actually became turned on by it. She was so glad he hadn't mentioned that part of their little escapade. She slowly curled up into the chair, Dom was the one for her, he kept her in line and yet wasn't cruel about it.

She began to work diligently as he did the same.

---

As the day rolled on, Dom was studying over a folder in-depth when he heard Alexa's stomach let out a loud rumble. He looked at the clock. Four o'clock, shit, he forgot to take Alexa to lunch.

He stood up from his desk, closed the folder and taking it over with him to Alexa. "Babe, why didn't you tell me to take you to lunch?" he demanded.

She looked up at him. "What time is it?"

"Four."

"Oh, I guess time slipped away from me. I'm sorry, Dom." She uncurled her body and began to stand up but let out a few groans. This time she laid her tiny hands against her bottom and let out another hiss.

He put his arms around her. "Sore?"

"Just a little bit," she grumbled, tilting her head up a little.

He leaned down to her ear. "Well, maybe next time you will think before you try to lie or do something dangerous, because there is plenty more where that came from, little one. Now, why don't we call it a day, go home, get some food in you and I can give you a rub down, or you could soak in the Jacuzzi." He let out a chuckle when her body trembled against his. "It's whichever one you want to do."

"Can I have both?" she asked sexily, those hazel blue eyes of hers pleading a little.

He let out a full hearty laugh. It was always going to be this way, certain things he would always give her her way and this was certainly one of them. As long as he could take care of her she could have her way. "I believe that can be arranged, come on, beautiful." He helped her gather some of her things then headed out to his car.

As they settled in, he began to head home. Alexa began to talk to him.

"Dom, what would a woman like me wear to a fundraiser?"

He shot her a look. "First off, what do you mean by a woman like you and second, anything you want, baby."

"Well, I mean, I am not high society, I don't belong at a function like that, and I don't even know what to do at a place like the Zeiss, I've never set foot in that place."

He reached out and took her hand pulling it up to his mouth and pressed his lips to it gently. "You'd stay as close to me as possible, and you would belong there, you have more class than most women who show up there."

She looked at him as he laced their fingers together, a smile played on her lips. "Fine, if we find something I like to wear then I will go, if not, I stay home."

Dom smiled wide when Alexa said home, hopefully, she was coming around to his place being her home because he was more than glad to share it. "Deal, we'll get us some food in us and then go shopping."

"You're going to go shopping with me for a dress?"

"Of course, it's my treat, and I want to see what I'll be holding you in most of Saturday night." He smiled wickedly at her.

She rolled her eyes at him as they pulled up to the gate. "Then my rub and soak in the tub?"

"Of course, baby girl." He punched in the code and headed up to the garage. "You won't have to be scared about going either. Brandon and I, both keep the place pretty well-secured during the event."

"I'm certain you won't let me out of your sight either way," she teased.

He got out of the car after parking and walked around to

help her out. "Now you're getting it." He smiled and pulled her to him, catching her lips with his.

She instantly let out that little moan of hers, which automatically made his body hard and ache for her. He continued to sip her lips slowly when her stomach let out another loud growl.

Dom pulled back. "I guess I better be feeding you," he teased as they headed into the house then to the kitchen. "What would you like to eat?"

"Grilled cheese sounds good, but you can go relax, and I can fix it," she began as she started to go to the fridge.

He pulled her hand and spun her around back into his body. "Or I could make it while you relax, or we both could since I know you won't relax."

"Okay, fine, I'll let you help." She smiled at him.

He reluctantly let her go, and she headed to the fridge while he grabbed the bread from the pantry and a skillet.

They began to make their sandwiches.

Dom put two sandwiches on one plate and two on the other once the grilled cheese was a nice golden brown.

He shut the skillet off, handed Alexa a plate, grabbed two bottles of water, and headed to the dining room.

They ate, made small talk with each other until Alexa only ate half of her second sandwich.

"What's the matter, Lex?" Dom laid a hand on her knee.

Her head snapped up and looked at him. "Nothing, just full."

He smiled at her. "Well, why don't you go freshen up while I clean up then I will do the same, and we can go pick out your fabulous gown for Saturday."

She smiled at him, but it didn't reach her eyes, but he let her head upstairs while he cleaned up.

---

Alexa stood in the room that was supposed to be hers. She was staring at herself in the mirror above the dresser. She grabbed some concealer and began to cover up the bruises on her cheeks. Was this a good idea? Maybe she should just stay at home? He couldn't really be proud to have her on his arm, could he?

## Chapter 16

Alexa was staring at all the dresses as Dom walked closely beside her. Honestly, all she wanted to do was snuggle into him and forget the whole dress shopping. But she had to give it a try.

She shot a glance at the strong, powerful man beside her, how could she want to snuggle up to a brute like him? She let out a sigh as she shoved the thought away and moved closer to the new protective man she had in her life.

Her eyes darted around quickly, becoming overwhelmed. She looked up at Dom a little but looked away just as quick.

"Hang on, Lex, I'm not good at this, and I can see you're starting to panic, let's go sit over here while I make a phone call." He led her over to a bench that was a dark color.

They sat down as he pulled his phone out. "Liz, I need some help, well we're at the mall. Alexa is trying to pick out a dress for the fundraiser on Saturday, can you come help? I'm not good at this, and she's never done this before either."

Alexa looked up at Dom, who was he talking to?

"Sure, bring Angelo, he can keep me company while you two pick out dresses, yes, Lizzie, just don't scare the girl." He ended the phone call and put his arm around Alexa and pulled her closer to him, laying his chin against her head a little. "Help's on the way, baby. I'm sorry, I thought this was going to be easier."

"Angelo is the head of security?" she asked, staring at the black tile flooring.

"Yes, Liz is his girlfriend, and she does the grocery shopping for me," he answered softly.

"Oh." She began to glance around at the dresses again. What was she really thinking?

---

Dom felt like an idiot. He didn't know how to help Alexa pick out a dress. He also hadn't thought she would have begun to stress out the way she had while trying to find one.

He was glad when Angelo and Lizzie walked in. He waved them over quickly.

He shook his head when Lizzie pulled on Angelo's hand and rushed over to them. Those two were something else.

Lizzie stopped right in front of them. "Hello, Mr. Mackenzie, Ms. Mills." She had a huge smile on her face.

Alexa pulled away from Dom a little. "Please, just Alexa is fine."

"Well, I'm Lizzie, come on, we'll find the perfect dresses."

Dom watched as Lizzie took Alexa's hand and pulled her up from the bench without letting Dom kiss her.

Angelo watched the girls start to go to the mass of dresses then sat down by his boss. "I apologize for Lizzie, Mr. Mackenzie."

Dom waved the apology off. "It's okay. I'm glad she can help. You're taking her to the fundraiser, right?"

Angelo gave a curt nod.

"Well, maybe Lex won't feel so awkward to go then if she and Lizzie hit it off."

"Liz told me about the conversation she had with you yesterday. I apologize for that as well. Sometimes she just doesn't know how to hold her tongue."

"It's okay, Angelo, she asked before we talked. I do have a request, make sure Alexa stays safe all night long on Saturday, keep an eye on her, especially if I am not with her that I don't plan on, but just in case. Still no word about Tate, is there?"

"No, sir, it's nuts, I've never had a man just up and disappear off the grid the way he has managed to do, I'm at a loss with him."

"Well, we can only hope for a fuck up from the bastard, I swear if he lays another hand on her I may kill him." Dom's voice hardened as he spoke.

He felt Angelo's hand on his shoulder. "You leave that to me, sir, if it comes down to that, but we will keep her safe, Mr. Mackenzie. I can tell you really care about her, Liz wasn't over-exaggerating."

"Seems obvious to everyone but her." Dom frowned as he watched Lizzie pull Alexa around the dress racks.

"Sir, she trusts you, that's a good start, although you were cuddled up pretty nice and close on the bench when we showed up."

"I seem to cuddle her a lot."

Angelo let out a laugh. "But you want more?"

Dom's eyes flashed to Angelo's. "I want her to know I'm serious."

"The famous cold-hearted player isn't so cold-hearted or playing at the moment, interesting." Angelo chuckled.

Dom narrowed his eyes at his head of security. If it hadn't been for the fact they had known each other most of their lives, he would have been upset at the comment Angelo just made. He just shook his head and punched Angelo in the shoulder a little. "Shut up."

"Yes, sir." Angelo sobered up quickly as his eyes landed on the girls.

---

Alexa let Lizzie pull her around the racks of dresses when she saw it. She pulled back on Lizzie's hand. "Can I have that one?" She pointed to the dress. It would come down to just above her knees, and it was navy blue, almost the same color as the ribbon for Child Abuse Awareness.

Lizzie turned to look, and she looked at the dress then back to Alexa. "Um, I don't know, Alexa, seems kind of short for a formal, and most go with a black dress."

"Oh, okay." Her face fell a little bit and tried to push away the deflated feeling that overcame her.

---

Dom nudged Angelo the minute he saw Alexa's smile fade. They stood up and headed over to their girls.

Dom touched Alexa's shoulder while Angelo wrapped his arms around Lizzie.

"What's going on, ladies?" Angelo asked.

Alexa shook her head. "Nothing."

Dom glanced at Lizzie and Angelo, Lizzie was biting her lip a little.

"It's all my fault, Mr. Mackenzie. She wants that dress, I didn't think it was too appropriate, and every other woman will probably be going with black, blue I am just not too sure about, sir, and it seems a bit short," Lizzie answered fear written all over her face and in her eyes.

Dom looked back at Alexa. How dare Lizzie tell his girl,

no, but he tried to keep his temper under control and tried to refrain from spanking Lex again. This was going to be one long battle. "Do you want that dress, Lex? No other dress has piqued your interest?"

She looked down at the ground and stepped away from him a little.

Dom tilted her head up gently. "Baby, do not lie to me, we just had this conversation. Now, do you want that dress?"

She nodded a little. "But if it's going to cause some problems, I'll find something else." She looked away again.

"Lizzie, Angelo, give us a minute?" He tilted his head to the side, gesturing them to leave him and Alexa alone. He pulled Alexa closer to him. "Baby, do you want this dress?" He rubbed her back reassuringly. "Don't think about what everyone else would want. What do you want?"

"I want the dress," she whispered.

"Then it's settled." He turned back to the rack and grabbed the dress then turned back to Alexa. "Go try it on, sweetheart."

"Are you sure?" She gazed up at him.

"Very." He smiled at her.

She jumped into his arms, throwing her arms around his neck and her lips landed on his. He held her up to him with one arm and kissed her back. He set her back down on the ground slowly and pulled back. "Go try it on, beautiful."

She took the dress from him and headed to the dressing room.

Dom smiled as he headed over to Angelo and Lizzie.

Lizzie stepped forward first. "I'm so sorry, Mr. Mackenzie."

"It's fine, Lizzie. It's fixed." He was bursting with happiness that was the first time she had made a move to hug him and kiss him without any hesitation at all. Progress.

"How'd you fix it?" Angelo asked, putting his arms around Lizzie again.

"Let her get the dress," he answered simply.

"Really?" Lizzie asked her voice full of surprise.

Dom shrugged his shoulders. "She never got a choice growing up, it was either her dad's way or she got beat. She doesn't make too many choices for herself either, or she waits for permission before doing something sometimes, so I've been trying to make her stand up for what she wants in her personal life, within reason, she wanted the dress, so she gets the dress."

"Wow, you're crazy about her, if anyone else tried to go against the dress code at the fundraiser you would be furious, she's changing you, Mr. Mackenzie." Lizzie smiled as she looked at Angelo. "I told you he was in deep."

The men just shook their heads.

---

Alexa got out of her matching sweats and put the dress on. She looked at herself in the mirror. She loved it. The straps came up to fasten around her neck, leaving her shoulders very bare. The blue was perfect, and it had some flowery designs made of lace around the top half of the dress.

She spun around no fabric covered her back at all, and she bit her lip as she stared at the little scars along her back, they were only noticeable if you knew to look for them.

The skirt of the dress was really flowy and barely reached her knees. She slowly stepped out of the dressing room and went over to Dom, Angelo, and Lizzie, who seemed to be in a deep conversation.

She let out a little cough and waited for Dom to turn around.

---

Dom turned the minute he heard the cough and froze when he saw Alexa. She looked gorgeous.

The dark navy blue made her eyes more of a deep blue. It made her skin look even more delicious and creamy. He walked up to her slowly and cupped her cheek. "Wow, you look amazing, so amazing, I can't wait to show you off."

She smiled up at him and hugged him.

His hands came into contact with the skin of her back. The strange primal need to cover her up was extreme, but he tried to control it. His hands slid up and down slowly and he pressed a kiss to her exposed shoulder. "Oh yeah, I love this dress," he murmured against her ear.

She leaned back and smiled up at him. "Thank you, Dominick, for everything."

He smiled and kissed her gently. "Anytime, beautiful, anytime. Now why don't you go change, and we'll find you some shoes."

"And a matching purse? Actually, no, I don't need a matching purse. I'm sorry, Dom." She stepped back from him and looked down.

He tilted her head up gently. "Yes, even a matching purse." He smiled as her eyes lit up. God, this woman was something else.

He shook his head, chuckling as she headed back to the changing room. He turned back to Angelo and Lizzie, who had dumb smiles on their faces. "What?" Dom demanded.

"Nothing, do you want me to help her with shoes?"

"Sure, only let her get what she wants."

"Yes, sir." Lizzie walked away, snatching a long, black dress and headed over to the changing room.

Dom couldn't wait to get this night and tomorrow over with so he could show Alexa off.

Alexa came out of the changing room and came face to face with Lizzie, she jumped back a little scared for a minute. "Lizzie, you scared me."

"Sorry, Alexa, Mr. Mackenzie wants me to help you with shoes and a bag, so let's go." She laced her arm through Alexa's, and they went over to the bags first.

Alexa found a navy-blue purse that matched her dress perfectly, and then they headed over to the shoes. Alexa took a little longer in that department. She finally found the perfect pair of open-toe navy-blue heels. The best part were the laces that wrapped and tied around her ankle. She never had owned such a sexy pair of heels. She wanted these. She tried them on, and they fit perfectly.

"I think I'm all good, Lizzie," Alexa stated as Lizzie grabbed a pair of simple black heels. Maybe she just wasn't cut out for a formal event. Alexa began to feel foolish again.

"What about makeup, are you good on all that?" Lizzie checked with her.

"I think I'm good." She reassured the woman who was helping.

They headed back over to their men. She stumbled for a moment, had she just referred to Dom as her man? No, no, no, this wasn't what was supposed to happen. Don't be so foolish. You jumped into his arms and kissed him first just a little while ago. She took a deep breath and managed to compose herself before they walked up to the guys.

Dom took everything from her and went to the counter and paid as did Angelo for Lizzie. She was losing this battle. If he kept doing these things for her, she would be his within a few days, and she didn't know if she wanted that or wanted to stay single. *Oh, come on, you've let him go further than anyone ever has. You're fooling yourself.*

She was so glad when they could finally head home. She

stayed quiet the whole ride home until they got to the gate. "Dom?" she whispered slightly.

He turned to look at her after putting the code in. "Yes?"

"Thank you for everything again, and you didn't have to do this."

"It was my pleasure, as will your massage and soak in the tub." He winked at her, and they headed to the garage then into the house.

Alexa took her things to her room and hung the dress up on the closet door, placing her shoes inside the closet along with her new matching bag. This was too much, and she took too much from his generosity, why had she done it? Her brows furrowed into a frown as she stared at everything. She was so selfish, what had she been thinking? She'd pay him back the minute she could.

She heard him walk into the room and felt his arms wrap around her. "You're overthinking again, Lex."

"I shouldn't have gotten so much," she whispered, feeling ashamed.

"Baby, it was fine, it didn't even cost me three-hundred dollars. You're fine, beautiful. I wanted to get everything for you that we purchased tonight. I wish you would have gotten more, but if that's all you feel you needed then that's fine, come on, let's go get you into that tub." He kissed her neck gently and led her into his room, then into the bathroom.

She watched as he filled the tub for her. She wondered if he'd have her take one by herself or if he'd join this time. She sat up on the counter as he filled the tub. She kicked her tennis shoes off as she stared off into space.

She felt a hand touch her cheek, and she jumped and cringed away quickly.

"Hey, baby, easy, it's just me, I'm so sorry, you okay?" Dom's eyes met hers.

"Yeah, I'm sorry. I'm fine." She closed her eyes and laid her head against his chest.

"Come on, babe, let's get you in this tub and get you to bed, little one." He slowly pulled her hoodie from her and then slid her sweatpants from her legs. He gently kissed her bare ankle, working his way up, when his lips touched a scar he froze, and looked up at her.

Alexa tried to pull away from him quickly, but he held her still.

"What's this?" His fingers ran over it slowly.

"Tate again," She whispered as she looked away.

"How many scars has he left on you, baby?" he inquired gently.

"Too many to count," she whispered.

"Well, I've seen two so far, where else?"

"My back," she mumbled and looked away.

He helped her off the counter and turned her around, and began to run his fingers against her bareback.

---

Anger filled him, how had he not noticed these before? He felt like a fool. He had just washed her this morning but never saw them, but he had to really strain his eyes to see them.

"I'm sorry, Dom."

"What are you sorry for?" Dom asked, turning her back around to face him.

"I have so many imperfections, and I am nothing but a scar covered freak."

"Hey, no you're not, the only prominent one I have seen so far is this one." He ran his fingers over the one on her arm. "All the other ones, I am sorry to say, I didn't notice. They aren't that bad, Alexa, honestly, and even if they were they do not define you. You're perfect to me, Lex, that's why I can look

165

past them. Maybe an ass for looking past them, but they just don't play a part in what made me want you the way I have."

She blushed as she looked up at him. "Really?"

"Really." He reached around and unhooked her bra, letting her beautiful full breasts fall free, then he pushed her thong down slowly. He began to press soft kisses against her skin as he lifted her back up onto the counter. "Perfect in every way," he whispered and took her nipples into his mouth, one then the other.

She whimpered as he did, but it didn't last long. He slowly scooped her off of the counter and placed her into the water. She looked up at him, and he couldn't help but smile back at her, she was his perfect girl, he couldn't be any happier than he was now.

## Chapter 17

Alexa pulled the blanket over her head, not ready to wake up. Friday at work had been a little stressful for both her and Dom. She rolled to curl up into Dom, but she came up empty. She peeked a little and saw he was indeed gone.

She rolled over, pulling the blanket around her tighter, wishing her eyes would close again, and she'd go back to sleep.

Yesterday was Friday that meant today was Saturday. "Ugh!" she groaned out. She was really thinking about throwing in the towel and not going. But Dom was so excited about it.

"What's the matter?" the deep voice asked.

Alexa jumped and moved the blanket a little, she glanced around and saw Dom was at the end of the bed. "Nothing."

Dom took a deep breath and got on the bed, pulling the blanket from her, he snuggled up beside her then covered them back up. "You're lying again, Alexandra, it was obviously something."

"I don't want to go tonight."

He pulled her on top of him. "Why not?"

"I won't belong there."

"Yes you will, Alexa, everything will be okay. I'll be there with you every step of the way, we'll be fine, and I can't wait to dance with you."

"Ha! You're funny, I do not dance."

He rolled them over, so he was nestled intimately between her thighs. "Why not?"

"Never have."

"Just follow my lead tonight, baby girl, and everything will be a-okay."

She shook her head, why could she never say no to this man. "Fine, Dom, I'll try."

He leaned down and caught her lips with his.

She pulled back a little. "Dom, why haven't we, well you know gone further?"

"Because you're not ready and I'm not going to try to make you ready, we have all the time in the world, plus I love pleasuring you more than anything else, want me to demonstrate?" His hand went down between them.

Alexa let out a squeal and closed her legs, shaking her head.

He chuckled and kissed her again, making her relax beneath him, letting his hand press against her folds. She let out a gasp and arched her back, pressing up against his hand.

---

Dom trailed kisses along her jaw to her ear lobe, taking it between his teeth nibbling and sucking on it. The next thing he knew, he was on his back with Alexa straddling him.

He looked up at her, smirking at the serious look on her face. She leaned forward to kiss him, his fingers laced in her hair gently as he kissed her back. She moved from his lips to his neck, pressing light kisses against his neck.

"Alexa," he moaned out, tightening his fingers in her hair. He jerked when she reached between them and stroked his already straining, rigid shaft through his sweatpants.

He pulled in a lung full of air as she moved from his neck down his lightly covered dark-haired chest, and down his toned abs. "Lex,." he hissed out as her hand moved under his sweatpants. "Lex!"

He almost shattered in her hand as her soft fingers wrapped around his bulge.

———————

Alexa's heart was fluttering in her chest as she gripped and stroked his straining flesh. She was so scared she would do something wrong, but from the way his breathing was becoming so ragged she assumed she was doing something right.

She pushed his sweatpants off of him then his boxers. She looked up at Dom wide-eyed when she saw how alert, thick, and long he looked.

His gaze seemed to soften as his eyes locked with hers. "Baby, you don't have to."

He made a move to pull her up to him, but her tongue left her mouth and slowly licked his tip, making him groan out, clutching the sheets in his hands.

She felt his hands then tangle in her hair and he eased into her mouth. She felt as if her jaw was going to break, but felt him twitch inside her mouth. He seemed to be guiding her as he moved her head slowly along his shaft.

Soon she got the hang of it herself and began to bob her head, making her mouth slide up and down him faster.

———————

Dom's toes curled as Alexa moved her mouth along him. He didn't know how much longer he could control himself as she took him deeper and deeper, as she moved on him.

His imagination never did her justice, he jerked his hips up, making her take him further. "Lex!" he cried out, feeling himself jerk inside her warm, tight mouth, then spilling into her. And she took all he had to give.

He almost got harder at the sight of her swallowing everything he released into her.

His breathing slowly came back to normal as he pulled her up against him. "Wow." He mumbled as he managed to get his boxers and sweatpants back up.

He collapsed onto the bed and cuddled her up against him until the rush of blood, heartbeat, and breath calmed. He began to pleasure her.

---

They lay on the bed, intertwined with one another, Dom gently stroking her back. "You didn't have to, you know."

"I know, I wanted to, though." She hid under the blanket a little.

He chuckled, pulling her closer to him, losing a little more of his heart to this special woman. If there was any more left to lose to her.

They lay in bed for a little while longer until both of their stomachs growled.

They made lunch and ate, then went to the couch where they cuddled together until it was time to get ready for the fundraiser.

---

Alexa got ready first, she slipped into her new dress after her shower, then began to apply some makeup. She decided to put her hair halfway up and halfway down.

She decided on gray eyeshadow, which made her eyes pop even more with the waterproof eyeliner's help. She was glad the scrapes she got the other day from her scuffle with Tate were healing and almost unnoticeable.

The bruises, however, were still a little prominent, but her split lip was healed. She managed to cover the bruises nicely then packed the makeup in the purse Dom had bought her.

She finished straightening herself up and went downstairs, her shoes in her hands. Her stomach kept getting butterflies and kept knotting up.

Dom started up the stairs as she was halfway down. They met, and Dom's gaze wandered over her slowly and he pulled her up against him. "I hope this night goes fast, I just want to be home with you, you look amazing, Lex."

Her cheeks heated. "Thank you," she whispered.

His knuckles brushed against her cheek. "Go relax. I'll be down in a little bit." He kissed her softly, then let her go.

Alexa sat on the couch, waiting for Dom to get ready. Her whole body was wound so tight, she couldn't help but bounce her foot like the first day at MAEP. She curled her hands into fists trying not to bite her nails.

Dom showered and dressed quickly. He put on his white buttoned-down dress shirt, and black suit, then his tie then got into his shiny black dress shoes. He headed down to Alexa, and she seemed to be getting a little tense. Never had he been so in tune with someone as he was with her.

When he walked into the living room from the stairs, he

wasn't too surprised that she was pacing back and forth instead of relaxing.

He walked over to her slowly. "Baby, everything's going to be okay."

"What if I embarrass you?"

"Never in a million years, come here." He held open his arms, and she walked over to him. He put his arms around her. "I will always be proud of you, little one." He kissed her forehead. "Are you ready?"

She took a deep breath. "As ready as I'll ever be."

He let her walk away to put her heels on. He hated the ghastly things, and he didn't know how she always walked in them. He pulled her into him, and they headed out to his Camaro.

---

Alexa's leg kept bouncing on the way to The Zeiss. She couldn't believe she was doing this. Dom tried to calm her down with some music and laying his hand on her knee, but then her other leg would start to bounce.

He didn't say a word, though. She didn't mind that he was staying quiet, she kept trying to keep calming herself down. It would work for a couple of moments, and then the nerves would start up again.

She stared out the windshield when they finally pulled up outside of The Zeiss. There wasn't very much going on yet. Maybe this year would be a dud. No, don't think that, if it is then so many kids who are like you won't get the help they need.

All of a sudden, a valet came over to them. The young, sharp-looking man opened her door first and then went to Dom's side, opening his door.

Alexa took a deep breath, she put both feet on the ground, but before she could stand a figure stepped in front of her.

She looked up quickly and saw Patrick Andrews. She tried to pull her legs back into the car, but he pulled her out just as Dom came around and pushed him away from her.

She clung to Dom's arm as she darted her eyes between both men.

"Patrick, don't touch her again." Dom glared at Patrick, making the older man step away.

"Sorry, Dom, I was just going to tell her she looked very different tonight and really stunning." Patrick dipped his head down, then proceeded inside.

Alexa looked up at Dom, who placed his other hand on top of the one holding his arm. He suddenly pulled from her arm, but then his hand brushed her back gently then landed possessively on her hip.

Her heart began to slow some as he held onto her. Her eyes darted around her, and they walked along a red carpet which was bracketed on both sides with gold stands and thick red ropes running between them. The building was at least four stories, not tremendous, but it was still magnificent. Two massive, white columns ran from the first floor to the top, and it was very lit up as well.

The steps they climbed to go inside were white marble, the sign above the entrance was white with The Zeiss printed in black in huge, bold, fancy lettering. The light fixtures were very abundant chandeliers, there were four pillars that went from the ground to the next floor that seemed to be holding it up.

There was a set of staircases on each side of the pillars in the middle. The stairs started out wide at the bottom then grew skinny toward the top. Everything seemed black and white, and the tile floor shined beneath the lights of the chandeliers. The stairs were white, but the railings along the sides were black. Dom led her to the stairway slowly. He leaned down to her. "Are you okay?"

She nodded her head as they climbed the stairs holding on to the railing. He led her across the hallway to a door where he took her on to a balcony that led down to another room with a round ceiling that was all skylights for the most part.

Dom took her down the other flight of stairs to the ground floor that was also black and white tile. There were chandeliers in there as well, about twelve to light up the whole room.

She shot a look up at Dom. "Wow," she whispered.

He smiled down at her just as an ear-splitting scream filled the mostly empty room.

"Lex!"

Alexa and Dom turned toward the woman running toward them.

Delilah looked beautiful. She was tan, and her blonde hair was up in a braid crown. She had on a long glittery black dress. She threw her arms around Alexa, the force making her teeter away from Dom.

"You came! I'm so happy you're here!" Delilah screamed.

"Delilah, can't breathe!" Alexa said, patting her sister on the back.

Delilah loosened her hold a little.

Alexa tried to get out of her grip, but she froze a little when she saw her mother, Noelle, and Brandon coming over to them.

Brandon was the first to get to her and made Delilah let go.

"Alexa, I'm so happy you are here." He leaned forward, kissing her cheek then hugging her. He then turned to Dom. "How are things going?"

Alexa stepped back to let the men talk, and Delilah pulled her up to Sabrina, their mother, and Noelle.

The three looked so much alike, all blonde, and taller than

her. She always felt like the odd one out. But they never felt that way, all three of them hugged her tightly.

"Oh, Lex, we've missed you." Sabrina kissed the top of her head. "You look so beautiful, who did you come with?"

Delilah broke into a laugh. "Mom, you'll never believe this, she came in on Mr. Mackenzie's arm!" She let out a squeal.

"Alexa, really, an old man?" Noelle asked, shock written all over her face.

Delilah rolled her eyes. "No, that Greek God that Brandon is talking to right now." She pointed over to Brandon and Dom.

Noelle and Sabrina both looked at Dom wide-eyed. "Wow," the two women gasped out.

---

Dom shook Brandon's hand. "Still nothing. He hasn't made any more moves to get to her."

"How are things between the two of you, though?" Brandon asked.

Dom scanned the ballroom quickly when he realized Alexa wasn't near him anymore. He smiled when he saw her with her sisters and mother. "We're making some progress."

"She has feelings for you, Dom. She has never given in to anyone helping her, until now." Brandon turned to watch his family.

"Eh, she's still reluctant, but I'm more stubborn than she is, I told Angelo to keep a close eye on her tonight."

"Good, well let's go get our women." They headed over to the group of sisters and mother.

---

Alexa blushed as her mom and sisters gushed over Dom. "It's not like that, he's my boss now, he needed a date, so here I am."

Delilah let out another squeal as another man began to walk toward them. "Speaking of dates, that's Charles Fitzgerald, Daddy introduced us a couple of months ago, he's way better than James."

Alexa's eyes widened as the man walked over to them, his sharp gunmetal eyes raked over her. She backed up quickly into a hard body, and she about jumped out of her skin.

A pair of arms wrapped around her shoulders. "You okay?" the deep voice whispered against her ear.

She looked back into Dom's eyes, but they were cold as ice as he watched the man walking over to them. She moved further back into him, wanting to feel safe. "I'm fine." She put up the brave front again.

Dom glanced down at Alexa and tightened his arms around her more, he looked up at Mrs. Adams. "Hello, ma'am, it's so nice to see you again."

"Likewise, Mr. Mackenzie, I'm glad you got my youngest daughter to come finally."

"So this is the famous Alexandra Mills, huh?" the man who joined Delilah asked casually.

Delilah supplied the answer. "Yes, that's my baby sister."

Charles held out his hand to her. "It's so nice to meet you finally."

Dom glared as the man's gaze raked over Alexa, but she managed to be polite and shook his hand.

He could feel how tense she was. She dropped the man's hand quickly. "Nice to meet you too, Mr. Fitzgerald."

Dom pulled her into his side, instead of in front of him, not liking the vibe he was getting from Fitzgerald. "I hate to part a family, but we have some other people to meet with soon, I'm going to get Alexa a drink before all the talking begins." He pulled her with him toward the beverage table.

He rubbed her arm slowly. "So, who was that guy?"

She looked up at him. "I guess she's been dating him for a couple of months now, his name is Charles Fitzgerald. She said Daddy introduced them. She was talking about Tate, she's never referred to Brandon as Daddy."

Dom's eye flashed to the man holding Delilah, he seemed happy with her, but the looks he was giving Alexa unsettled him. He spotted Angelo and waved him over.

As soon as Angelo walked over Dom pointed with his eyes. "Find out as much as you can about that man, his name is Charles Fitzgerald, Tate introduced him to Delilah."

Angelo gave a nod and walked away.

Dom laid his hand possessively against Alexa's back and pulled her into him. "It'll be okay, Angelo will figure that guy out, just stay close to me or Angelo the rest of the night, okay, babe?"

Alexa nodded her head as a sharp voice came from behind them.

"Nicky, I am so glad you are here. Oh, you're with her?" the woman asked when they both turned to see Carla rushing up to them, then stop dead in her tracks. "What's she doing here?"

"She's my date, Carla, how many times do I have to tell you not to be disrespectful to her, she is still an employee." Dom glared at the woman. Man, this night was going to be nothing but drama.

"Your father told me you weren't bringing anyone this year. I thought maybe we could hang out together." Carla narrowed her cold eyes at Alexa.

"Well, he never asked me what I was doing this year so he wouldn't know now, would he? Just back off, Carla. I am not interested, and I have never been. I've tried to be nice about it, hell Alexa put you in your place, too. One more wrong move and you will not have a job, am I understood?" Dom glared back at Carla, whose face paled as she walked away quickly.

Alexa let out a sigh. "I want to go already."

"It'll be okay." Dom rubbed her back gently.

"Sure doesn't feel like it, first Patrick, then that man my father knows, now Carla. I am not a drama kind of person, this is why I have always kept to myself. Tate was enough drama to last me the rest of my life, if not more."

"I know, baby, it'll stop now, I promise."

"Nicky." Another voice interrupted them. He turned to meet his mother and two sisters. "Mom, Collette, Arielle, how are you guys? Miles here too?" He pasted on the fake smile, this just gets better and better. Miles was Patrick's father and currently his mother, Mary's, new man interest. "It's great to see all of you."

"Dominick, how are you this evening?" Miles smiled at him and held out his hand. "And who is this pretty lady you seem to be very protective over this evening?"

"Mr. Andrews, I'd like you to meet my new consultant, Alexandra Mills, she just started at MAEP about a month ago." Dom smiled as he pulled Alexa closer to him.

She held out her hand. "Nice to meet you, Mr. Andrews."

"Ah, so you are the new young woman Calvin has spoken highly of the last couple of days, he says you are great for the company. I may have to come to take a look for myself, but I am pleased to have you onboard and having you here this evening." He grasped her hand gently and placed a soft kiss against it.

She blushed. "Thank you, sir, I'm just thankful Dom gave me the opportunity."

"Well, I hope you won't let my lug head son scare you off, he's always been jealous of Dominick here, but who could blame him? I wish these boys would get along better, Cal and I never had these discrepancies with each other."

"No, I'm here to stay for a while. I really am loving what I am doing for the company, and it's an amazing new opportunity."

"Mills?" Mary finally interrupted. "As in Sabrina Mills, who's married to Brandon Adams?" She narrowed her sharp blue gaze at Alexa.

"Yes, Mother, we've already discussed all of that, she was working for Brandon before she came to work for me, so it's all out in the open. She was given Brandon's blessing to come work for me, so we are all good in that department."

"Miles, you're going to trust a woman whose stepfather is your main rival?"

"Mary, let the men discuss the business, you just go eat to your heart's content." Miles dismissed Mary quickly.

Dominick was shocked at first, but his mother walked away without another word. He cleared his throat. "It's okay. I keep a very close tab on Ms. Mills here, and she's not going to be doing any sneaking around me."

Alexa smiled up at him. "Or so you think," she teased.

Dom just laughed at her and kissed her temple. "You are something else, woman."

Miles looked between the two and laughed. "Are my eyes deceiving me or has a woman finally landed the infamous Dominick Mackenzie."

Dom smiled and pulled her closer. "Maybe, still trying to win her over." He watched Miles walk away and the dirty looks that Arielle and Collette gave Alexa, but he glared at them, and they scurried away.

"Can we go now?" Alexa asked, looking up at him.

"Not yet, I'm getting a dance from you, baby." He pulled her up to him and kissed her in front of everyone, and she let him.

"You are a terrible, terrible man," she accused him as he pulled back from her.

"So terrible you want me." He kissed the spot below her ear, and they began to walk around saying hello and thank you to their clients who had shown up so far.

---

Alexa was holding onto Dom tightly, not wanting to lose him in the fast-growing crowd. They were bombarded by the press, who was usually always there. Only they usually focused more on Brandon.

They seemed to swarm Alexa instantly. "Ma'am, how does it feel knowing your stepfather created this fund in honor of you five years ago?"

Alexa was frozen. She didn't know what to say.

The questions kept coming like lightning. "How does it feel to be on the arm of the most eligible bachelor and playboy?"

"How do you deal with the memories of being abused as a child?"

"Do you hold any grudges toward your sisters who were never beaten growing up?"

"How come you've never shown up before?"

Dom shoved the people away from Alexa. "If you don't back off, you'll be thrown out of here, now go." She knew that glare, and he dared any of them to challenge him.

One tried to, but soon Angelo was between the press and Dom, ushering them away.

Alexa was a stuttering fool while trying to answer the questions. She felt like an idiot, such an idiot, she pulled away from Dom and strolled away from him as quickly as she could trying to pick her way through the crowd. How could she be so stupid?

She felt a hand grab hold of her arm, and she turned around, but it wasn't Dom, she pulled back from Charles quickly and stumbled a little but stayed upright. "What do you want?"

"That attack didn't look too friendly, are you okay?" he asked, sounding sincere.

"I'm fine, I just need a minute, if you'll excuse me." She headed out to the empty deck, just needing some air. She leaned against the wall as she stared out at the lit-up garden. This was not her life, never going to be her life, how did any of those reporters know who she was? She hugged herself tightly as the tears threatened to fall.

*No, you can't do that, not today, you're hiding too much. What a lot of good it did, they still knew who you were. Just keep it together, Lex, you're stronger than this, although lately, it doesn't feel that way.*

She turned to go back in when a shadow fell from the lighting of the ballroom. She moved back against the wall as Carla came out. "So sorry about all those newscasters, they really wanted a juicy story, how could I not tell them about Brandon Adam's long-lost stepdaughter being at the fundraiser?"

Alexa glared at Carla. "You did that, on purpose? You are one inconsiderate bitch."

She felt the slap across her face as another shadow rushed out. She looked and saw Brandon.

"I'm an inconsiderate bitch, huh? What about you? Coming in acting like no one else could have wanted Nicky, and then suddenly, you have him wrapped around your finger. He'd do anything and everything for you. I wanted that, it's not fair, so if anyone is the inconsiderate bitch, I believe it would be you." She went to slap Alexa again, but Brandon caught her hand.

"I think you need to leave my daughter alone if you know

what is good for you." Brandon hardened his voice as he squeezed her wrist and tossed her away from Alexa.

---

"Angelo, did you see which way Alexa went? She took off after you got the news crews away from us, but I lost her in the crowd, damn her being so short." He strained to see if he could spot her. No luck.

"Mr. Adams rushed out on the deck, shortly after Carla went out there, and it looks like he just threw her back inside." Angelo motioned with his hand to where Dom needed to look.

"Thanks, Angelo." Dom felt the fear ease a little bit, but he couldn't make it all go away until Alexa was back in his arms. He flew out past Carla and heard the tears.

---

"I want to go somewhere else where no one knows me, and no one knows what happened to me, Daddy, I just want to disappear. Why is everyone either just cold-hearted or feel threatened by me when I do nothing? I didn't ask for the attention from Mr. Mackenzie. I didn't ask him to save me. I'm an idiot." Alexa slid down onto the bench outside up against the wall, as she laid her head on the shoulder of the only man she knew as a father.

Brandon hugged her close to him and rocked her. "I know you didn't ask for it, and I can't control Dominick. I warned you about him, but he's changed for the better for you. Almost everyone sees it, he cares for you, and he would do anything in the world to protect you, sweetheart. Dry your eyes, you're going to ruin your makeup, and it looked so beautiful."

"But he doesn't need some stupid, insecure, jumpy, scared pansy who can't even sleep with a light off," she sobbed out.

"But I know why you are those things, Alexa and I don't care. I still want you." Dom broke into the conversation.

Brandon looked over and kissed his pride and joy on her forehead. "I love you, sweetheart, don't put yourself down so much. You are an amazing woman. I'll let you two talk."

Alexa watched Brandon leave, and she looked away from Dom. "I wish you didn't try to understand, is this what it's going to be like if we are official? Constantly attacked by that woman who clearly wants you? Or any other woman who feels like they've had a claim on you?"

Dom let out a sad sigh and sat down beside her. "Well, if you wouldn't have left me, this wouldn't have happened, but no, it's not always going to be like this. Once we are official and I talk you into everything I want to do, then everyone will know I am beyond serious about you and they will back off. And, if not, then you will always have a bodyguard on you. No one is going to hurt you emotionally or physically and get away with it."

"She told those reporters who I was," she sobbed out.

"Fuck," He gritted out, making her jump a little. "And here I thought the problem was going to be the Fitzgerald guy." He tilted her head to look up at him. Surprisingly, her makeup didn't run with the tears she was letting fall. "I'll take care of Carla, I promise, you just have to trust me and trust what I feel for you. She's the only one who has been making a scene lately. Every other break up I have ever done was a clean break, and nothing was left to even think there'd be another chance."

"I wanted to rip her hair out of her nice perfect bun." Alexa sighed out as she leaned against Dom.

"Why didn't you?"

"We're here for a fundraiser against abuse, I couldn't really do that, I have better standards than her apparently."

He wiped her tears away slowly, and helped her stand up

when they heard the music start to play. "How about a dance, baby, then I will take you home?"

"Okay," she whispered and let him pull her from the bench.

As they headed inside, he stopped her quickly and gently grabbed her chin. "She hit you?" he demanded, seeing the ugly red mark on her cheek she was sure was there.

She looked away and tried to shake her head, but he was already off across the room. She could only stand there and watch Dom walk away, she felt an arm wrap around her shoulders, and she looked back to see Lizzie and Angelo standing behind and beside her.

"What's going on?" Lizzie whispered in her ear.

"He's upset."

"Well, we can see that, what happened, Alexa?" Angelo asked, laying a hand on her bare shoulder.

"Carla slapped me," she whispered as she looked down at the ground.

"Oh no. Lizzie, stay with Alexa." Angelo was off after his boss.

---

Dom found Carla with ease, she was with Patrick, which was obvious. "Excuse me, Carla, but didn't we have a meeting a few days ago about bothering Alexa after what happened?" His voice was calm at first.

She looked up at him, trying to play innocent. "Yes, sir, and I've stayed away from her."

"Oh, have you now, have you really?" His voice got louder, making everyone look his way. "Why don't you remind me again what my words were that day in our meeting?"

"That if anyone messed with her, they would no longer have a job, but I didn't."

"Really, then why is there now a red mark on her cheek? And why did I find her crying and Brandon consoling her a little bit ago?" He glared at the HR manager whom he had wanted to do away with for a while now.

"I don't know. Maybe she stupidly ran into a wall." Carla glared back at Dom.

"I think you made her cry because you can't get over the fact that I care about her and not you. I also believe you slapped her since Brandon did throw you out from the deck area, and my head of security saw you go out there and be tossed away. Now did you make my girl cry and did you slap her?"

"No." Carla glared at Dom.

"You are a liar, Carla." Brandon came up beside Dom. "Now admit you slapped her and put her down."

"I didn't." She folded her arms over her chest, glaring at the two men.

"I mean, I can just get the video surveillance if you don't want to tell the truth."

"Fine, I slapped the dumb bitch, she deserved it, she has no reason to be with you," she yelled and glared.

"Carla, you are fired!" Dom shouted loud enough for everyone to hear.

---

Alexa stood there frozen as Dom just fired Carla. She let out a gasp and went to step forward, but Lizzie pulled her back against her.

"I wouldn't, Alexa." She rubbed her shoulder gently.

"He just fired her because of me."

"Well, she had no right to slap you, or bad mouth you."

She watched as Carla left the fundraiser and then watched as Dom came back over to her. She stepped back from Dom after seeing him the angriest she had ever seen him. She was a little afraid of him.

The music began again, and he pulled her into him gently. She let him pull her out on the floor, but she hid her face as everyone kept staring at them. "I wish you wouldn't have done that, Dom."

"She hurt you. Everyone at MAEP was warned the day you were attacked by Tate. I told them all if they ever did anything to you after that day they would be fired. I am not condoning it since we are at a fundraiser against abuse and you are the main reason Brandon made this event. She wasn't getting away with it, and I am not having a stupid idiot like her around to make us look bad." He leaned down and nuzzled her neck gently. "I'm taking you home after this dance," he whispered and pressed his lips to her neck. "After this morning, all I can think about is getting you undressed again."

She looked up at him and shook her head. "You really scared me, Dom."

"I'm sorry. I will never get that angry with you, baby, I promise. You are everything to me, and you deserve protection. I was getting really tired of Carla anyways, first she had an attitude lately, then she started in on you all the time, fired you, then tonight, so I am glad she is gone," he explained and kissed her passionately, pulling her up against him.

She let out a moan and whimper as he did, and she wrapped her arms around his neck tightly, kissing him back with as much passion. Might as well tell the world they were together after that kind of a kiss. But that didn't mean anything in the playbook of Dominick Mackenzie, although he was never caught kissing in public, except for her.

He hoped Tate had a better plan than what he was thinking, this woman was going to be really hard to get to now that Dominick Mackenzie was involved with her. She was untouchable, as was just displayed with the firing of his HR manager. He let out a sigh as he pulled the woman beside him into his arms and began to dance with her.

## Chapter 18

Dom spun Alexa around and pulled her back into him, and he leaned down, claiming her lips deeply as he stopped dancing. One hand was splayed against her back while the other cupped her cheek. He smiled down at her when he pulled back from her, rubbing his thumb against her cheek softly.

He was shocked when she pulled him back down to her and kissed him, he dragged her off her feet and kissed her back. He set her down slowly. "Are you ready to go home now? I think everyone will understand why we want to leave already."

She smiled up at him, but it faded. "I want to talk to my mom and Brandon, can I do it alone, though?"

"You're killing me, woman, but okay, I'll take you to them. When you are done, call me, so I can come get you." He placed his arm around her shoulders as they searched for her mom and Brandon.

"There they are." Alexa pointed over toward a corner, and sure enough, Brandon and Sabrina were eating in the corner.

Dom walked her over. "Brandon, Mrs. Adams, Alexa

would like to talk to you privately, I told her to call me when she is done, and I'll come get her."

Brandon threw his plate away. "Of course."

Dom pulled Alexa to him and kissed her softly. "My phone is on sound and vibrate, so call me, I'll answer this time." He brushed her cheek with his hand. He hated leaving her but made himself go.

The minute Dom left, she wanted him back with her, but she had to do this herself. She turned to Brandon and her mom.

Brandon ushered her up the stairs with Sabrina behind them, and they found a private place to talk. "What's going on inside that brain of yours, dear?"

"Why is Delilah with someone Tate introduced to her? Aren't either of you worried?"

"Alexa, your father never hurt them. I have to tell you I am sorry I let it go on for so long, but I don't think he'd hurt Delilah or Noelle, they were his pride and joy and still are," Sabrina began.

"But."

"Alexa, they're fine, you just worry about staying safe and away from him, I'm sure Dominick will keep you safe, it'll be okay." Sabrina kissed her forehead and began to walk away.

She turned to look at Brandon. "Do you feel the same way?"

"No." He pulled her further away from the people who were walking by. "I didn't know about him until tonight, they may be Tate's pride and joy, but you are mine. I actually couldn't stand the way he was looking at you. It also worries me that even the famous Dominick glare didn't make him stop, I want both of you to stay alert from now on, both of you need to be careful."

She wrapped her arms around Brandon. "Thank you for everything, Dad."

He hugged her back. "Come on, let's go find Dom."

She pulled her phone out and called him. "Hey, we're done, we're heading back into the ballroom."

"I'll meet you at the stairs, okay?"

"Okay, that's fine, thank you, Dom."

Brandon wrapped his arm around her protectively and took her up the steps slowly. They walked into the ballroom, Brandon kissed her cheek. "If you or Dom need anything just let me know, I promised I would protect you the day I married your mother, and I stand by that promise."

"Thank you, Dad, I love you." She hugged him tightly and watched him walk down the steps. She scanned the room to try to find Dom she wasn't seeing him. She frowned as she scanned the room. He said he'd be here.

She backed up a little and ran into a hard chest, she spun quickly and met the gunmetal eyes. She moved back to the wall of the steps. "Mr. Fitzgerald."

"Hello, would you care to dance? I've already given Delilah a few dances and Noelle one. I'm afraid I've missed you, though." He smiled, but it didn't reach his eyes.

"No, I'm waiting for my boyfriend, he should be here any minute." She tried to move further away. There was something about him she did not trust. She tried to step around him, but he pulled her up against him. She pushed back against his chest.

"Sorry your boyfriend may be a little delayed, I sent Delilah to talk to him about you." He pulled her against him harder.

Her head whipped around, scanning the crowd again and saw Delilah indeed talking to Dom. He was trying to push her out of his way, so was her older sister in on this? She struggled in the arms of Fitzgerald. He began to drag her out the door, but she slammed her fist into his face quickly. He stumbled back but took her with him.

She let out a scream trying to get everyone's attention, his hand slammed over her mouth before she could finish the scream, and he picked her up with ease. She kicked and struggled then bit his hand.

He let out a yell and went to smack her when he was shoved back from her quickly, and she looked up, seeing Dom she moved backward, quickly tripping over her heels and landed on her butt. She moved back further, pressing herself against the wall behind her. She could only watch as the men struggled.

***

Dom was angry as Delilah had walked into his path, preventing him from getting to Alexa. She just kept going on about their relationship, to see if they really were a thing and that he had better not hurt her sister. Blah, blah, blah.

The minute he heard the little scream, he knew Alexa was in danger. He looked to the balcony steps to see Alexa struggling with Fitzgerald. He pushed past Delilah and took the steps two at a time. The minute the man raised his hand to hit her, Dom shoved him back, breaking his hold on Alexa.

"So, interested in my girl, huh? Did you forget the scene I made with the last person who touched her?" Dom hauled him up and slammed him against the wall. "I see you around her again you're in trouble, I don't think your girlfriend will like that you were trying to get to her sister."

He felt a hand on his shoulder, he looked back to see Angelo there. "I'll handle him, Dom."

Dom tried to calm his anger and let the man fall to the ground turning around to Alexa. Before he knew it, she was in his arms, her arms around his neck tightly and kissing him.

"Come on, babe, let's get you home." He wrapped her in his strong arms and headed out of the ballroom and out of the hotel. He set her down as the valet took his ticket and went to get his car. He glanced down at her as she clung to his jacket tightly and shivered a little.

He took his jacket off and wrapped it around her gently. "You okay?" He rubbed her arm gently.

"I think so." She pulled the jacket around her tighter.

He kissed her temple, pulling her closer to him, he wondered if he could talk her into going away until they fixed all of this. If Tate could get one man involved who knew how many others he could get. If he couldn't convince her to go somewhere else, he may lose her yet.

He led her to the car once the valet showed up with it. He opened the passenger door and helped her sit down.

He got in on his side and took off.

———

Dom flew home faster than he should have. Ten minutes after leaving The Zeiss, he was already in the garage, getting Alexa out of the car. He took her in and stripped her of her shoes and laid her purse on the counter.

He began to go upstairs, his heart aching at the way she clung to him. He went to the bathroom after turning the lights on, he sat her on the counter and turned the shower on.

He undid his tie and pulled his shirt from his pants, unbuttoning the first few top buttons. He turned back to Alexa and cradled her face in his hands gently.

"Dom, don't ever leave my side again, I need you," she whispered. "I'm so sorry. I was so stupid to want to talk with them alone. If you hadn't—"

He silenced her with his lips in a frenzy. "It's okay, if I hadn't gotten stopped by Delilah, I would have been up there." He laid his forehead against hers. "As long as we are out, I will be stuck to you like glue."

"Dom, he put her up to talking to you, I don't know how, I'm wondering if she's part of it, but she's my sister, would she really hurt me like that?" She wrapped her arms around him tightly as she trembled against him. He held her tightly, rubbing her back.

"Why don't you jump in the shower, sweetheart?"

"You too?"

"I'll take one after you're done, okay? I'm going to call Angelo, I won't leave the bedroom, though."

She drew in a shaky breath but nodded her head.

He made sure she got in the shower okay and made a call as he headed to his bedroom, where he discarded his shoes. "Anything?" he asked when Angelo answered.

"Made the motherfucker sing like a canary. Tate introduced him to Delilah to try to get close to Alexa. Tate sold him on the idea when he found out how much money could possibly be involved. He gave me an address of where they have been meeting, they met in a bar one night while Tate was very drunk and complaining about you. Before that, Fitz never came into contact with any of the Mills, he just wanted to try to get laid and come into some easy money. As for him getting Delilah to distract you I am not too sure about that yet, I'll keep working on it, Boss."

"So a lot of the problem is me, but now everyone is going to know exactly how I feel about her, so even if I distance us from each other, she's still in danger."

"I advise against leaving her alone, Dom, she will come to harm if we do not keep tabs on her. Fitz says if she's left alone once and Tate finds out, she'll disappear until he is ready to bargain for her."

"I think we got lucky he didn't have stronger men who wouldn't sing at the first sign of trouble. Well, we know what we have to do now, one of us must be with her at all times, I want this bastard locked up, dead if that's what it comes down to."

"Yes, sir."

Dom ended the call on the verge of throwing his phone. He raked his fingers through his hair roughly, not sure what to do for Alexa. Even if he hadn't come into her life, she would still be in trouble because Tate kept coming back for any money she would give him.

He headed into the bathroom, and he watched Alexa stand motionless in the water from the showerhead. She asked him never to leave her side again, was she having second thoughts? He finished stripping and joined her in the shower. He ran his hands against her back and over her shoulders. "What are you thinking?" he whispered against her ear.

"How lucky I am to have you on my side. Mother wasn't worried about that man, and she's not worried about Tate hurting Noelle or Delilah, she threw them in my face. They are his pride and joy, and I was the fucking mistake."

Dom's heart shattered, and he was close to actual tears because she was hurting so bad. He turned her around toward him to look at her. "You are not a mistake, baby, you were made for me, made to come into my life and change me for the better. The minute you tumbled into that conference room I knew you would tame me. You think I call every person hours after an interview? No, little one, just you."

She gazed up at him and wrapped her arms around his neck tightly and stood on her tiptoes to kiss him. He made it easier by pulling her up into his arms, wrapping her legs around his waist.

He pressed her back against the shower sidewall as his tongue dove into her mouth, circling with her own tongue. He thrust his tongue in and out of her mouth in the same rhythm he wanted to take her. His hands moved to her ass, cupping her cheeks in his hands, squeezing them hard.

"Dominick, please," she begged as she squirmed against him.

"Please what, Lex?" He moved to her neck, nipping and sucking on it.

"I want you." She gasped out, lacing her fingers into his hair tightly, making him groan.

He shut the water off quickly and walked out of the shower with her still wrapped around him, he sat her down on the vanity top and grabbed a towel, first drying himself off then her.

He picked her back up and slammed his lips down onto hers, hungry for her. He laid her down on the bed and leaned over her to grab a foil package. His mouth found her already rock-hard tips and rasped his tongue against them repeatedly as she squirmed against him. He pulled back a little. "Are you sure?"

She didn't answer just pushed him onto his back and took the package from him and opened it, she slowly rolled it over his long, thick, hard shaft. She moved to straddle him, but he pulled her to him, looking into her eyes.

"Are you sure?" he whispered on the verge of losing himself already.

"Yes, please, Dom," she whispered, trying to move back down to his straining flesh.

She squirmed against him as he ran his hands from her ass up to her back slowly and let her do what she wanted. She leaned down, and he met her lips just as she slowly lowered herself down onto him.

She let out a tiny groan of pain as she sank down onto him a little bit.

He pulled her back up a little. "Take your time, beautiful.

I'm not going anywhere, I promise. Just go as slow as you need."

She nodded her head and slid down a little more. He tried his best to stay still even though he wanted just to roll her over and take her, but he reined his desire in yet again so she could take her time and adjust to him.

He leaned up and cupped one breast and found the other with his mouth, he slowly tortured her rosy tips, and she let out a scream of pleasure and pain as she slipped the rest of the way down on him. He groaned in pleasure as she took all of him. He moved his hands to her ass, squeezing, trying to let her adjust to him.

---

Alexa couldn't believe how much he stretched her, and she let out a sharp breath as she sank down onto him. She took all of him but didn't know what else to really do. She looked at Dom, scared of doing something wrong.

He leaned up and caught her lips slowly. "Are you okay?"

She nodded her head a little.

"Baby, it's okay, just move when you're ready."

"I don't know how," she admitted and hid her face against his shoulder.

He slowly began to move her up and down his still very rock-hard shaft. "Just like that, baby, you control how fast you want to go, it's okay."

She let out a moan as he moved her against him and managed to take over, he began to push up into her as she came down on him. "Dominick," she gasped out, as she clutched his shoulders in her hands, and continued to move and picked up speed. She couldn't believe how much he filled her, he leaned up and began to suck on her ear, which practically pushed her over the edge. She dug her fingers into his hair with their chests pressed together as she rocked against him more.

"Dominick!" she screamed, leaning her head back.

She was shocked when he rolled them over, and began to rock against her gently at first as she wrapped her legs around him. He moved into her a little faster, making her arch her back pushing herself up into him, meeting his thrusts. "Dominick, please!" she screamed, not feeling enough of the feeling build yet.

"Lex, are you sure?"

"Yes, please." She tightened her legs around him and pulled him down into her as deep as he could go.

He thrust into her urgently as she shivered beneath him and clung to him, he slammed into her.

She screamed at the feel of the harsh loving he was giving her, it felt so amazing. She began to feel herself come undone as he continued to thrust into her hard, making the headboard hit the wall. "Dominick!" she screamed, feeling the pressure build and spill and shatter her world into thousands of different colors. She bit down on his shoulder, trying to muffle her cries of release, and she felt herself tighten even more around him.

He thrust into her a few more times, letting her ride out her moment of bliss along his steel-hard cock, and at the last moment of her coming down from the stars, she felt him jerk and slam into her one more time spilling himself into the protection she had put on him. His hands gripped her ass, holding her close to him as he reached the end of his wave of pure blissful relief.

He slowly pulled from her making her jerk and feel empty, she wanted him back the moment he slid from her. He discarded the used condom and pulled her up against him tightly. "You okay?" he whispered, pressing his lips to her forehead.

She let out a giggle and curled into him, an arm over his hard abs and a leg over one of his. "Perfect," she whispered as her head fell to his chest.

---

Dom let out a chuckle as he ran his fingertips down her back slowly. Man, she was so worth the wait. So worth it. He kissed her forehead again as he felt her fall into a deep sleep. He was never letting her go. God, he loved her for crying out loud. Of all the things he had felt in his lifetime, this was such a new feeling, and he loved how it took over his whole body.

He began to fall asleep, his lips still against her forehead. No one would ever hurt her again.

## Chapter 19

Dom and Alexa walked into the office building with their coffee and her blueberry muffin. They headed straight to his office, like every morning. He had chosen a light gray suit today, and he looked so good in it.

She went with an aqua blouse and a black pencil skirt with a pair of black flats.

As soon as Dom walked in behind her, he closed the door and pulled her back around, pushing her up against the door and kissed her senseless.

He slowly pulled back from her and smiled at her as she rolled her eyes at him. "Can't even let me finish my coffee?"

"Nope, sure can't." He smiled wickedly.

"Yesterday wasn't enough?"

"Baby, I could have you every day for the rest of my life, and it wouldn't be enough." He kissed her again, but their coffees were getting in the way.

She giggled as he finally let her go. She headed over to the table to finish her muffin and coffee. She began to remember most of the day before. She was sure they had done it on almost every surface in his house.

She smiled, but it faded when she began to think it would end once she could finally go home. She didn't want to, though.

She glanced over at Dom under her dark eyelashes. Could she be okay without him once things went back to normal? She had lost her heart to him, she loved him so much, but that didn't mean he loved her as much, or if at all.

---

She began to open her email on her tablet when Dom walked over to her. She glanced up at him. "What's up?" she asked, scrolling through her emails again.

He placed a finger beneath her chin. "How do you not mix both?" he whispered and pressed his lips against hers.

"Because I know you will mix business and pleasure and if I start, we'd never get anything done."

"Smartass, well I need to try to find a new HR manager today, so I'll be busy with that most of the day, will you be okay by yourself?"

"I may need you to check up on me later, but I will be okay, don't scare anyone today."

"No promises, I'm a real hard-ass, you know."

She kissed him and let him leave the office. She settled back into doing what she did best. Search and read.

---

A few hours went by, and Alexa slowly got up from the table, grabbing a folder to make copies of some forms she had been putting off for a while. She hated doing it since the copier was down in the basement.

She grabbed a bottle of water from the break room fridge

and made her way down the basement steps. She turned the light on and began to make her copies.

She took another drink of her water as the copier ran when the lights went out, and the door shut loudly. She spun around quickly, dropping the bottle of water.

Fear hit her hard. Dom knew her fear of the dark, and he wouldn't have done this to her. Her eyes weren't adjusting to the darkness.

"You may have gotten rid of Carla, but I'm still here, and you will not ruin the plans we made," the rough voice began.

Alexa tried to back away but ran into the copier, almost tipping it over. "I didn't get rid of her, she made that happen herself." Her voice trembled as she spoke.

A hand reached out and grabbed her chin hard. "You were something we never expected, never expected Dom to fall so hard for you, but making you disappear will crush him. He won't be able to run the company anymore. Then I'll take over with the blessing of both my father and Calvin."

Alexa tried to shove his hand away from her. "You're wrong, so wrong, he won't give up this company like that, he's worked too hard to let it go."

Patrick gripped her harder then slammed her up against the empty wall behind him. "He'd give up anything to keep you away from dear old Dad, and I think I'll deliver you to him."

"You're an idiot to think he'd do that." She shoved his hand away from her face, but he caught her hands tightly, pushing them up onto the wall above her head.

"Want to say that again?"

"You're an idiot!" She wished her eyes would adjust to the darkness, but it just wasn't happening. She felt the sharp slap across her cheek and was slammed down onto the floor. She began to struggle, but her arms were yanked behind her back hard, making her yell in pain.

She managed to yank a hand free and slammed it back, hitting something on his body. It threw him off balance, and she managed to scramble away from him. She tried to think where she was in the room to try to get to the door.

She got up but stumbled over her own feet and landed right into another wall in the room. She felt around, and her fingers brushed against the cold knob. She twisted it, but it wouldn't budge. She managed to throw the lock, and the door fell open.

She took off up the steps quickly then a hand wrapped around her ankle, pulling her down onto the steps. She looked back, and it was indeed, Patrick. She slammed her other foot back into his face making him let her go, and she ran.

Her heart raced in fear. She wouldn't let him get away with trying to take the company from Dom or trying to give her to Tate to make that happen.

She glanced at the clock when she saw Ashley wasn't at her desk. Lunchtime.

Her gaze darted from Dom's office door to the conference room. His door was still open while the conference room door was closed. She heard Patrick yell at her.

"You dumb bitch, you messed up my face, now I'm really giving you to dear old Daddy."

She glanced back, and he was almost on top of her, she hated to interrupt an interview, but she didn't have a choice. She ran to the closed door and she shoved the door open and jerked away from Patrick, falling through the door landing on the floor hard.

---

Dom was up the minute he saw Alexa falling through the door yet again. He rushed over to her as Patrick stepped in.

"Patrick?" Dom asked, as he pulled Alexa up to him. "What happened?"

"That bitch just started to attack me for no reason, and I think her stupid ass broke my nose," he screamed, now holding his nose.

His nose and mouth were bleeding, and he had a bruise on his face and a couple of red marks.

Dom looked down at Alexa, she had a bruise on her face, and her clothes looked like she had been in a struggle. "Alexa?"

"I'm quitting and going back to BAP," she answered, glaring at Patrick.

Dom pulled her closer to him. "What, why?"

"Because I was better off there." She tried to pull away from him, but he held her against his body tightly.

"Patrick, what really happened?" another voice asked. Dom turned to look at Miles, who was standing up from his chair along with Cal.

"D-dad?" Patrick stuttered out.

"Yeah, I've been here for a while now, what really happened?" the old man demanded.

"As I said, she attacked me for no reason." Patrick grew defensive.

"Yeah, because shutting the lights off on me, then shutting the door wasn't a good enough reason to get your ass handed to you, he was trying to–" She stopped talking when Patrick moved closer to her.

"Alexa, what are you talking about?" Dom asked, tilting her head up to look at him.

Her eyes grew wide as if something had just dawned on her.

No one would believe her. She pulled away from Dom and started to rush out of the room. She was yanked back around. Hazel met brown.

"I think you owe me an apology," Patrick demanded.

"I don't think I do." She yanked her arm away from him and slammed her foot down on his, then stormed away.

She rushed to Dom's office and began to gather her things. She turned to leave as Dom, Miles, and Calvin walked in.

"Alexa, talk to me, babe," Dom pleaded.

"Why? No one will believe me," she muttered as Calvin shut the door.

Miles stepped forward. "What did my son do?"

"Like I said in there, he shut the lights off on me while I was in the basement making copies, he also shut the door locking us inside." Alexa moved back from Dom when he went to move toward her.

"Baby, why would he do that?"

She closed her eyes tightly. "He was trying to use me to make you lose the company. I don't belong here, Dom, I don't belong in your life, nothing is going to get better until I am out of it."

"Alexa," Calvin came forward, shouting a little. "Sit down!"

She flinched and sat down in the chair at the table like a good girl was supposed to do.

"Dad, don't yell at her," Dom scolded. He knelt in front of her. "Honey, talk to me, please?" He looked into her eyes as he laid his hands on her knees. "You can tell me anything."

"He wants you gone, Dom. He wants the company to himself, he was going to hand me over to Tate."

"Who's Tate?" Miles asked, looking between herself and Dom.

"Her abusive sperm donor," Dom answered then stared into Alexa's eyes. "What did he think that was going to do?"

"Force you to pay a lot of money to Tate to get me back. I'm assuming he'd ask for so much you'd have to sell out, possibly to Patrick," she whispered. "I have to go. I can't keep doing this." She went to stand, fighting the tears, but Dom pulled her down into his lap.

She struggled to get away from him until his lips landed on hers, and she instantly relaxed in his arms. He slowly pulled away, and she laid her head on his shoulder, her hands pinned between their chests.

---

Dom believed her but couldn't believe Patrick was that far gone. "So that's what he and Carla were up to?"

She nodded. "He mentioned something about just because I got rid of her didn't mean his plan was over."

Dom began to think. This could work to their advantage. "Keep Patrick from leaving and let's hope it's not too late to stop him from making a phone call," Dom demanded of his dad and Miles. "And bring him in here."

He stood up, still holding Alexa tightly, he kissed her forehead then sat her back in the chair, and he sat down beside her as he pulled his phone out. "Get here as soon as you can, thanks Angelo." He ended the call and wrapped an arm around Alexa.

He would finish all of this today, here and now.

He waited for Cal and Miles to bring Patrick back. They finally walked in. Dom stood quickly, grabbing Patrick by the jacket, shoving him on the couch. "Where were you meeting Tate?"

Patrick scoffed. "I don't know, he never said where, I'm supposed to call him when I get her."

"Then, by all means, go ahead, call him, tell him you've got her, I want to know where you're supposed to meet him." Dom glared hard at Patrick, he was ready to beat Patrick.

"Why should I?"

"Because either way, you'll probably go to jail, aiding a man who's being searched for by the cops for breaking and entering, and aggravated assault doesn't look too good." Dom turned to see Angelo walking into the office as he answered Patrick's question.

Angelo placed his arms over his chest with a glare that could kill. "Or we could maybe get a deal for you if you find out where to drop her."

Patrick sat still as Dom and Angelo continued to glare at him.

"How'd you even get involved with Tate?" Dom demanded.

He was still silent.

"Hmm, maybe he needs the same treatment Fitzgerald got?" Angelo pondered as Dom locked eyes with him.

Dom began to think about that. Would it get Patrick to talk? His gaze went back to Patrick, was the man really that jealous of him that he'd try to send a woman like Alexa into harm's way so willingly?

He looked over to Alexa. She was the most important thing in his life, and he'd never let her go once he knew for sure they could really be something great.

He moved his gaze back to Patrick. "You want to make this harder?"

"I'm not doing anything for you or her, and she's just a stupid–"

"I'd watch myself if I were you, Andrews, we are nothing anymore. I used to look up to you, but you just wanted everything for yourself. You hated how much I've made this company succeed instead of you, and honestly, you make me sick, get him out of here, Angelo," Dom ordered.

He watched Angelo yank him up and pull him out of the office. Maybe Angelo could get him to talk yet. He turned to Miles. "I'm sorry, Miles, I'm not letting him hurt her, try to strip this company from me, nor am I playing his games."

Miles laid a hand on Dom's shoulder. "I wouldn't expect anything less, I will make arrangements today, he's no longer a co-owner. I'm sorry for what he's done, Dominick, but I'm glad we have this all cleared up for the most part."

"Thank you, Miles, I'm sorry it came down to this, though." He turned to his dad. "You understand, right, Dad?"

"Of course, this woman is very important to you, I wouldn't expect anything less from you, the poor thing has been through enough," Cal answered.

Dom looked at Alexa, she had pulled her legs up against her chest, her head lying against her knees. "Can you guys handle the HR interviews, I want to take her home."

"Yeah," Miles and Cal answered at the same time.

"Thanks." Dom made his way over to Alexa as Cal and Miles went out the door.

Dom held his hand out to her. "How about we go home, baby?"

She looked up at him blankly but took his hand. "I'm scared, Dom, really scared."

"I know, baby, but I'm here to help and protect you. Miles and Dad will take care of the interviews, I'm taking you home."

"How did my life get so fucked up?" she whispered.

"Because you have a man now who could get almost anything in the world, and Tate is a sick bastard who would try to use that to his advantage, but it won't work. We'll find that dickhead and put him away for good, then we can get on with life." He pulled her up against him, grabbed her things, and headed out the door, then the building.

He put her in the car and headed home. He pulled into

the garage. No matter what, he would do whatever it took to keep the woman he loved safe. He took her into the house, and up to the bedroom, where he sat her down on the bed, pulling her shoes off slowly. "Sweats?"

She shrugged her shoulders. He kissed her gently. "I'll be right back."

He went to the room next to his. He might as well get Lizzie to move everything to his room. He found a black hoodie and black sweatpants. He headed back to his bedroom.

Dom walked in and let out a sigh when he saw Alexa curled up into a small ball on the bed. He crawled up to her, made her sit up, and began to strip her. Before he could get her hoodie and sweatpants on her, she leaned up and kissed him with urgency.

---

Alexa just wanted to forget everything that had happened today. She wrapped her arms around his neck, as he laid his hands against her back, kissing him with as much urgency as she felt. Maybe they both realized if she hadn't fought, she'd probably be in Tate's cruel hands. She moved to her knees as she pushed his jacket off, then began to undo his shirt and also pushed that off. She reached for his belt quickly and unfastened it.

His hands slid up her back to the clasp of her bra, making her tremble with need and want. She felt his body move as he shoved his shoes off. He pulled her up against him and wrapped her legs around him. He laid her back against the bed as he knelt between her legs. His lips left hers. She let out a whimper as he moved away but moaned when his mouth found one of her tightly beaded nipples while his thumb and forefinger rolled the other.

"Dominick," she moaned, begging, and his fingers slid

beneath her lacy boy shorts and slammed into her, making her scream even louder. She felt herself clench around his fingers tightly as he thrust them into her. She laced her fingers through his hair, arching her hips into his touch. He pulled back, pulling her panties off of her and kissed his way up her leg slowly. She felt her muscles clench in anticipation, she felt his warm breath against her aching center, and his fingers pushed back into her, making her let out an ear-shattering scream. Then his tongue stroked her sensitive, sweet jewel.

She dug her fingers into his hair, pulling him closer just before everything shattered. Colors exploded behind her eyelids as he continued thrusting into her and she rode the wild wave of pleasure. He worked everything up inside of her all over again, not letting up the pressure of his tongue or fingers. Just when she felt herself going to lose it again, he pulled away undoing his pants and shoving them down quickly, then slammed his hard shaft into her.

She dug her fingers into his back at the feel of him stretching her. She almost instantly clamped around him again. He rolled his hips into hers and then rolled onto his back, pulling her with him. His hands cupped her ass tightly as she settled onto him.

She began to rock her body on top of him as he thrust up into her. He leaned up and kissed her hard. "Do you trust me, baby?" he whispered against her lips. She moaned but nodded her head. He rolled them over again, but he pulled out of her and leaned back on his knees. "Bend over," he whispered.

She sat there, frozen for a moment before she did. She felt his hands rub her ass, then spread her legs a little more. She arched her back as his tip slowly worked its way into her aching center. She screamed when he buried himself to the hilt. It was so different from what they had done before. He began to thrust into her, sending her senses reeling at the different movement. After he thrust and pushed her forward, he would pull her back against him by her hips.

"Dominick!" she screamed as his hand came around the front of her and stroked her over sensitive button, and she shattered, screaming his name even louder.

She felt him lean over her kissing her back as he thrust into her and felt him jerk inside her spilling himself into her. She collapsed onto the bed as he lay down beside her, but pulled her back against his rock-hard abs and chest.

"Are you okay?" he whispered.

"Umm-hmm," she mumbled as she moved even further back into him.

---

Dom kissed her shoulder as he gently ran his fingertips down across her stomach. He held her close to him as he felt her start to drift off to sleep. He managed to pull the blanket from behind him and over them and wrapped his arm around her tighter, kissing the back of her neck. How was he going to keep her safe?

He didn't even want her to go to work the next day. He wanted her to stay here in the fortress he had created that he never thought he would have to use. His mind kept running a mile a minute as she slept tucked up into him and the blanket.

## Chapter 20

A lexa jerked awake and pulled away from whatever was holding her down. As she moved away she rolled and fell onto the floor, landing hard on her side.

She let out a yelp of pain.

---

Dom felt Alexa jerk and pull away, then heard the loud yell. He leaned over the side of the bed seeing her sprawled out on the floor, naked.

He got up slowly and scooped her up into his arms, pulling her close to him and laid them back down on the bed. "What happened?"

"Just a bad dream, I'm sorry I woke you."

"I wasn't asleep, sweetheart, I was just cuddling you while you slept, are you okay?"

"Yeah, I guess."

He rubbed his fingertips up and down her back slowly. "Are you sure?"

She nodded her head and tried to move closer to him shivering a little.

"Cold?" he asked gently.

As she nodded her head he pulled her closer to him and pulled the blanket over them again. He kissed her forehead as she began to fall asleep again.

He stroked her back slowly, the nightmares seemed to be getting worse. He hoped once they got Tate off the streets the nightmares would stop. He tightened his arms around her as he thought about what would happen to them once she was safe from Tate. He didn't want her to leave him or his home. He didn't think he could sleep without her ever again.

Her hand tightened on his shoulder. "Dom?" she whispered so softly he almost didn't hear her.

"What, baby?"

"I'm getting hungry," she mumbled, rubbing her cheek against his chest.

"Well, what do you want to eat little one?" He laid his cheek on top of her head.

"Pizza?" she asked softly still.

"Okay, your wish is my command." He kissed her forehead. "But I need you to let me up, love, so I can get my phone."

She whimpered tightening her grip on his shoulder. "But you're so warm, Dom."

"Well, how will you get the pizza you want?"

"They should be able to read minds and poof just show up with it."

Dom closed his eyes, and shook his head as he chuckled. "If only it was that easy, baby girl."

She sighed and let go of him, he found her clothes he had gotten for her earlier and handed them to her.

He found his pants, pulled out his phone grumbling a little when he saw two missed calls from Angelo.

He called the pizza place, ordered, then went to get his boxers on and a pair of sweatpants.

He then called Angelo back. "What do you got?"

"Absolutely nothing, Dom. I made him call Tate but Tate got angry when he couldn't talk to Alexa, he wanted proof that Patrick had her, he's not as stupid as we thought."

Dom's gaze went to Alexa, who was dressed and getting under the blanket right away. "Fuck, now what?"

"I don't know. I took Patrick to the police station, my buddy locked him up, we'll see how long he stays locked up. They don't have any breaks about Tate either."

"Damn it, okay. What's Lizzie doing tomorrow?"

"I'm not sure, I'll have to call and ask her. Why? What's up?"

"Tate's somehow managed to get too many people on his side. I want Alexa to stay home until we get things figured out, see if Lizzie will stay with her. It'd be better for Lex to have someone she knows, and honestly Lizzie is who I trust since everyone else is tied up trying to find the dirt bag."

"Okay, Boss, I'll figure things out and let you know."

They ended the call and Dom's blood was boiling, he was so angry, he couldn't believe a jackass like Tate could out smart his security team.

He went to the bed and kissed Alexa gently. "I'm going to go wait on the pizza downstairs."

She sat up and grabbed his hand tightly. "I'll go with you."

"Okay, babe." He kissed the back of her hand then headed downstairs. He led her over to the couch and pulled her down onto his lap. "If we don't find Tate soon I want to take you away from here, somewhere he won't look for you, also I want you stay here at least for tomorrow, if Lizzie will come over to stay with you."

"What about work?" Alexa asked as she looked into his eyes.

"Work from here, please, babe, he can't get into this house and I want you safe."

She sighed as she laid her head on his shoulder. "Okay."

"If you get worried or scared just call me."

She nodded her head.

A loud buzzer rang through the house, Dom kissed her forehead. "That'll be the pizza, I'll be back." She moved from his lap and he made his way to the door, he checked the camera to make sure and he put the code in to open the gate.

He watched the car drive up to the house slowly. Dom stepped out on the porch and took the pizza since he had paid over the phone along with the tip. He headed back inside locking the door, he watched the deliveryman on the camera and made sure the gate closed before he went back to the living room.

As he walked into the living room he smiled when he saw her curled up in a ball on the couch. She was just too adorable but he wasn't liking how she was breaking down inside.

Before, she had the brave front, now she wasn't even strong enough to pretend. He wanted her to be open with him, not completely shattered. He went down the steps to the couch. "Baby, food's here."

She sat up and smiled at him. "Thanks, Dom, for everything."

"Any time, what do you want to drink, baby?"

"Do you have any more strawberry wine?" she asked looking so innocent.

He leaned down and kissed her. "I'll have to check, we finished the one bottle off the other night." He headed into the kitchen, he found another bottle of wine. He grabbed two glasses then headed back to Alexa.

He placed the glasses on the table behind the couch, he filled them with the cool, crisp, light red liquid. He handed the glasses to Alexa when she turned and looked at him.

He went around the table and jumped over the back of the couch and sat down beside her.

They ate in silence, they managed to finish all of the pizza and she downed three glasses of wine.

After, Dom lay back on the couch taking her with him, he cuddled her close to his body. His phone began to vibrate in the pocket of his sweatpants. He managed to get it out of his pocket and answered it. "Yeah, Angelo?"

"Lizzie will be there tomorrow before you leave for work, sir, I still can't find anything on Tate."

"Damn, all right thanks, Angelo, tell Liz thank you too."

"No problem, Boss, see you later."

Dom ended the call laying his chin on top of Alexa's head. "Baby, how does he always disappear?"

"I don't know, after the divorce he had to sell the diner. I don't know where he went after that or what he started doing. He left us all alone until I turned sixteen and got a job, he'd take money, disappear and the cycle would just repeat. Then when I got older and got a better job it'd be more money every time."

He rubbed her back gently. "Has he ever tried kidnapping you before?"

"No," she answered shortly.

Dom pondered a moment. "I wonder why."

"I don't know. Maybe he wasn't so desperate before, I mean he used to be able to get money from me all of the time, now you have me locked away from him and he can't get the money he wants." Alexa paused for a minute. "You don't have to do all of this, Dom."

He smiled and hugged her. "Yeah I do, come on, let's get you to bed." He sat up as she moved off of him. He went to put the wine away, placed the glasses in the sink and threw the box out.

He walked back into the living room and picked Alexa up

as she seemed to be struggling to get up the steps. "I think three glasses of wine were two too many," he teased as he started up the steps.

"Probably," she whispered as she snuggled into his chest.

He smiled as he headed to the bedroom, he laid her down on the bed, made sure both their phones were plugged in to chargers, then leaned over to kiss her.

She kissed him back, and just as she fell asleep she whispered, "I love you, Dom." And out like a light she went.

He had a huge smile plastered to his face as he got into bed with her, laying an arm over her hips and kissed her forehead gently. "You'll never believe me, but I love you too, Alexa," he whispered.

She snuggled into him closer and let out a soft sigh.

He wondered if he could ever get her to tell him she loved him again. It made his heart soar.

He slowly closed his eyes and sleep overtook him as well.

## Chapter 21

Dom grumbled as his alarm went off, he leaned back and turned the annoying buzzing sound off with the palm of his hand. He rolled back into Alexa.

He heard her mumble as she grabbed the sheet beneath them. He rubbed her arm softly. "Lex, it's okay." He leaned closer pressing his lips to her forehead. "I'm going to jump in the shower, you're safe here, baby, you'll always be safe."

"I know," she mumbled.

He smiled and rolled out of the bed to go to his bathroom. He took a short shower then dried off. He headed out to get dressed. He smiled as he saw Alexa curled up under the blanket. Adorable even when she wasn't trying.

He went to his closet and decided on a light blue suit, and light blue shirt with a black tie. He pulled his pants on over his boxers then got the shirt on, and did his tie. He grabbed his socks, sat in the chair in the bedroom and slipped them on.

He got up heading over to the bed throwing the jacket over the frame at the end of the bed. He sat down beside Alexa and uncovered her slowly. "Baby, I'm getting ready to leave, do you need anything?"

Her eyes opened slowly and she ran a hand across her face. "No, I'm okay, I have a bit of a headache but I'll take care of it later, I wish you'd let me go with you."

He leaned down kissing her passionately. "Not today, baby, I want you to stay home, and if you don't want to you don't have to work on anything today." He smiled as he brushed his knuckles against her cheek softly.

"Can I sleep a little longer?"

"Sure, I'll tell Lizzie to let you sleep as long as you want, I'll call you when I go to lunch too." He kissed her again then got up, grabbed his jacket, and felt empty as he headed downstairs without her.

He wondered if she remembered she'd told him she loved him and that he told her he loved her too last night. Part of him hoped she did, part of him hoped she didn't.

He may be being stupid but he wanted the words exchanged when she wasn't in the middle of a buzz. He had never said those words to a woman before, never planned to either until her, he could tell her it a million times a day and it would never be said enough. How he knew he loved her and what love was, was beyond him.

He walked past the couch just as Lizzie walked in through the front door and closed it quietly behind her. He stopped, waiting for her to finish coming in.

Her gaze finally landed on him and she jumped. "Good morning, Mr. Mackenzie, where's Alexa?"

"Upstairs, still sleeping, she wanted to sleep a little longer, the bedroom she was supposed to stay in is available if you're still tired, she's in my room."

"Thanks, Mr. Mackenzie, do you need or want me to do anything besides hang with Lex?"

"Maybe move some of her things into my room, it gets a little annoying to go to that room if she needs something, but other than that I can't think of anything else, I'll get my dry cleaning before coming home tonight."

"Yes, Mr. Mackenzie."

Dom slipped into his shoes then left to start his day, that he couldn't wait to be over, so he could be with Alexa.

---

Lizzie glanced around the house, Dom had to be the cleanest man she knew. Angelo wasn't even this bad, and he ran a tight ship.

All she ever had to do for Dom was grocery shop, pick up, and drop off his dry cleaning, he would even do his own laundry.

Although, at the moment, it looked like it needed doing. She headed closer to the laundry room and began to throw the clothes in.

Finally, something she was getting paid to do. She got the clothes in the washer and started it. She let out a yawn, maybe she would take up the offer and use the empty bedroom.

This was way earlier than she was used to waking up. She made her way toward the stairs but stopped. She turned back to use the couch instead. She plopped down once she reached it and turned the TV on and out she went.

---

Alexa's eyes slowly peeled open, she glanced at the bedside clock, seven, ugh, really? She yanked the hood on her hoodie up onto her head and buried her head into Dom's pillow taking a deep breath as she pulled the blanket up around her.

His scent rolled through her making her relax a little. She wrapped her arms around the pillow, pulling it close to her chest. She wished he was there holding her, she missed him so much. She snuggled the pillow harder when something, all of a sudden, dawned on her. She had been feeling a buzz the night before, she pulled her bottom lip between her teeth. She told him she loved him before she passed out.

What a fool she had been, why would she tell him that? Because it's true. Her brain mocked her. Well just great, what if he went running for the hills and decided he didn't want her anymore because of her foolish buzzed outburst she had shared with him.

She finally realized she wasn't getting back to sleep, she rolled out of the firm, big bed, and headed to the bathroom. She opened the glass shower door, got the water on and adjusted it, then got in after she undressed. She stepped under the almost scalding water, she let out a moan as it slid down her body. She pushed her head beneath the steady stream wetting her hair.

She smiled as she wished Dom were in there with her. She finally got out, dried herself off and wrapped the towel around herself tightly. She headed to the bedroom she was supposed to be staying in.

She decided on a pair of dark gray sweatpants and an aqua tank top along with a matching bra. She got dressed and headed back to Dom's room and began to clean it up a little, not that it was a huge mess. How did the man find time to protect her, love on her, take care of her, and clean? Well, she supposed they didn't really make that big of a mess.

After she picked up the few clothes that were on the floor, she grabbed her phone. She went to her messages and began to text Dom. She just stared at the screen, what did someone say to someone after they had said I love you with a wine buzz? She let out a sigh and pushed the lock button, she felt so awkward. She shook her head and headed downstairs a little surprised Lizzie hadn't shown up yet.

As she went toward the kitchen she soon found Lizzie,

snoring unladylike on the couch, her body spread eagle as she slept. Alexa shook her head trying not to laugh as she went to the kitchen for breakfast. She began to search the pantry. What even sounded good?

She found some cinnamon raisin bread, she took out two slices and popped them into the toaster. She went to the fridge and found a tub of butter. She stared out the window above the sink as she waited for her food. There were some pretty nasty looking clouds rolling toward them. She bit her lip, at least the house was mainly windows, it wouldn't be too bad if they lost power. She shivered a little. Why was she all of a sudden having a bad feeling? She heard the toaster pop and grabbed a plate and knife, she began to butter the two pieces then headed to the dining room table.

She stared longingly at the spot Dom would usually sit at. She missed him but this was for the best. She began to eat and Lizzie came walking into the dining room.

Alexa smiled at her. "Good morning, Lizzie."

"Hey." She let out a yawn. "How long have you been up?"

"Hmm, not long honestly, what are we doing today?"

"Well, Dom asked me to move some of your things into his room today, so we could do that." Lizzie sat down on a chair across from her.

Alexa about choked on the bite of toast she had just taken. "I'm sorry, what?"

"It's okay, Alexa. Angelo and I have worked for Dom for a while now, Angelo longer than me but we know you've been staying in his room, he's also so different with you, Lex."

"Why would he want this?" She frowned not eating anymore.

"He said it was getting a little annoying basically running back and forth when you need something, so we'll just move the stuff you really need and go from there." Lizzie smiled at her.

"Is there a point, though? I mean once they find Tate, I'll just have to move everything back home." Alexa sunk back into the chair as she stared at the table.

"Is that what you want to do, go home?" Lizzie asked softly.

Alexa glanced up at her, but bit her lip. Did she want to go home? She shrugged her shoulders. She had wanted that a few weeks ago, but now that she had gotten so used to having him around all the time she didn't know if she'd be okay away from him.

She let out a sigh running her fingers through her hair agitated with herself. She pushed the plate away, losing her appetite.

Lizzie let out a sigh. "Well it doesn't need to be decided now. Why don't you head upstairs, I'll be there in a minute. I just have to put the clothes into the dryer." Lizzie stood up and headed to the laundry room.

Alexa sighed and headed up to the bedroom that had her things in it. She grabbed her phone and went to text Dom but changed her mind and sat on the bed as she stared at the screen again. She didn't know what to do, what if he did hear her say she loved him before she stupidly passed out? She cradled her chin in her hand as she tossed the phone on the bed. Was that why he wanted her stuff moved? Did he love her too? She felt her heart flutter at the thought.

She smiled but it faded when the lights seemed to flicker a little bit. She got up from the bed and headed over to the window. Why had the lights flickered? The storm seemed to still be quite a distance away from them. Her eyes darted around outside the back of the house.

She began to walk away when all of a sudden the lights went out in the hallway and bedroom then she heard a short scream.

Lizzie, oh no. She grabbed her phone and began to call

Dom while she went to try to find Lizzie. Maybe the power going out scared her, she didn't blame her.

Dom finally answered her call. "Good morning beautiful."

"Dom, where's the fuse box?"

"Sorry, what?"

"The fuse box for the house, where is it, we just lost all the power here, we haven't even been hit by the storm yet." She began to panic a little as she raced down the steps.

"Oh, hey where's Lizzie, she knows where it's at, but it's in the closet by the front door." Dom answered easily.

"Well she was doing the laundry, I was upstairs, I haven't seen her yet, hold on, Lizzie?" She called out but no reply. Her eyes darted around the silent house. "Lizzie? Lizzie, where are you?" She got louder. "Dom, I'm not finding her, something doesn't feel right."

"Okay, listen to me, I'm on my way. I'll call Angelo, he'll probably be there before me but trust me I'm on my–"

She didn't hear anything else he said as she felt something crack her upside the head. She let out a groan as she landed on her hands and knees, dropping her phone. She reached her hand up when she felt something warm slide against her temple.

She pulled her hand away and saw the blood. She tried to stand back up but her vision was beginning to blur. She shook her head trying to get her eyes to clear. She tried to feel around for her phone when something slammed down on her hand making her scream in pain.

---

Fear ripped through Dom. "Alexa? Alexa, answer me, what happened, Lex!" He began to dial Angelo's number on the phone at his desk.

"Hello?"

"Angelo, my place now, something's wrong. Alexa couldn't find Lizzie and it sounded like someone attacked her, I'll be there soon."

Oh why did he leave her alone? Why didn't he have someone better than Lizzie stay with her? Fuck. Fuck. Fuck. No one was able to get into his house without the code. Fuck.

He rushed out of the office and to his car, why, oh why, oh why? He should have been home with her. She'd be safe right now. All of this was his fault.

---

Alexa pulled her hand up against her chest. All she felt was pain and dizziness. She couldn't focus on anything. She was pulled up roughly and thrown over a shoulder. She tried to push, kick, and punch the person holding her. It had no effect. She felt herself being slammed down onto something else, which wasn't that far of a drop. Then she was engulfed in pitch black.

She heard something slam. She felt rough carpet beneath her face. She tried to get up and bashed her head on something above her. Anxiety began to claim her as she couldn't see in the dark. She let out a small cry as she slammed her feet up against whatever was above her. This couldn't be happening.

She heard an engine start and then she was thrown sideways into something as what she assumed was a car took off. She must be in the trunk. Tears began to well up in her eyes, how was she going to get out of this?

## Chapter 22

Dom couldn't believe the sight he drove up to in his driveway. The gate was bent and almost off the hinges. He raced up the driveway, his heart beating so fast he thought it was going to explode. All he could hear was the thud in his ears. He threw the car in park and ran through the open front door. "Angelo?" he yelled and saw him come out through the living room. "Angelo, they okay?"

"I don't know, Dom, I can't find them." Angelo shook his head in disgust as his sharp gaze darted around the room.

"Neither one of them?"

"No, I've searched everywhere." Angelo's hair wasn't slicked back like usual. He looked disheveled.

"Fuck, what happened?"

"The mainline to the house was cut, I'm assuming he got in then cut the line. He had to ram his car through the gate, there's no other way it would look so destroyed, I don't know why he took both of them unless Lizzie tried to stop him."

"Fuck, fuck, fuck, when I get my hands on that bastard, I'm killing him." He flew to the kitchen as he began to call an electrician to fix the power, and called someone to replace the gate with the most substantial steel money could buy. He leaned against the counter, his arms folded tightly over his chest brooding.

Angelo walked over to him. "I found this in the middle of the living room." He held up a baggy with Alexa's phone in it.

"Great." Dom cursed again, raking both hands through his hair, making it stick up from different angles.

All of a sudden, they heard a thump.

The men looked at each other. "What the hell?" Dom asked. Then another thump and a thud. "The laundry room." He flew across the kitchen and into the laundry room with Angelo behind him. Dom pushed in on the hidden closet door, and it popped open, they heard a muffled scream.

"Oh my God, Lizzie!" Angelo moved in front of Dom and picked his girlfriend up carefully. The poor girl had her hands tied behind her back. Her ankles were tied too, along with a rope around her mouth with a wadded-up piece of cloth. She had tears streaming down her cheeks and a trickle of blood falling from her forehead.

Angelo hauled her out of the hidden closet and rushed to the bar Dom had in his kitchen. He untied her quickly. As soon as he got her free, she threw her arms around his neck, crying hysterically.

Angelo held her, muttering soft words of reassurance to her until she finally calmed down.

"Baby, what happened?" Angelo asked as he cupped her cheeks and checked out the gash on her forehead a little.

"I was changing the laundry over when all the lights went out. I was attacked, they tied me up and threw me into the closet, I was hit over the head with something and they demanded to know where— Oh God, Lex, no, where is she, is she okay?" Lizzie's blue eyes darted from Angelo to Dom then back to Angelo.

"I don't think she's here, baby, her phone was in the

middle of the living room," Angelo explained, he glanced at Dom and turned back to Lizzie. "Baby, do you know who did this to you?"

"No, it was too dark, but also my head hurt so bad and my vision blurred so badly, I didn't even know where he put me." Her eyes darted to Dom. "I'm so sorry, Mr. Mackenzie."

"It's okay, Liz, we'll find her," he reassured her, they just had to. He had to tell her he loved her. He had to hold her again. Hell, he had to marry her, he saw no way of getting around his feelings for her. He loved her, and he couldn't face a day without her. He fucked up.

His gut was churning, and his heart was breaking, he wanted his Alexa. He turned away, pulling his hands down over his face, what was he going to do?

Dom heard Angelo on the phone. "Come on, bro, we got to figure this out, and now. He managed to get in Dominick Mackenzie's home and take her. Come on, Bryce, help me out."

Dom turned to look at Angelo. He had a deep scowl on his face as he kept talking to whomever he was talking to on the phone.

Dom pulled out his own cell phone and managed to pull up his security camera footage. He figured out the make and model of the car, a dark maroon, Chevy Malibu, two thousand to at least two thousand six. But he couldn't get a plate number. He showed Angelo what he found.

"Bryce put an APB out on a Maroon Malibu, two thousand to at least two thousand six, it looks like a bit of a rust bucket, thanks, bro." Angelo ended the call and looked Lizzie over again.

Dom shook his head. He wanted to break something, punch anything. He let out a scream and slammed his fist into the wall beside him, making a loud bang and sending drywall and dust flying.

He had to find Alexa, her being in Tate's hands was unacceptable. Who knew what he'd do to her before demanding the money?

---

The hyperventilating was starting to settle into Alexa. She just wanted out. She wanted Dom. She tried to calm her heart rate. She wasn't going to be a sitting duck. She had to try to think of something.

She moved her hand and felt something long, cold and metal? What was it? She ran her hands down it a little, it felt like a tire-iron. Maybe it would come in handy. She pulled it in front of her when she felt the car come to an abrupt halt. Then she heard the engine cut out. She took a deep breath, she could do this, she had to do this.

A loud thud came from above her making her jump. She was ready, she heard the sound of the key enter the lock on the trunk. It lifted slowly. She pulled her legs up and kicked open the trunk fast.

There was a thud and a series of curses. She didn't try to figure out who it was. She scrambled out of the trunk from the side, keeping ahold of her new weapon. She took off running, thinking she could figure out where she was once she felt safe.

The concrete bit into her feet as they slammed down on the sidewalk as she ran. She thought she couldn't handle much more of the pain when she was tackled to the ground. She screamed loudly, trying to get away.

She was yanked back and flipped over hard, the bare skin of her back and shoulders pressed against the concrete hard. Hazel-blue met brown, almost black looking eyes. Him. She began to struggle and tried to get her leg up to kick him when she was punched in the face hard.

She felt the blow, her head began swimming again but she managed to scream out in pain. She couldn't get him off her, this was it, either probably die trying to get away or just give in.

She choked back the tears as he hauled her up and threw her over his shoulder. She looked around, begging to see someone who could help her. No one did, her eyes landed on the tire-iron. Stupid, stupid, stupid. She lost her hold on it when she had been slammed to the ground.

What to do, what to do? She leaned up a little and saw his neck was close to her mouth. She didn't think, she just did and sunk her teeth hard into his neck. He let out a scream of pain and pulled her off his shoulder.

She landed hard on her back on the concrete. She groaned in pain as she felt tiny rocks dig into her skin. She then saw the fist flying toward her. First, there was so much pain and then nothing but darkness.

---

Dom had had about enough waiting, he kept pacing the floor. He was surprised he hadn't worn a hole in it yet. He was Dominick Mackenzie for crying out loud, and he always got what he wanted. Now he had people telling him what he could and couldn't do.

He got more agitated with each passing minute he was without Alexa. He was waiting for Tate's demand for money, waiting on news that someone found the piece of shit car. For all they knew, he'd dump the car once he got Alexa far enough away.

He heard Angelo's phone ring, and Angelo answered it.

Dom hated hearing only Angelo's side of the conversation, which only consisted of grunts, rights, and okays.

Dom stared at Angelo as he ended the call.

"Sir, they got a call of an older man chasing a young woman. Lizzie, what was Alexa wearing?"

Dom looked to Lizzie, who was curled up into a ball on the couch. Her blue eyes darted to him then Angelo. "A blueish tank top, and black sweatpants."

"Dom, we've got her, she was struggling with Tate near his old diner, by a mechanic garage." Angelo turned to Lizzie. "Babe, will you be okay, or do you want me to stay with you?"

"I'm going with you." Lizzie stood up from the couch and walked over to Angelo.

Dom was out the garage door with a set of keys in his hands to one of his SUVs. He was getting his girl back.

## Chapter 23

Alexa groaned in pain as she slowly came to. She glanced around slowly, her head still spinning a little. She tried to move but felt the ropes around her torso. She was sitting in a chair. Her legs were tied to the legs of the chair. Her arms were tied to the back of the chair, her hands behind her.

She glanced around more. It looked like a garage of some sort. She didn't hear anything but saw a table with a bunch of items on it. Tools, knives and car parts. No, no, no. Not here, not again. She hadn't been in this room since she was fifteen. Tate had tortured her so many times in here. She began to try to move the chair when she heard the door slam. She froze and searched the room again.

"So happy to see you're finally awake, dear daughter." He yanked the chair over to the table with ease even with her on it. He leaned the chair back against the table. He grabbed a knife holding it against her throat too close for her comfort. She tried to pull away, but all it earned was another slap. She closed her eyes as tears stung them. Don't give in to him, don't give in to the pain. She opened her eyes and glared at him.

"How much do you think you're worth to the famous playboy Dominick Mackenzie, or are you really just another whore to him who fell for his charm?" Tate laughed as she glared at him. "Will he just throw you away? Will he not come for you and not care what happens to you?"

She glared at him more. Dom may be a player, or at least was until he met her, but he would never be so cruel as to forget about her.

"I'm thinking if you mean so much to him, maybe two million will be a sufficient amount for you to return safely to him, but what if I'm wrong?" His eyes turned darker with anger. "Am I wrong, little whore? Do you mean anything to him, I mean he didn't have you locked away very well. All I had to do was destroy that gate, and pick the lock on his house after I disconnected the power, seems to me he doesn't care too much about you, and the girl he had staying with you wasn't tough to overcome just like you, easy targets. Maybe he doesn't care about you."

She cursed at him behind her gag, but all it got her was a sick laugh and another slap to the face. She wondered about Lizzie, what had he done to her, she hoped he didn't hurt her too badly.

"Or maybe more? I think I have to contemplate this a little to decide." He slammed the knife down on the table beside her and leaned toward her, gripping her chin hard. "You be a good little girl or suffer some harsh consequences." He slapped her lightly and began to walk away.

She watched him leave and slam the door shut. She looked back to the knife he slammed down on the table. It was hanging off the edge a little.

Ha, and she was the idiot? She rocked the chair forward and began to make the chair hop, by bouncing her body up and down, over to where the knife was on the table.

She worked her hand up enough that it bent her elbow,

and she knocked the knife down to the ground, but she missed catching it. She closed her eyes tightly. What now? She turned around to try to find the knife, and it had landed right behind her.

She made the chair move back toward the way she had come from. She began to rock the chair side to side. She took a deep breath. This was going to hurt. She braced herself for the pain as the chair tipped over.

She screamed out in pain as her arm hit the cement floor and was pinned between the floor and chair. She began to move her hand, fighting through the pain. Her hand closed around the handle. She pulled it the best she could toward the rope around her wrist and began to cut through it. She felt the rope slacken around her wrist. All of a sudden, it was free. She managed to work her arm free from in between the floor and chair, pulling the knife with her. She started to work on the rope around her torso.

It loosened and fell from her, she could now lean down, and she started on her ankles. She had to hurry up. She got to her feet quickly and began to work on her last wrist. She tried to make herself hurry. She looked around the room, trying to remember the ways out beside the huge metal garage door. Her eyes landed on the regular-sized house door beside the garage door. She ran over to it and tried the knob. It didn't turn.

She heard the door Tate walked out of a little bit ago slam again. She jumped and turned quickly. She was in trouble if he found her. As he stormed over to the overturned chair screaming, she rushed over to the door he just came out of glad she was hidden from his view.

She flinched when he yelled again and threw the table over, making a loud crash echo throughout the empty garage. Her hand reached the knob and pulled the door open and she ran. She ran to the door that had light spilling through the glass window.

She went as fast as her feet could carry her. Her lungs were starting to burn, but she had to get away. She almost screamed when she heard the door behind her slam again. She froze for a second when something flew past her and smashed the window beside the door.

Alexa glanced behind her as she finally reached the door. He was almost on top of her again. Alexa twisted the knob and flew out the door. Just as her feet hit the biting concrete, she was snatched by her hair and pulled back into Tate's body.

"Let her go, Tate!" a voice yelled.

She looked up. She knew that voice. Dom. He came. He found her.

She felt her head snapped back even more as the hand tightened in her hair, making her scream out in pain. Her eyes locked on Dom, what could they do now?

---

Dom stood there staring Tate down, she was so close to being in his arms, but she had been pulled up short.

Dom made a step toward them, but Tate yanked her back harder.

"You-Stay back! You want her alive, I want money. I'm sure we can reach some sort of agreement."

Dom glared at Tate harder. "How much are we talking?" he demanded.

"How much is she worth to you?" Tate challenged.

"A lot, whatever you want, just talk to me, and I'll make it happen." Dom tried to look Alexa over, but she kept struggling against Tate.

Everything seemed to happen so fast. Tate let out a scream of pain and shoved Alexa away from him, making her fall to the ground. She stood up, still holding the knife, and ran away from Tate just as Angelo and his buddy Bryce rushed forward and grabbed Tate taking him to the ground.

Alexa ran to Dom, dropped the knife and threw her arms around him, and he caught her with ease pulling her close to his body.

He felt her body tremble against his. He made his way to his SUV still holding her. "You're okay, baby, I've got you. I'm so sorry, you're safe now, though," he whispered against her ear. He opened the passenger side door and sat her down on the seat.

He pulled back a little and cradled her cheeks in his hands gently. Anger filled him when he saw the bruises along her face and the blood along her cheek. More anger flew over him, and he started to turn and go beat Tate, but she pulled him back toward her, he gazed into her beautiful eyes.

"Don't leave me," she whispered as those eyes began to fill up with tears.

He put his arms around her. "Never again, I'm here, baby, I'm right here." He laid his chin on top of her head as Lizzie came running over to them.

"Alexa, I'm so sorry," she cried out and moved between Dom and Alexa. "Are you okay?"

---

Alexa glanced at Dom, praying he wouldn't go far. "What are you sorry for, he wouldn't have hurt you if it hadn't been for me."

"I'm okay though, I'm glad you are okay too." Lizzie hugged her tightly and kissed her forehead. "I'm sorry, though, because I couldn't keep him away from you, I didn't even have a chance."

Alexa smiled. "I got away, though, that's what matters."

She looked back at Dom, all she wanted was to be in his arms, but now that Tate would be off the street, would she still be welcome?

"Lizzie, can you give us a few?" Dom asked, looking back at Alexa.

Lizzie scurried away back to the other SUV.

Dom wrapped Alexa back into his arms. "Are you sure you're okay, little one?"

She nodded her head a little as she wrapped her arms around him, pressing her hands against his warm, toned back. "I want to go home," she whispered.

He nodded his head and adjusted her so she was sitting on the seat correctly and fastened her seatbelt for her. He went around to the other side after he hollered toward Angelo, who nodded his head. He got in the car and started to head home.

She wanted to reach out and take his hand. She didn't know if she should, though. *He was going to pay anything to get you from Tate,* her brain began a mental battle. *Yeah, because he's not a total cruel bastard and knows what Tate put you through before.* She stared out the window as they left the crappy part of town. She shivered and looked over at Dom. "How'd you guys know where I was?"

"Someone called the police and told them about a scuffle between a young woman and an older man, we discovered it was the old diner Tate owned," Dom explained and reached over, taking her hand like she ached to do.

She clutched his hand tightly. "At least someone spoke up," she whispered.

"How'd you manage to get out of that mechanic garage?" he whispered, stroking his thumb against the side of her hand.

She relayed everything that happened to her and how she got free, clutching his hand tightly.

"God, babe, I'm so sorry I wasn't there, he never would have gotten to you," he whispered as he squeezed her hand.

She ached to tell him she really did love him. "It's okay, either way, I'm free now, he won't bother me again." She laid her head back against the headrest and slowly closed her eyes.

"We should probably take you to the hospital, you know."

"I don't want to go. I'm fine, trust me, today was nothing compared to what he used to do to me, I'm fine, I just want to be home."

"Okay, if you say so." He pulled her hand up to his mouth and kissed it gently.

She felt him slow down and opened her eyes to find them outside his home.

He parked in the garage. "Why don't you head inside." He stroked her cheek gently. "I'm going to get my car and park it in here also."

She nodded her head a little and began to slide out of the SUV, then headed into the house. Well, she might as well start packing.

She headed upstairs to the bedroom she was supposed to have and began to get her clothes folded and placed them in the suitcases that Angelo brought her stuff in. She heard Dom yelling for her, she called back to him. "I'm in here."

He walked into the bedroom and froze as their eyes locked. "What are you doing?"

"Getting my stuff packed so I can go home. Tate's locked away, I shouldn't be in trouble anymore." She broke eye contact and continued to pack her things.

"Is that really where you want to be?" he asked her as he stepped into the room more.

Was it what she wanted? Did she want to go back to her lonely life without him? She stared at the clothes. "Where else am I supposed to go?"

"You don't have to go anywhere. You could stay here with me."

"Is that what you want?" she whispered.

"Baby, it's up to you, if you want to go home I'll take you home, if you want to stay then you can stay with me." He came to stand behind her but didn't touch her.

"Why would you want me to stay here? I've ruined so much already, and I'm safe now, I mean this was the only reason why we did this and why everything got out of control between us, right?"

"I've always been in control, Lex, and no, that's not the only reason why everything between us happened."

"Then, why did it?"

"Oh you stubborn woman, because we care about each other a lot, when I found out you were gone today and that I might never see you again, my heart broke, my anger broke, everything broke, I don't want to spend another day, hour, minute, or second, for that matter, without you."

She turned to look at him a little. "So, what are you saying?"

"I love you, Lex. I've loved you for a while now, and I don't want to lose you, when you told me you loved me last night, my heart soared. So what you had a buzz; you still said it, and I know it's what you feel."

She turned more toward him as she stared into his hazel-green eyes. "Dom, I-I do love you," she whispered as she searched his eyes. "I love you so much." She jumped into him and threw her arms around his neck.

"I want you to stay with me, Lex. I want you for the rest of my life." His mouth clamped down onto hers, then his tongue slid between her lips, meeting her tongue, sweeping and swirling together.

She whimpered as she tightened her arms around his neck, and he stroked her mouth to pure ecstasy. She moaned as he lifted her, wrapping her legs around his waist. He took her toward his room and went into the bathroom.

He walked them into the shower and turned the water on,

never once breaking their kiss. He set her down on the floor and pulled back from her. She looked up at him as he began to strip her clothes off of her quickly, throwing them up and over the shower door, and he did the same with his and lifted her back up, moving them beneath the water.

The water slid down their bodies, making them slip against each other. He drove his tongue back into her mouth, and she let out a loud moan. He lifted her a little and then settled her burning center onto his hard, thick shaft, making her scream out, leaning her head back into the water.

"Dominick, yes, please," she screamed and begged him as he slammed her back and forth along his hard male heat. She gripped his shoulders tightly as she felt herself coming undone, and she shattered when he took first one hard beaded nipple, then the other into his mouth.

She screamed as she laced her fingers through his hair, and she felt him jerk inside her and spill into her as he growled out her name almost as loud as she had screamed for him. He leaned her back against the wall as he laid his forehead against hers.

They both were panting heavily as they came down from their high. He gently stroked her ass in his hands. "I love you," she whispered.

He moved and kissed her softly. "I love you, too. God, I thought I really lost you today."

She hugged him tightly as the tears almost began again. She choked back a sob. "I knew you'd come for me, though."

"Yeah, but you showed you didn't really need me for the most part, you got away from him, even managed to stab him in the leg with a knife, I failed you today, baby."

She slowly shook her head. "No, you gave me the power to want to fight; if he had me and I didn't have you, I would have just given up and wouldn't have tried to get away."

He kissed her again. "You are never going to be out of my

sight ever again, baby, never again." He began to wash her up then himself, and he dried them off and scooped her up into his arms and took her to his bed.

She curled into him, her body hurting a little from every-thing she had been through for the day, but she was home. Safe, where she belonged. With Dominick Mackenzie. Her eyes slowly began to close as exhaustion overtook her body.

## Chapter 24

Dom felt Alexa fall asleep in his arms. He didn't know how he was going to fall asleep. He was scared he'd close his eyes, and she would be gone again. He didn't want to leave her ever again. This was going to put a damper in his plan of asking her to marry him.

He wanted to pick out the ring, but he wanted her near him at all times after today. He kissed her forehead gently and finally began to fall asleep himself.

He was yanked out of sleep when he felt hands pushing against his chest and heard crying. He grabbed Alexa's wrists gently. "Baby, hey, it's okay. I'm right here, you're okay, shhh."

"Dom?" she sobbed out a little.

"Yes, little one, I'm right here, shhh." Dom kissed her forehead and rubbed her back gently. "I'll always be here."

"How do I know that?" she whispered, her voice husky from sleep, and her tears slowing some.

"Well, one because I love you so damn much, I would have given that bastard anything under the sun to get you back, and two, marry me?" he whispered as he continued to rub her back.

"W-what?" She pulled back and looked up at him confusion written on her pretty face.

"Marry me, Alexandra, and I'll never stop loving you. You are my world, Lex, you've become so important to me, marrying you is the only option for me." He kissed her nose softly.

She laid her hand against his slightly roughened cheek since he had decided to forgo a shave that day. "You better ask Brandon," she whispered.

He pulled his phone off his bed stand and began to call him. "Brandon, can you stop by before you go home for the night?"

"Um, sure, MAEP or what?"

"My house."

"Okay, I'll be there around, five."

"Great, see you then." Dom hung up and kissed Alexa. "I'll ask him when he comes over."

"Really?"

"Yes, I'll do anything for you, baby. I love you that much."

"Even with all my bruises, scars, and the whole mess I've caused?"

"I love every inch of you. I thought I showed you in the shower, want me to show you again?" He smiled wickedly at her.

She giggled a little as he rolled on top of her.

"I know none of this is enough to show you how much I love you, but you won't let me do much of anything else."

She leaned up and kissed him, she laid her hands against his cheeks and stroked them with the pads of her thumbs. "You came to save me today, you always try to calm me when I'm afraid, you've believed in me when no one else really did, you've been there to protect me for a couple of months now, you'll keep my attitude in check, you'll keep everything about me in check, even if you punish me I know it'll be out of love, that you care about me and want what's best for me.

"Honestly, I never thought this would be the kind of relationship I would ever have or want to have but I want it with you, Dom, I love you." Her cheeks flushed as she paused for a moment. "You told me before that there was more to it than the spanking and punishing me when I misbehave, what did you mean by that?"

Dom let the silence linger for a moment before he chose his words carefully. "I won't really expect it from you right away after all you've endured, but I'd love to deny you an orgasm, I would also love to see you tied down to our bed while I pleasure you or punish you, and will want to blindfold you as well, amongst other things, Lex, but we can wait for now, I have your trust and I never plan on breaking that trust."

She gazed up at him slowly, searching his eyes. "You're serious?"

"Oh, I'm very serious, Alexandra, you have no idea."

"Can I ask you something?"

"Anything, love."

"How come you haven't lectured me about escaping on my own from Tate and putting myself in harm's way by doing so?"

"Oh, part of me wants to, but I think you've been through enough for today."

"Dom, what if I want you to? If you hadn't been out there with Angelo I would have been in deep trouble and I feel so guilty."

"Sweetheart, there's no reason to feel guilty, I have known you're independent since the day I met you and today I am glad you are."

Alexa wiggled beneath him slightly. "Please, Dom, I know I took a huge risk, please punish me," she begged him softly.

Dom didn't know what to do at first, he was speechless for

the first time in his life. His wonderful love was asking to be punished for getting away from her 'father' and putting herself at risk, he never expected this.

He slowly sat up and pulled her over his lap, her ass in the air, her face against the mattress. "Are you sure, baby?" He gently stroked her perfect, spankable ass.

"Please, sir."

He pulled his hand back and swatted her round ass, hard. He couldn't help the smile that fell upon his lips at the sound of Alexa sucking in a deep breath. "Do you know why you're being disciplined right now, baby?"

"Because I put myself in danger by not waiting for you, even though I knew you'd find me today, Dom." She let out a cry when he swatted lower and caught both cheeks hard.

"And why didn't you wait for me, Alexandra?" he demanded harshly.

"I just couldn't take being in that garage, too many horrible memories. I couldn't be in there for very long. I'm sorry, sir, for putting myself at risk," she sobbed out as he cracked her ass again only harder. Her body jerked and her hands flew to cover her already reddening ass.

Dom caught her wrists tightly and held them at the small of her back and spanked her again. "And what are you going to do next time you have to wait for me?"

"I'll wait, sir, I promise. I won't do anything stupid, I promise, please, Dom, please." She tried to pull her wrists from his hands.

*Whack!* The crack echoed through the room and she cried out again.

"Do not fight me, Alexandra, you did ask for this. Didn't you?"

"Yes, sir, I did," she sobbed out.

"And what are you going to be from now on?"

"I'm going to be a good little girl, sir, I promise."

Dom cracked her ass hard five more times before he finished her punishment she had asked for. He slowly began to rub her bottom gently. "Tell me what kind of bad memories, Alexa, please I want you to tell me." He kept her pinned across his lap and she lay there on top of his lap like the good little girl she promised him she would be.

He continued to rub her ass gently as her body trembled terribly before she began to speak.

Alexa shivered again but Dom continued to rub her ass soothingly. She lay across his lap still, how could something that stung and burned so much make her feel this relaxed after?

"Sweetheart, come here." Dom's deep voice interrupted her thoughts.

She slowly adjusted herself and sat in his lap as he continued to stroke her fiery bottom. She let out a moan at the feel of his huge hands basically playing with her butt.

"It belonged to a friend of his when he owned the diner next to it, he'd take me there if I broke something at the diner or screwed something up, he'd tie me to anything he could find, he'd tear my shirt off and whip me with anything he could find, his belt, a belt from a car, anything." She shivered again.

Dom rolled onto his back, taking her with him. "He will never touch you again, my love, never again, I'm so sorry."

"You're here now, you've taken care of me the past couple of months, that means everything to me, what do you think Brandon will say?"

"I don't know, babe, he may check my temperature, you've awakened a side of me I didn't even know existed."

She looked into his eyes. "Why didn't you ever want to get married before? Why were you always so unattached?"

He slowly sat up in bed, leaning back against the head-board, wrapping one of his strong arms around the small of her back. "Seeing how destroyed my father was after finding out my mother was running around on him hurt. I promised myself I'd never let that happen to me, give a woman my heart and let them have the power to destroy me like that was never going to happen for me. He spent a lot of time in a bottle after the divorce, and then my sisters also had failed marriages."

Alexa laid her hand against his cheek, he closed his eyes soaking in her touch. "And you're going to let me have that power?" she asked unsurely.

"Yes, I am, I'm hoping you won't use that power to actually destroy me, you're too innocent for that, although I've turned you pretty naughty." He smiled as she blushed and hid her face against his neck.

"I'd never run around on you, Dom. I love you, so much, honestly, I was terrified that we would be over after Tate was caught," she admitted.

"Oh no, baby, we can finally start." He smirked as he laid her down on her back and began to kiss her soft creamy skin.

As he rained kisses along almost every inch of her body he had her squirming so bad, he almost chuckled but refrained from doing so. He slowly made his way to her neck and attacked it. "Lex, do you trust me?"

"Of course, Dom," she answered and writhed beneath him.

He left the bed and headed over to the chest he had on the other side of the bedroom and began to rummage through it. "There we go." He mumbled as he finally found the two pairs of cuffs.

He strolled back to Alexa who was sitting up a little, watching him carefully. He climbed on to the bed and had her lay down again, she went to touch him but he caught her wrists and pinned them to the bed. "Let's see how naughty I can make you, little one."

She gasped as he claimed her lips again and he continued as he placed a cuff on one of her wrists then cuffed it to the bed frame above her head. He slowly pulled back and gazed down at her. "Okay?"

She slowly nodded her head and he cuffed her other wrist in the same manner.

"If for any reason you're not okay, you have to tell me, baby, okay?" he asked sternly.

"Yes, sir."

He smiled, loving hearing sir come from those sexy lips of hers, ever since she fell into his conference room. He smacked her ass a little. "Good girl," he encouraged as she let out a tiny moan. He leaned down and kissed her passionately then pressed soft kisses to her cheek. "You can't come until I say you can this time," he whispered against her ear.

---

Alexa swallowed, she was already on the verge of an orgasm, how could she not? She glanced up at him, but nodded her head. "Yes, sir."

"God, what that does to me." Dom groaned against her neck and began to make his way down between her spread legs.

Alexa moaned loudly as Dom kissed along her body. She about shattered when his fingers entered her deeply. "Dominick."

"Don't come," he warned. "There will be consequences."

Her stomach fluttered at the thought but wasn't sure she could hold out, it seemed impossible as he drove his fingers into her hard then buried his face between her parted lips, his tongue licking and twirling around and around her sensitive button.

She wanted to run her hands through his hair and yanked on her wrists and moaned louder when she couldn't, but it just sent her closer to the edge. She felt so close when he would slow down or completely stop then he would work her up all over again.

By the fifth time, her body was wavering so close she couldn't stop and the bliss of her release shattered and wracked her body so deeply, she screamed as her arms and legs turned to jelly.

Dom pulled back quickly and she immediately knew she was in trouble.

"Did you just come?" he demanded.

She nodded her head shyly.

"I told you not to, Alexandra."

"I'm sorry, Dom," she whispered, ashamed of herself for letting go. She averted her gaze from him, knowing she disappointed him.

She let out a gasp when Dom rolled her over quickly, her arms crossed in front of her and he pulled her to her knees, giving her a swift swat against her ass, making her groan at the pleasure she felt all over again.

She felt him lean over her a little. "I'll let it slide this time, this is a work in progress, we'll get better," he said gruffly against her ear, his voice laced with straight desire, which caused goosebumps to fly across her skin. He suddenly slammed into her, burying himself to the hilt.

She screamed out his name instantly and tried to move her hands but, of course, she couldn't, she could just kneel there and take what he was giving her, and she wasn't complaining at the sensations Dom stirred inside of her.

He continued to pound into her harshly and quickly but it felt so amazing and different than before. She felt one hand slide to her breasts and he pinched each nipple in turn making her scream again.

She couldn't believe what he was doing to her. She felt the pleasure build and build then the whack came quickly to her ass, pushing her further to her peak again and his other hand moved to her sensitive little jewel and began to twirl his fingers around it quickly which made her completely lose herself and scream into the pillow as she felt him jerk inside of her and fill her full with his hot seed.

She collapsed onto the bed as Dom reached above her and undid the cuffs. She whimpered a little as Dom gently rolled her to her back and began to massage her wrists as they lay there in the wonderful afterglow.

---

Shortly after they relaxed and cuddled with each other they took a quick shower, dressed, and headed downstairs to wait for Brandon.

Dom let him in the gate when he hit the buzzer for entrance and already had the front door unlocked. He was ready for the long talk he was probably going to get from Brandon.

But, after Tate, nothing was scaring him off. He wanted Alexa for the rest of his days. No one was going to stop him. He reached out a hand as Brandon got to the door. "Thanks for coming, Brandon."

"No problem," Brandon began as Dom led him into the house. "So what do you need to talk to me about?" His voice slowly trailed off as his gaze landed on Alexa. "Lex?" he gasped out.

Brandon rushed over to her and cupped her cheeks gently. "Sweetheart, what happened?"

Alexa grabbed his hands. "I'm okay, really. Tate got to me,

but he's locked up now." She slowly moved closer and wrapped her arms around Brandon tightly.

Brandon hugged her and looked back at Dom. "Is this what you needed to talk to me about?"

"No." Dom smiled at the sight of Brandon and Alexa. "Let's go to my office."

Brandon went to turn with Alexa, but she laid her hands against his chest. "What, sweetheart?"

"Just you and Dom need to have this talk, I'm going to stay here, maybe watch some TV." She hugged him again and sat back down on the couch.

Dom headed over to Alexa, he knelt in front of her. "Are you sure?"

"Yeah." She smiled at him. "I'll be okay."

He kissed her passionately, then stood up and led Brandon to his home office. Dom went around to sit in his leather office chair. "Please sit, Brandon."

Brandon did as Dom instructed and laid his ankle on top of his other knee. "Dom, what's going on?"

"Brandon, I love Alexa, a lot, she's turned me into someone I never thought I'd be, I want to be in her life for a very long time."

"Well, I assumed you two were already together at the fundraiser, I was happy then, so I guess I am still happy for both of you if you still want to be together."

"Well, yeah I guess we've been together for a little bit, but I want her to be more than my girlfriend, I want her in my life for the rest of my life, I need to know if I can marry her."

Brandon sat there in silence for a minute. "Is that what she wants?"

"I think so, Brandon, she's special, I thought I was going to lose her today and that pain almost killed me. I never want to feel what my life was like before she came into it ever again."

"Well, I guess you have permission to ask her, but if she says no, you have to accept that, Dom."

"I will, Brandon, thank you." Dom stood up and leaned forward to shake Brandon's hand. "Also, I want to offer to combine our companies, Patrick is no longer a part of MAEP, he was arrested for trying to help Tate get Alexa."

Brandon's mouth dropped open. "Dominick, I will have to think about it, but I will let you know." He said goodbye to a sleeping Alexa and left.

Dom headed out to Alexa. He smiled when he saw her curled up on the couch. He shook his head, kissing her forehead, then headed to the kitchen. What could he prepare her for dinner?

He looked in the fridge, but nothing sounded good. He opened the freezer and chose macaroni and cheese. He pulled it out and began to preheat the oven.

He went to the laundry room to check the clothes and started the dryer, when it dawned on him. He pulled out his phone and called his dad.

"To what do I owe the honor to hear from my son today?" Cal answered.

"I'm asking Alexa to marry me," Dom answered as he sat at the bar in the kitchen.

"Oh, really now? Wow, took you long enough. Congratulations, Dom."

"Thanks, Dad." Dom chuckled a little, go figure his dad had known before he probably did. "I was wondering if you still had grandma's ring?"

"Of course I do, it's been sitting here waiting for you."

"Good, can you drop it off tonight? I'd come get it, but Lex had another run-in with Tate, and I don't want to leave her alone right now."

"Sure, give me about fifteen minutes."

"Thanks, Dad."

"You're welcome. See you soon."

Dom hung up, this was nowhere near romantic, but it had to be better than asking her while they had been lying in bed.

He headed back to the living room after he put the macaroni and cheese in the oven. Alexa was still asleep. The poor girl. At least she was safe after today.

He heard the light knock on the door, he went to answer it and stepped outside. "Thanks for knocking so quietly, Dad, and bringing the ring over."

Cal handed him the pink velvet box. "No problem, so tell me, is the ass locked away now?"

"Yeah, he is, and I'm making sure he stays that way."

"Good, I'm happy you've found a woman who's won your heart, Dom. I'm sorry for the pain your mother and I caused to make you harden your heart for so long."

"It's okay, Dad, it wasn't your fault. I just needed the right one to come into my life, and she's it."

Cal smiled and hugged Dom tightly. "Good luck." He turned to leave, and Dom headed back into the house.

He slipped the box into his pocket and went to sit on the couch. He sat next to her head and moved her hair behind her ear gently, and rubbed her cheek with his thumb slowly.

She stirred a little and let out a small sigh as she laid her head on his thigh and clutched his pants in her hand.

He smiled and placed his hand on her shoulder.

They stayed like that until the oven began to go off.

Alexa woke up with a jerk, but Dom pulled her into his lap. "Hey, it's okay, just the oven."

"Sorry, Dom."

He kissed her gently and stood up with her arms around his neck and her legs around his waist. "It's okay, one day at a time." He sat her down on one of the barstools and began to get the mac and cheese out.

He didn't know how to make the moment perfect, and it

was killing him inside. He didn't have a romantic bone in his body.

He got the plates out and began to dish each of them a plate. He placed the plates in front of her and another stool.

"Hey, Brandon left without saying goodbye," she commented as her brows furrowed together as he got two forks out of the drawer.

"He did say goodbye, but you were sleeping so peacefully, he didn't want to wake you up."

"Oh, well, what did he say?"

"Why don't you eat first, then we'll discuss it, baby."

She pouted a little but gave in and began to eat.

Dom chuckled at her pout and kissed her temple as he came around the bar and sat beside her. He began to eat also.

Once they were done, they both cleaned up and went out to the back patio. They sat in the two lounge chairs.

Dom carefully pulled out the ring box as they watched the sun begin to set a little. "Lex, I love you, so damn much," he started. "I don't know how to do all of the romance or the relationship thing, but I want to try to make you so happy for the rest of our lives, I wasn't very prepared when I asked you in bed to marry me, but this time I am."

He slowly stood and knelt in front of her. He presented the box to her. "Will you marry me?" He opened the box.

---

Alexa let out a gasp as she stared at the ring. It was rose gold with a clear circular diamond and the band twisted about a quarter of the way down.

"Wait, what did Brandon say?"

He smiled at her. "He gave me permission to ask you."

"Yes, Dom, I love you so much, how'd you manage to get this though?"

"It was my grandma's, Dad came by and dropped it off. If you want your own ring I'll get you one."

"No, this is perfect, it's beautiful, Dom." She threw her arms around his neck and kissed him passionately.

She couldn't help but smile as he slid the ring onto her left ring finger, this man was something else. She never expected any of this to happen the day she fell into his office, and he helped her up, but at this moment, she was so glad she had.

He slowly sat down beside her in her chair as they lay back and finished watching the sunset.

She curled up into him, laying her head on his chest and holding onto his shirt as if her life depended on it. Where would she be without the man? He made her feel so wonderful and loved. It didn't matter if there wasn't a huge crowd to see them get engaged, it didn't matter if there were millions of flowers or not. All that mattered was he was giving her a chance with his heart.

And she wouldn't ruin that chance.

## Epilogue

Alexa held tightly onto Brandon's arm, the man she loved and had grown to call Dad. She looked up at him, feeling so many knots and twists in her stomach.

"Are you okay, sweetheart?" Brandon asked as he looked down at her.

"Yeah, I'm okay, just nervous, thank you for saying yes, Dad, to letting me marry Dom and for walking me down the aisle."

"Honey, even if I had said no you wouldn't have listened, you would have married him anyway, you love him so much."

"Yeah I do. God, he looks so handsome standing up there," she whispered as she stared at Dom, who was wearing a dark black suit, a white dress shirt, and a purple flower boutonniere on his lapel that matched the bouquet she was holding in one of her hands.

"Yeah, and he's standing there just for you, love." Brandon was fidgeting a little.

"Are you sure you're okay?" Alexa teased as she looked up at him.

"Perfectly fine." He reassured with a huge smile on his face.

"Well then, I suppose we should start this glorious moment." She tightened her hand on his arm, and they began to proceed to Dom. She couldn't wait to be Mrs. Dominick Mackenzie.

---

Dom turned a little more toward the entranceway that Alexa and Brandon would be coming out of as the music began. He had never thought he'd be here. This was crazy and exhilarating all at the same time. A huge smile broke over his face as he saw his beautiful bride start to come down the aisle.

It had been a long but short ride to get to where they were today. It had been worth it, except for the pain she had gone through. But today, she was so gorgeous, no bruises, no cuts, she was perfect in every way.

Her dress was actually blue, like the one she had worn to the fundraiser, it showed she had gone through abuse multiple times, survived and came out on top. It was longer than the dress from their first date. It came a little past her knees. It had straps that went up around her neck though, it was tight around her breasts but then fanned out toward her waist, thighs, and knees. It was perfect for hiding their little secret they had discovered shortly after he had asked her to marry him.

They were going to be husband and wife along with parents. They weren't sure when they were going to share the news with their families yet. Maybe during the reception since they also had another announcement to make.

As she glided down to him, she was smiling, and it was sending his heart fluttering. God, how he loved this woman.

Brandon was smiling too, and Dom was glad he had

agreed to let him and Alexa get married and accepted when Alexa asked him to walk her down the aisle. He was a very good man to her, just like Dom himself promised to be.

As they got there in front of the preacher and himself, the preacher asked, "Who gives this woman to this man?"

"Her mother and I," Brandon answered. He turned to Alexa. "I love you, sweetheart." He hugged her gently and kissed her forehead. He went to sit by Sabrina, who was crying her eyes out at the sight of her baby, finally taking a chance on a man.

Dom took Alexa's hand as the preacher began the ceremony. They kissed passionately in front of everyone and broke away from one another. She laid her head against his chest and whispered just for him to hear. "I love you, Dominick Mackenzie."

He smiled and tilted her head up to look into her beautiful eyes. "I love you, Alexandra Mackenzie." He smiled wider as they made their way down the aisle.

Everything was cleaned up so they could actually have the reception out on the stone porch. He had tried to tell her money wasn't an issue, but she wanted to do it where they had finally admitted they loved each other. And him being him and her being her, he couldn't tell her no.

As soon as everything got arranged and the music got set up, they began their first dance as husband and wife. He had gotten to choose the song, and he had picked 'Never Gonna Be Alone' by Nickelback. And the song rang true, he was never going to let her down ever again nor let her fall no matter how rough life got for them.

When their dance was over, Alexa and Brandon danced to 'I Loved Her First' by Heartland. As soon as everyone began to settle down and the meal was served, Alexa, Dom, and Brandon stood up and clinked a knife against one of the Champagne glasses.

Once they had everyone's attention, Dom began, "We are glad you all could be here today to celebrate the joining of two people, but it's not just us who are joining together today, it is a blending of two families, and it's going to continue to grow and flourish. As of today, BAP and MAEP will be combining together as well."

Brandon laid a hand on Alexa's shoulder. "And I am handing the BAP part of the company over to my wonderful daughter, Alexa. She's proven herself more than once and overcome so many obstacles, more than anyone else could ever know, and hell, she landed the most eligible bachelor as well. She is strong-willed and confident, and I am happy to make her the owner of the BAP part of this union between us."

Alexa's mouth dropped open at the news. She whirled to look at Dom. "You knew?"

"Eh, maybe." He smirked at her and bent down to kiss her passionately. "Do you want to tell them the other news?"

"I suppose so." She smiled up at him and turned around to face everyone else. "As Dom said, we are going to continue to grow and flourish, Mr. Mackenzie, Mrs. Mackenzie, Dad, Mom, you all are going to be grandparents, Arielle, Collette, Noelle, Delilah you all are going to be aunts."

Everyone clapped and whistled and gave a round of applause, Sabrina, Noelle, Delilah, and Cal all came forward to hug the happy couple tightly.

Arielle, Collette and Mrs. Mackenzie stayed still as their eyes widened in shock.

Alexa didn't care, and nothing was going to ruin this day, she was so happy.

They had found out Delilah had nothing to do with the

whole Charles and Tate fiasco, and she soon found someone who was actually into her. Noelle had found a new man as well.

Everything was slowly falling into place, and Alexa wouldn't change it for the world.

## The End

## Blushing Books

Blushing Books is the oldest eBook publisher on the web. We've been running websites that publish steamy romance and erotica since 1999, and we have been selling eBooks since 2003. We have free and promotional offerings that change weekly, so please do visit us at http://www.blushingbooks.com/free.

## Blushing Books Newsletter

Please join the Blushing Books newsletter
to receive updates & special promotional offers.
You can also join by using your mobile phone:
Just text BLUSHING to 22828.

Every month, one new sign up via text messaging will
receive a $25.00 Amazon gift card so sign up today!